In *The Scent of Safety*, Sue Bingham Herring engages her readers with a true-to-life story of loss, pain, faith, hope, and redemption. Her novel serves as a vehicle for valuable self-help in surviving today's stresses. She breathes life into her characters and pulls you into their world of learning to live beyond the pain. I look forward to following her "Raveled Tapestries" series.

Gaye James, author of *Living Beyond the Silence of Selective Mutism*

I can't say enough about Sue Bingham Herring's new novel, *The Scent of Safety*. Readers will find it easy to relate to her characters and will likely identify with elements of their personal struggles. As they recognize similarities to their responses to events in their lives, they will see their responses as not only normal but understandable, and they will see that they can heal. The most meaningful aspect of this book for me is the author's clear demonstration of the importance of compassion and faith in God for trans-formational healing.

Holly B. Suber, founder and artistic director of Hope Street Missions, Uganda

The Scent of Safety pulled me in with the very first line and had me caught up with the characters' lives. There are always twists and turns in real life and the author does an excellent job weaving life's intricacies into the lives of the characters. Very thought provoking, I'm still pondering on the book weeks later.

Esther Julianne McDaniel, author of *When Memories Leave*

Sue Bingham Herring's debut novel, *The Scent of Safety*, provides a fresh look at how to maintain faith when facing adversity. Her characters' personal battles show the power of rising above trials while also identifying opportunities based on their faith in God.

Kary Oberbrunner, CEO of Igniting Souls,
author of *Unhackable, Day Job to Dream Job*,
and *Elixir Project*

The Scent of Safety

A Novel

Raveled Tapestries
Book One

A weaver sees potential in the colors and textures of
individual threads that, when woven together,
may become a beautiful tapestry.
Once it has become worn and raveled, she has a choice:
she can toss it aside carelessly, or she can use
her gifts to find the broken threads and
strengthen it, making it even
more precious.

The Scent of Safety

A Novel

SUE BINGHAM HERRING

AUTHOR ACADEMY elite

This book is a work of fiction.
All characters, organizations, businesses, and events portrayed in this
novel are used fictitiously or are products of the author's imagination.

For the benefit of the reader's interests, references for several of the
books, quotes, and songs mentioned in this book are listed by chapter
after the Author's Note.

The Scent of Safety - A Novel © 2020 by Sue Bingham Herring. All
rights reserved.

Published by Author Academy Elite
PO Box 43, Powell, OH 43065
www.AuthorAcademyElite.com

Identifiers:
Library of Congress Control Number: 2020914891
ISBN: 978-1-64746-433-2 (paperback)
ISBN: 978-1-64746-434-9 (hardback)
ISBN: 978-1-64746-435-6 (ebook)

Available in paperback, hardback, and e-book

All Scripture quotations, unless otherwise indicated, are from
the King James Version.

For Apple, as she rises from the ashes and
spreads her wings . . . it is her turn

And ye shall know the truth, and the truth
shall make you free.

John 8:32

Mind Your Words.   Proceed With Care.
We don't know what lives in the Hearts and Minds of Others.
All are Unique. Every Event is Processed Differently by Each of Us.
Memories and Words have Great Power. The Challenge is to
Separate   Memories Worth Keeping   from those
Unworthy of Godliness. Keep Precious Ones Safe and
Bind them to your Heart. Use Them to the
Benefit of Others, Giving
All Glory to
God

Preface

Wouldn't it be nice if the streets of life were smooth? It would make things easier if the streetlights stayed lit and directions were always clear—with warnings for every twisting road and washed out bridge. I wonder though, if we always knew what to expect, would we forget the importance of awareness? Life is full of surprises that come in many forms and may feel chaotic; but they often serve as opportunities that lead to greater things. Sometimes these surprises come as people, sometimes as places, and sometimes they come from the shadows of the past. Like threads in a tapestry, once woven together they become the landscape of our lives. It is important to pay attention; to recognize and appreciate each thread. Their individual beauty and significance can be missed, because sometimes we close our eyes when they come from the most frightening places imaginable.

Trauma, even with all the studies and therapies which have become popular over the past several decades, continues to be one of the most challenging issues in the understanding and treatment of mental health. The definition alone is under continuous scrutiny and transition. There are no simple answers to explain the complexity of the nature of man. It is my belief that the determination of modern society to keep science separate from faith only creates more confusion. This book is intended to be an argument for the necessity of faith for survival.

The following is a brief, overly simplified explanation of the impact of trauma; it serves to aid the reader in understanding the purpose of the book:

For mammals, the sense of smell is the first to reach the brain. The brain records and imprints learned experiences, then uses the stored information to ensure survival. When the brain detects a situation that it perceives to be harmful, alarms are activated. These alarms exist in the form of physical pain and/or emotional distress, which puts the human organism on high alert. When the brain sees a threat, it *will* get your attention, even if the threat is only implied or is based on misinformation.

Most people know this as fight or flight. It involves the activation of the Sympathetic Nervous System and prepares the body to protect itself. An entire cavalcade of physiological preparation including things such as muscle tightening, jaw clenching, increased respiration and heart rate, and the release of adrenaline and neurochemicals can be involved. For some people, an alarm is a frequent occurrence; for others it may not happen for years. We don't always recognize an alarm for what it is, especially if the brain makes a delayed connection after an event. Left unchecked, this unnecessary physiological arousal can lead to fear-driven decision-making and can result in emotional imbalance and/or stress-related health deterioration.

The behavioral and physiological effects due to traumatic events which take place between conception and the first several years of life are known as Complex Trauma and/or Developmental Trauma. Memories at this stage of life are registered in relational and sensory terms, as the language necessary to explain an event has not yet been acquired. Explanations added after the fact are often influenced by emotion and are seldom, if ever, grounded in objectivity.

This book is about ordinary people—people like you and me—who have experienced various traumatic situations. For some the events took place earlier in life than for others. I pray their stories will allow those of you who struggle or are seeking answers for yourselves or for a friend or family member to make connections and recognize relatable issues.

Traumatic events happen. The reactions to trauma can be seen daily all around us. We can choose to believe they happen *to* us and adopt a victim mentality, or we can choose to see them as opportunities to grow and gain wisdom. We always have the option to look for the good hidden in the most devastating circumstances.

As always, my goal is to help individuals who question the quality of their lives to become enlightened, to find solutions, and to be encouraged to seek and receive help. On a broad scale I hope to inform and to educate through sharing an entertaining story as a reminder that we are in this life together—together we can increase the awareness of the importance of compassion for our fellow man.

1
South Alabama 1937

Etta Mae Williams was ironing in the midday light on the screened porch off the Francis' kitchen. She shivered at the chill of the breeze from the ceiling fan on her neck that was damp with perspiration while she unconsciously kept time with the old fan's unbalanced thumping and the monotonous rhythm of the steadily dripping faucet. A movement in the bushes caught her eye at the same time a whisper from outside grabbed her attention. She stepped off the little stool she used to get leverage over the heavy iron to turn in the direction of the sound. Her neighbor's son was in the bushes, motioning to her to come closer with wild eyes—his finger to his lips. She cautiously glanced back at the doorway, then took a step toward the screen.

"What you doin' out there, Jerome? You know you not spose t' come here." She kept her voice at a low whisper.

"Etta Mae! You gotta come on home! That law man Ben an' his boys done come an' took Jesse! Mama say come fetch you. Moze was playin' in the yard an' now he ain't nowhere aroun' an' we done been lookin' *everwhere*, but we ain't foun' him. Mama say you gotta come on home an' fine yore boy!" Jerome was breathless as he looked around frantically.

She jumped when she heard a creak from the kitchen floor. "Etta Mae, is there someone out there with you? You know you aren't allowed company at this house." Etta Mae shooed Jerome away when she realized Mrs. Francis was moving in the direction of the porch across the old hardwood floor. She hopped back onto her stool beside the ironing board with her back to the kitchen doorway.

"Oh, *no* ma'am, I was just talkin' to the Lord while I'm ironin', Ms. Francis. I'm sorry, I guess I was gettin' too carried away." Etta Mae scanned the bushes to make sure Jerome was out of sight. She needed this job, but where was Moses? When she sensed the presence of the large woman behind her, she spun around, iron in hand, and almost lost her balance on the stool. Hilda Francis stood in the doorway with her hands on her hips. She looked down her nose through her wire-rimmed glasses, pinched her lips tight, and surveyed the porch and yard with her squinty eyes. At barely five feet tall, even when up on her stool, Etta Mae's employer towered over her.

As Mrs. Francis turned and headed back toward the dining room, she corrected her young maid as she shuffled away, "Use correct English, Etta Mae, you've been taught proper diction. Your mother spoke clearly and I know she trained you to pronounce your words."

"Yes ma'am, Mrs. Francis, you're right. My mama said she was lucky to have you to teach her. I guess I was getting lazy. She would be scolding me, too, if she was here, God rest her soul." Then she spoke a little louder, "Mrs. Francis, little Moses wasn't feeling too good when I left for work today, that's what I was praying about. I wonder if you could do without me this afternoon so I can go check on him . . . *after* I finish these last two shirts for

Mr. Francis, of course." Etta Mae was looking for a quick way out. She had learned the power of a compliment and knew how proud Mrs. Francis was about being a teacher. She thought about her mama's words, 'you catch more flies with honey,' and thought to herself, "Yessum, that lesson comes in handy."

"Proper grammar, Etta Mae, he wasn't feeling *well*. I suppose that will be fine, but make sure you are here tomorrow. Come a little early and wear the uniform I bought for you with a clean apron. The ladies from the church are coming for luncheon, and I'll need you to serve." Etta Mae could practically hear Mrs. Francis feeling proud and imagined her standing even taller as she walked away.

"Yes ma'am, he didn't feel *well*." She shook her head and finished the two shirts, thankfully without a scorch.

By the time Etta Mae left for home she felt like she might have shook hard enough to turn white. As soon as she rounded the trees and was out of sight, she took off running for home. All she could think of was her four-year-old boy and that crazy Ben, the meanest man on the face of the earth. She ran like her life depended on it. She ran like she did that night almost five years ago from Ben and the other two demons.

"Lord God, why you keep puttin' that devil in my life? I can't handle any *more*, Lord! You got to send me some help. You can't let 'em take my boy. Ben knows, Lord, he knows, and he watches. Lord, I swear on this, they hurt my boy . . . I'll kill 'em and it don't matter what you do to me for that, 'cause I can't do it anymore, Lord."

When Etta Mae made the turn in the dirt road at the edge of the shanties she stopped, panting and gasping. She lurched forward to get her breath and grabbed her knees to keep from falling. She looked up and stared at her little place and then at Jesse's across the road. She felt the heat rising in her face. His screen door hung off the hinges, his rocker was out in the yard on its side, and the rail had been busted off the porch. Evelyn spotted Etta Mae and ran out to where she stood in the road.

Etta Mae searched Evelyn's eyes.

"We ain't found him yet, Baby . . ."

Etta Mae dropped to the ground and let out a deep moan that escalated into a shrieking scream. She began to sob and beat the dirt with her fists. Evelyn tried to hold her, but Etta Mae swung and thrashed as she cursed the man she wished she could have killed the night he left her for dead in the ditch. Evelyn had been with Etta Mae's mama when they found her that night, just a girl of fifteen, thrown naked and bloody from the truck. Finally, Etta Mae fell onto Evelyn's waiting bosom, heaving, and whispered with resolve, "One day I just might *kill* that bastard."

"No one would blame you, chile. We'll find Moses though, and you don't need no more trouble brought on you. Oooh Laud, it was wild over there. Yo boy's smart, though. I bet he hid hisself so good we just gonna have to wait 'til he feels safe to come out."

They sat there in the road, rocking while Evelyn hummed, her arms around the slender girl who, at twenty, still looked fifteen. Etta Mae's eyes were fixed on Jesse's place. She watched as his old bitch hound came out from under the porch. "Bluebell's pups are under that porch . . ."

Evelyn shook her head sympathetically. "No, baby, we looked there."

Etta Mae was intent. "I *know* he's under there," she whispered, shaking her head with renewed determination. She pulled herself away from Evelyn and ran to the side of the porch where she saw the dog come out. She could hear the pups whining. It was dark under there and the air was cloudy with dust. "Moses? Baby? You under here?" Nothing. "Moses! If you're under here you *better* answer me, boy!" She strained to see as her eyes began to adjust to the dark. Something moved; there was a faint whimper that wasn't a pup. Her voice softened and she coaxed, "Come on out, Baby, Mama's here, you're okay, come on." She watched as his little hands and feet came out from under the pile of puppies that licked him as they rooted around in their blindness for a ninny. He slowly crawled out to her. She grabbed him, pulled him close, and pressed his head to her heart as she rocked. "Thank you Lord, thank you Jesus, thank you," tears of relief and gratitude streamed down her face, cut trails through the red clay that coated her cheeks, and dripped from her nose and chin.

Little Moses clung to her. Dust and dirt were caked in his hair and stuck in clumps to his runny nose. "Oh, Mama, I been wantin' you! Mama, you *cryin'* on me! You know what? Jesus made me imbisable, Mama! I was imbisable an' nobody couden see me. They took Jesse, Mama! They was mean an' they dragged him, an' he say, 'please no *please* no,' but they tied him to the truck an' dragged him. I wanted you, Mama, I wanted you so bad, an' I 'memberd what you say if I'm scared. I 'membered an' I called Jesus an' I tol him 'I'm scared,' just like you say, Mama, an' I got imbisable."

"Shhhhh . . . shhh, you did good, Baby, shhhh, no more . . . shhhhh you're okay now Moses. Mama's here. You're safe, Baby." Etta Mae rocked and consoled her whimpering child as his body shivered while his brain processed what he had witnessed, depositing it into his senses and his developing beliefs. In a deep place in her heart she doubted they would ever be safe.

Jesse Thatcher's body was found in the river a few days later. According to the story, Jesse failed to say "Sir" to a white law man, and his fate was sealed. As was typical after a lynching, no witnesses came forward. No one was charged even though it was known what had been done. It was a time in America not far enough gone. The pain continues today.

The men who took Jesse didn't care who saw. They were protected by their own kind, and they let it serve as a warning to anyone else. Even though no one admitted what happened, the boy knew. He was there. He had watched through the steps from under the floorboards. He had heard the hate and the fear as the men dragged his friend Jesse away. The memory became embedded in his senses and the meaning of it was interpreted from the perspective of a four-year-old child. From that moment on, he would remember it on many levels. The safety he felt in his invisibility in the dirt under that porch would dictate his life's choices for the next eight decades.

2

Moses

When Etta Mae's baby was born, she followed her mama's instruction to see it as a gift from God despite how things came about. Since it seemed to her it was God's plan for her to raise this boy, she named him Moses and added her father's name, Jedidiah Williams. After her mama died from a fever a year later, she didn't know what else to do but to stay in their little place with her one-year-old son. Her mama's friend, Evelyn, helped look out for them. Not long after, Etta Mae went to work for Mr. and Mrs. Francis, her mama's long-time employers. Etta Mae had worked for them for over two years when Ben and his men took Jesse.

Mrs. Francis loved Etta Mae's mother, and had taught her and Etta Mae to read. When Mr. Francis heard what happened out in the shanties, he was worried about Etta Mae's safety. He and Mrs. Francis suspected the truth about Ben. Mr. Francis got in touch with some people he knew near Birmingham. He found an attorney up there who was looking to hire some help. His wife had taken ill, and he needed someone who could cook and care for her and for their three children. The attorney, Mr. Bradley, liked that Etta Mae was a young Christian and could read well. The good reference from Mr. and Mrs. Francis sealed the deal. He hadn't planned on hiring someone with a child, but he felt called to give her the job after he learned about her circumstances. She and the boy needed the safety he could provide.

Getting away from the community where they were known before Moses got old enough to question his light skin was fine with Etta Mae. So far, Moses accepted her explanation that God had reasons for making people different colors. She didn't need anyone running their mouth. She and Moses moved into the cottage on the back of the Bradley's property where she figured her boy would have a chance for a better life.

Except for their relationship with the Bradleys, they stayed mostly to themselves. As the years passed, Moses did well in school. He read every book his mama's boss man's children brought home and he studied the Bible with his mama at night. The gardener took Moses under his wing, impressed with the boy's intelligence, quiet manners, and his desire to learn about plants. Moses especially wanted to know how to grow his own food. No one was interested in why these things were important to him, but if anyone asked, he simply said he didn't like to be hungry.

Like *all* children, eight-year-old boys who weren't rebellious schemers were fine if they showed respect and knew their place, regardless of color. They were seldom the subject of concern among wealthy white businessmen in 1941, even in Birmingham. Moses learned the Golden Rule from his mama, "Do unto others as you would have them do unto you." She said it was no guarantee because some people have the devil in them no matter what, but if he showed respect, most likely he could earn respect and stay safe. That was just the way it was in the white man's world. She prayed the world would change, but it had been like that for a long time. Change for the good wasn't something Etta Mae believed she could count on, at least not in her lifetime on this earth.

Etta Mae had already lost her ability to trust in the fairness of the world before she was fifteen years old. She taught Moses that fairness only existed in Heaven and told him she'd be ready to go when her Lord Jesus sent for her. She believed everything else was meant to be a lesson for improvement, and not just for herself; there was much a person could learn to do to help others survive this world. She did come to trust the Bradleys, though. They were fine people. She was loved and respected and considered a member of the family.

Etta Mae died at the age of ninety having lived a good life in her own cottage. Mr. Bradley deeded it to her long before his death. Shortly after his father passed on, the oldest child, David, came to live in the big house. David was only thirteen years younger than Etta Mae, so to him she was more like a big sister. Few outsiders grasped what she was to Mr. Bradley, or what he was to her, for that matter. Etta Mae devoted her life to raising three generations of Bradley children. Soft-spoken and demure, she was known to all as Big Mammy. The stark contradiction to her stature spoke volumes about her character. She was Moses' inspiration.

Moses possessed an innate wisdom. As a child he listened, paid attention, and kept his opinions to himself; then he applied what he learned to his life. What he experienced at barely four years old hidden in the dirt under the porch was an important lesson. The meaning it took on was what only an innocent child could imagine. While he didn't want to remember, it walked through his mind more often than he liked. His mama told him his heart could never forget things that hurt, even if his mind was determined not to remember. You just couldn't let it work you up into a snit. It was more important to make sure the good memories were sealed on his heart. She told him to match the good ones with the bad to snuff the bad ones out.

It occurred to Moses most people who had been afraid the way he and his mama had been afraid ended up bitter and angry. Fear twisted itself into hatred that became a seething invisible demon that lurked, waiting for an opportunity to strike out. His mama told him about a boy they knew before they went to live at Mr. Bradley's. He was too little to remember very well. The boy's mama was named Evelyn and he was there the day bad things happened that Moses tried to forget. That boy grew up angry and ended up joining a gang. He got killed out in California and it broke his mama's heart. Moses didn't want to live that way.

One night in a dream an angel came and sat on the end of Moses' bed and said, "In a *flash*, God's plan will be known to you, and once apparent, it cannot be denied." Then the angel smiled and told Moses to be patient and wait, to forget the past and look to the future. The dream was one of those that makes you think you're awake because it's so vivid and bright. Now he was waiting for the flash. He hoped he'd know it however it might come. He had been taught to ask in order to receive, so Moses made it his habit to ask the Lord to show him His plan every day. Somehow, he knew there was something important for him to do.

Moses felt sorry for people who were afraid of each other. He was sad when he felt fear. He didn't like to admit being scared when he thought of what people he didn't even know might do to him. He had never done anything against a single person—not on purpose anyway. He knew what could happen even when nothing had been done with a plan to provoke it. You never knew when the demon was going to come flying out. Dealing with all the possibilities overwhelmed Moses. He decided early on to find a way to live in peace while he waited. If that meant spending his days alone, then that would have to be alright. He believed his mama and took comfort knowing Jesus was looking out for him all the time.

Sometimes, while Moses was still learning to understand his gifts, he came close to getting in trouble by trusting the wrong person. Being friends with the Bradley children, especially David, got people who might hurt Moses to back off. David was bigger and three years older than Moses. David learned from his daddy to respect and stand up for hardworking people no matter what color they were. Sometimes people weren't quite sure if Moses was white or black, but he was proud to be his mama's son. David didn't seem to care if other kids called him names for being Moses' friend. David lived the way the Lord told him to live, just like Moses did. That's why Moses loved David Bradley.

Moses loved David's little sister, Leah, too. There was something different about her big hazel eyes that sparkled when she laughed and her freckled cheeks that dimpled when she smiled. She was smart and sensitive. She loved her doll, but she liked to play rough with the boys, too. Leah was almost two years younger than Moses, but sometimes she seemed older than all of them.

Etta Mae had to have a long talk about the rules of life with Moses when he was ten. He wasn't allowed to go to the lake any more with David if his sisters were along because they would be wearing swimsuits. People might think bad things about him. Moses was haunted the rest of his life by the thought that if he had been at the lake with the family that day, he could have saved Leah from drowning.

They said no one saw her go under. Moses believed if he had been there, he would have been watching to keep her safe. He wished he could have been invisible. It changed how Moses chose to live.

Moses traveled different routes wherever he went, and he went at different times. This was the ordinary way he practiced invisibility, and the idea of the possibility pleased him greatly. He planted vegetables and fruit trees in places where he could tend them without being noticed. He traded what he grew, like cucumbers, asparagus, berries, and apples, for other supplies he needed. He believed it was important to learn patience as he waited for the fruits of his labor to ripen. He had learned from Psalm 128 that if he labored faithfully and was patient, he would be blessed.

Moses befriended a man named Hank; a widower who ran a little car repair business called Red's Garage. Hank told Moses he enjoyed his company and offered him the use of the shed behind his business, not realizing the size of the area Moses considered his home. Hank never told Moses that he had planned to end his life the day they met. He didn't have to. These were the things Moses simply knew. Something Moses said had changed Hank's mind—that, and the light that seemed to shine through Moses' eyes.

Hank's generosity was repaid with much appreciated produce. Acquaintances who thought they knew Moses nicknamed him Willy and found him to be *different* and *interestingly odd*. He was inclined to agree with a smile. They had no idea what an anomaly Moses Williams truly was. The shed at Red's became the place anyone who *thought* they knew him believed he lived, and when he wasn't around, no one worried about him or questioned where he was.

Over the years Moses' domain grew, unnoticed by the rest of the world, exactly the way he liked it. If hikers or campers saw a few fruit trees or plants which looked out of place, it didn't seem to matter. Moses spread his efforts across about two square miles. The best part of it was the feeling of peace he had when he was alone in nature. It wasn't just peace though. It was more a sense of safety. It felt much like being held by his mama—the softness of her skin and the scent that seemed to come from her pores.

Civilization came dangerously close several years back, but for whatever reason, the area that was slated to be developed was abandoned mid-way through the project. Moses heard rumors about the financial troubles of the developer. Once the construction stopped, Moses contacted David Bradley's daughter, Ruth, who had followed in the family tradition as an attorney. She helped him make sure the development would never start back up. Moses lived his whole life doing what he felt led to do, slowly creating a cultivated wilderness that served to camouflage his network of hidden structures and gardens. As far as Moses was concerned, God had him there to do His bidding. He felt responsible for the care of the land and for the people the Lord put there for him to help.

He welcomed the cryptic messages he received. Often, they came in his dreams and sometimes from random strangers, but he was still waiting for that flash. He felt good and strong, but time was going by. He had said good-bye to his mama back in 2007, then he recently had said goodbye to David Bradley. Moses was beginning to wonder how much longer he would have to wait; he was hanging onto the promise.

As summer grew close, Moses looked forward to his yearly work for a little Christian camp for girls up on the mountain. About twenty years before, David had left a note at Hank's place for Moses to come see him about a job. As soon as he could, Moses had found a way over to David's. After a nice visit with Etta Mae, David had taken him to the church to meet with Pastor Matthews. The church had been given a piece of acreage on the mountain and they needed help laying out plans to start a summer camp. Each year since he was hired, Moses had spent the month of May getting things ready for the summer.

Recently, Pastor Matthews' wife had taken ill and a new man had been chosen to run the camp. Moses went to meet with the new Pastor. He worried he might lose that job. After their meeting, he was asked if he could stay up at the camp all summer as the maintenance man and grounds keeper. When they agreed he could have several days off every few weeks to tend his property, the deal was done. The idea swelled up in Moses as he walked around grinning like a fool.

3

Tina

Ron's Office   Two Weeks Before graduation   May 2001

Tina sat deep in the mushy couch. Her fingertips moved along the finely cracked leather while she examined her feet, assuming she looked nonchalant. It had been a while since she came to see Ron. This time was at her mother's insistence. She was late, as usual. He was the same as ever: laid back, wrinkled shirt, drinking a cup of coffee, staring at her and waiting for her to start the conversation. He always remembered what she had said at her last session and how she expressed what she felt. He seldom wrote anything down, at least not while she was there. He was so damn matter of fact and it seemed he could read her mind. That pissed her off and left her feeling small, but it also left her wanting more. She figured that must be how this worked for teen-agers whose parents thought they were out of control. She sat. He sat and waited. Her mind went back to Monday when she stood in the hall in front of her locker; she knew what was inside, but she didn't want to see it.

It looked like he was leaving it up to her to talk first, so she gave in. "I guess Carol called you."

"She did." Ron nodded as he spoke.

"What did she tell you?"

"She said her daughter needed to come back to therapy."

"What else did she tell you?"

"Nothing."

"I have a hard time believing that."

"That's all she said. I guess she thought it should be up to you to tell me what's been going on." Ron rocked back in his big office chair, took a long sip of his coffee, then got up to adjust the blinds and sat back down to wait.

There it was. He was so good at throwing the ball right back at her. A few minutes passed. She could hear the ticking of his very cool blue Zoloft clock the drug rep gave him. Tina had tried to get Ron to give it to her. One of the few bright and cheerful things in his office—she smiled at the thought. *Perfect*, since it's a drug for depression.

The air in the room felt heavy despite Ron's oddly entertaining assortment of décor. She was sure you'd have to be odd to want to do his job. She glanced up at the shelf with a gargoyle working on a laptop and the small carved angel with an expression of tormented pain. Then there was his obvious delight with *The Wizard of Oz:* his framed poster of Glinda the Good Witch with her wand that said "You've always had the power my dear . . . " and the little "Don't make me get my flying monkeys " sign hanging near his chair. That one was her favorite, but today it failed to brighten her thoughts.

Tina avoided conversation by adjusting herself as she sank too deep into the doo-doo brown worn-out sofa and grabbed the needlepoint pillow with Einstein's definition of insanity on it. She read the words and silently asked herself, "Do I really do the same thing over and over? I'm not just *expecting* things to change . . ." She laughed as she studied a few new drawings likely done by other crazies, thinking somebody got brownie points. Tina looked up at Ron's crystal ball blue eyes and the mustache that, even though it was small, somehow camouflaged what his mouth was doing. As usual, he studied her. She wondered what he was thinking. It was unfathomable to her how he could stay that calm and quiet for so long. Then a thought crossed her mind and a dark smile slid onto her face that shifted her strained expression.

"I guess this is what could be described as a pregnant moment," she said with a smirk. He looked curiously at her and read her eyes. She knew he got it when he choked a little on the coffee he was sipping, and sat up, chuckling.

"Are you?"

"Yes. Are you *laughing*? That's not very nice of you. Why don't you look surprised?"

"Oh, you caught me by *surprise* alright, but what does it matter what *I* think?" He shrugged with a crooked smile and shook his head. "Have you told your parents?"

"Carol and Jack? No. I haven't told anyone, not even Jimmy. I haven't decided anything. I have to be sure before I let them push me into something."

"This is the same Jimmy? The mechanic?"

"Yes." Tina squinted at Ron, ready for his response. Nothing. Damn.

Another moment of silence passed while he looked thoughtful.

"How long have you known?"

"Only a few days for sure, but I guess I've been sure I was for over a month. It's wonderful and terrifying at the same time. It's such big deal. I need to know how I feel before I let the wardens make decisions for me. They'll want to send me somewhere and make me give it away. I need time to be ready. I've always known I'd have kids one day. I just didn't think it would be so soon. A girl at school got rid of hers before it was too late this year. She hasn't been the same since. Everyone thinks she's going to do something drastic, maybe even kill herself. It's really tragic. I don't believe that's an option, but I have to have a chance to think. I'm glad my mom insisted I come back to see you. I need to be able to sort it all out."

Ron shook his head. It was obvious he was formulating a response. "What's been happening to cause your mother to think you need therapy?"

"Carol being Carol—always eavesdropping. I guess she heard me throwing up. Her knee jerk reaction. You know, the Bulimia thing, her fear there's something seriously wrong with me. Listen, now that you know, are you going to have to tell them? I'm almost eighteen, Ron, and this *is* private, right? I'm not planning to hurt myself or any of those other reasons you're supposed to tell like you told me the first time I came, right? If you are, I need to know before you do."

"We can wait. It's private, except it would be an ethical dilemma for me if they were *never* told. They pay the bill, after all. We can talk to them together if you want. I think I know you well enough to trust you aren't going to do anything dangerous. Other than morning sickness, have you had any problems? You know it's going to be important for you to see a doctor."

This was the Ron she loved. The one person she could talk to who listened and at least acted like he respected her. He allowed her to think for herself and encouraged her to look at things clearly without flying into batshit crazy like Carol. She could imagine her mom wringing her hands and crying and having a spaz attack, and no telling what Mr. Unpredictable would do. Dad could do anything from turning and walking quietly out of the room to throwing his prosthetic at her. She knew how to avoid triggering her dad.

"I already went to the Health Department. So, I guess I have told someone. My bad. Bet you didn't expect that, huh? I did a drugstore test at school Monday. I know, I waited a long time. It was hard buying the test and I couldn't ask anybody else to get one for me. I think I didn't want to know in time to be tempted to do what Gwen di . . . oops, you didn't hear the name. I had made an appointment for Tuesday afternoon and I wanted to be sure before I went. I'm fine. They were nice. The nurse said it would be due in December. That makes me ten weeks. I've only got a few weeks until graduation, and my birthday is two days after. Thank God I already got through exams and my grades are good. I'm not showing, and nobody knows. Whatever happens, I'm okay for now."

"You always have an idea of what you want and how to get it, Tina, and you have a real gift for rationalizing your decisions."

"That sounded pretty sarcastic."

"Not *really*, but it wasn't meant to be a compliment, either. Sometimes, like most everyone, some of your ideas are questionable and won't necessarily go as planned. How's Jimmy been doing with the drinking? I thought you were ready to break it off last time I saw you after the way things went at Christmas."

"Hmmm, you *are* a mousetrap. I was, and I *did*, but we got back together right before Spring Break and went to the beach. I'm pretty sure that's when *this* happened. Jimmy's different. He had shit-for-brains parents. He doesn't mean it when he goes off. It's not all his fault. He says I'm good for him and he'll do better."

Ron leaned his head back with his eyes closed, then reached up and pinched the bridge of his nose. She watched him, knowing he must want to say something. This was how he acted when he was worried about her. She had been here with him before. He had told her after Christmas he saw a dangerous future for her and he wished she wasn't so naïve.

"Did you ever read the book about co-dependence I gave you? I'm quite sure I gave you *Codependent No More*." He was still leaning back with his eyes closed.

"You did, but no, it's not like that."

"Well, I beg to differ." Ron sat up, shook his head, and looked all stern. His raised voice startled Tina, "It is *exactly* like that. I'm serious about this, Tina. *Read* it. Pay attention to it. You owe it to yourself and especially to this baby. Behaviors like Jimmy's don't simply go away. If anything, without him admitting he needs help, they'll only get worse. I wish I could get you to understand the seriousness of your circumstances."

Silence. Her face flushed as she felt the tingling heat in the back of her neck. She studied the crazy drawings again, then Glinda, and the Zoloft clock.

"Wow look at that. My session is just about up. Time flies when you're having fun. Can I come for the next few weeks, so she'll get off my back? Can I bring you a grad-uation invitation?"

"You know you can, and yes, bring one by. Check with Barb on your way out to make sure about the time. Listen, you have my number. If *anything* comes up, it's okay to call, alright?"

"Sure. I will. I promise."

Ron gave her shoulder a squeeze and winked. The usual sendoff. She wanted to throw her arms around his neck and give him a bear hug. Instead, she turned and gestured a thrown kiss as she went out the door.

4
Penny's Misery Tina's Lament
Monday April 16, 2018

Tina McKenzie stood gazing out the kitchen window and watched a pair of Cardinals as they splashed in the birdbath. Their wet feathers glistened in the afternoon sun. She had spotted the returning Hummingbirds earlier as they darted about and sipped nectar from the long-awaited Rhododendron blossoms. As the breeze played in the trees, the afternoon sun created a dance of light across the deck she and her husband had enjoyed building. They had been overjoyed when they found the perfect home for their growing family, and the addition to the backyard made it even more special. She closed her eyes, wrapped her arms around herself, and drifted into a warm memory of a springtime afternoon a decade before when John's loving arms were around her. After finishing the deck that day, they had basked in the joyful laughter over a belly-full of kicking baby while the soon-to-be big brother and sister giggled playfully. Her memory was so vivid she could practically smell the blooming lilacs her husband had planted for her. It seemed then that the rainbow after the storm in her life had finally come, even if the lilacs never survived the summer heat.

Jolted by the rattle of the window above the sink, Tina was so deep in her daydream it took a moment for her to reorient to the present. When she realized she hadn't heard the bus, she checked her watch, sighed, and turned to face whatever came home from school today.

"Penny? What have I told you about slamming the front door?" She expected her young daughter to bounce into the kitchen for an after-school snack, but no sound came from the front of the house. She left the kitchen and turned the corner toward the entryway. A blue jacket and a worn-out emoji backpack lay abandoned on the floor.

"Penny? Where are you?"

"I'm here." The response came from a sniffling voice on the stairs.

"Oh Honey, what's wrong? Are you hurt?"

"Everything's wrong Mom. Nothing's right. My life stinks! I *hate* Bobby Taylor. Boys are so *stupid!* And why didn't I ride my bike today? I had to get on the *stupid* bus. Mom, *please* don't make me go to school tomorrow. I think I'm getting sick," she pleaded with her wrinkled brow, red eyes, and an artificial cough. Her freckled forehead dropped onto her arms that were wrapped around her knees and she began to sob dramatically.

Tina looked up at her with concern and with a little annoyance, bothered by yet another extreme performance. Her approach softened as memories of her own childhood crossed her mind. It broke her heart when one of her children was struggling, and it was happening too often with her ten-year-old. She studied Penny as she took several steps up the stairs and sat a few treads below her. When

Tina reached for Penny's hand, she quickly moved it farther away.

Deep breath. "I know boys can act like jerks sometimes,
but *Sweetie,* they don't always know how to get a girl's
attention without being obnoxious." Tina knew Penny and
Bobby had arguments, and it hadn't only been fifth grade.
The feud had been a hot mess throughout elementary
school, and he could be an unmerciful bully. Tina went to
middle school with Bobby's mother and didn't think saying
something to her would make any difference. In Tina's
opinion, Rhonda Taylor ended up with her just deserts;
raising five wild boys while their father worked on the
road. "Okay, tell me what Bobby did this time."

"He made a joke about my nose. We're learning about
birds in science and he said I had a beak. Then he said
I'm more like a bird than a girl since I'm so small and he
chirped at me, and then his friends started doing it, too.
Mrs. Jenkins told him to stop, but she was busy. She didn't
do anything about it. Why is he so mean to me, Mom? I
need to make him stop."

"Whoa . . . okay . . . I've told you before, I don't think
Bobby gets much attention at home with all those brothers.
I'll bet *he* gets teased a lot, too. Every time you react, he
gets exactly what he wants. He's going to keep on doing
it as long as you flip out. You're *letting* him control you
and he wins when you get upset. At some point you'll see.
When you ignore him, he'll find someone else to tease. I
know I've said all that before. I guess you'll figure it out
eventually." Tina waited for a response. She wasn't sure if
Penny was listening or if she had tuned her out. Nothing.
"If you aren't going to listen, then there's no reason for
me to sit here and talk."

Tina began to stand, but Penny grabbed her hand and
pulled her back down.

"I'm listening." Penny's eyes reconnected with her mother's, but only for a moment.

"Then look at me." Tina waited for eye contact. "Are you a bird?" Penny looked at her like she was crazy. "I asked you a serious question. Are you a bird?"

"No, and that's a stupid question, Mom."

"Penny, if you know you aren't a bird, what does that say about what Bobby said?"

"It's a *stupid* comment. I know *that*, Mom. But it still hurts for everybody else to think it's funny and laugh." There were the tears again.

Tina thought she almost had her. She decided to try a different approach.

"Okay, so you know you aren't a bird, and sometimes people laugh and don't even realize how bad it hurts you. You *could* remind yourself that's about them. What people say only tells you about *their* character. And the nose thing . . . we've talked about this so many times. You have a perfectly lovely nose, Penny. There are lots of famous people, like *movie* stars, who are *beautiful* and who have unusual noses, like Meryl Streep, or Sarah Jessica Parker, or . . . how about Barbara Streisand? The shape of your nose is simply the way God made you. Just like people, no two are exactly alike."

Tina stumbled through words searching for a way to say something meaningful. No matter what came out, it all sounded boring and wrong. She couldn't stop trying, even when she told herself it was time to shut up because she *knew* Penny was cringing. At least now her daughter looked like she was listening. Her words poured out.

"It's like being small. I was the shortest person in my class until eighth grade, but I grew. And look at your brother; nobody would look at Carson today and think he was *ever* a little bitty guy. You'll grow when your body is ready to grow. People said mean things to *me*, but they don't anymore. I finally learned that the people who say mean things are the most insecure. The things kids like Bobby say can't *really* hurt you. One day his friends will figure him out and they'll think he's rude." Tina did her best to make sense, but this wasn't the first time she had to tackle this issue and she was looking for a fresh approach. Even though she knew she had said most of it before and her words were probably wasted, she couldn't make herself stop. She needed to be able to help.

Penny rolled her eyes and groaned, then slapped her hand down on the step. "Why do you do this, Mom? You say all that *stuff.* Who *are* those people with the wonderful noses? And what do *their* noses have to do with *me?* What Bobby says does *too* hurt, and his friends don't think he's rude, they think he's funny. I'm just a big joke. No, wait, I'm a *little* joke, and my nose isn't the only problem. *Nobody* understands, *nobody* cares how I feel, *nobody knows how hard a time I have.*" After a moment of silence, she shrieked, "I want to change my name. I have a *stupid* name. I *hate my name!*" Penny was beginning to scream as she stood up.

Tina could see the situation was quickly going from bad to a full-out disaster. The tension in the air was thick and Penny's small fists were clenched.

Penny hovered over Tina. "Why did you do this to me, anyway? Cathy told me the truth about how I got my name. She said I was a funny-looking baby, and when you saw me for the first time you laughed and decided to give me a funny name." Now the tears poured from Penny's big hazel eyes and she gasped for air as her nose was beginning to run.

This new twist hit Tina like a punch to the gut. Stunned by the turn things had taken, she stood and reached for Penny's arm, but she wasn't fast enough. What could Cathy have been thinking? How could she have said something so cruel to her little sister?

Penny bolted up the stairs. "I hate my life! Why was I even born?" Her bedroom door slammed shut.

Tina was tired and frustrated, and to be honest she wondered what the point was. With a look of total exhaustion, the visibly shaken mom appeared much older than her thirty-four years. She slumped back onto the step, ready to surrender. Dishrag limp, she fell into the rubble of the slow-motion avalanche falling around her. She wished she knew why things were so wrong.

As was her habit, Tina turned things around and looked for something or someone to blame. It was easier to be a victim even though she would deny that was how she felt. She couldn't imagine who would be stupid enough to choose this life. On days like this she wished she could ask John why—why did he leave her to handle all this by herself? She knew it was an accident, but he promised to be here for her. Too many people had broken that promise. What had she done to deserve it?

Tina pressed her back against the wall. Tipping her chin up, she squeezed her eyes closed and wiped the tears from her face with her slender fingers. She reached behind her head, pulled her short ponytail tighter, and took a long, deep breath. Straightening her back, she gathered herself as she stood and said loud enough to be heard through the closed door at the top of the stairs, "Penelope Esther McKenzie, *we* gave you a *beautiful* name, and I will not have any more of this nonsense. You know none of that is true. I suggest you wash your face and get ready for supper. I'll bet you have homework. When your sister and brother get home, we *will* have a family meeting."

Tina lied about words not hurting and she lied when she said she had gotten over the emotional torment she endured in middle school. Those cuts had gone deep into her heart, and she couldn't imagine *ever* being completely free of them. Penny's insecurity frustrated Tina to no end, because her little girl was smart and adorable, but Penny couldn't see that. It occurred to Tina she had felt much the same about herself when she was ten. Words couldn't fix the problem.

Tina went back down the stairs and walked into the living room. She needed to start dinner but didn't want to do anything. Some days she felt life slapping her so fast she kept her eyes closed and missed most of what happened. Eventually, the past was the only thing she could bring into focus whether she wanted to remember it or not. She looked back over the last seventeen years and the progression of horrible events. From her perspective, she was the common denominator.

All those visits to Ron's office in high school and the counseling after John's death didn't teach Tina how to stay calm when Penny got wound up. Once it was this chaotic, every muscle in her body tensed and her nerve-endings set off screaming alarms. She winced as she eased herself down into the recliner. She didn't want to give up, but she felt helpless no matter what she had learned. All she remembered to do when it hit her was to get busy with something else and stuff the things she couldn't fix into a box. She kept those memories stored away. If she never opened that box, she could keep them at bay.

Tina thought about Ron as she lowered the back of the chair. She wished he hadn't moved away. It would be so helpful to see him again, to have his help to find her strength. Her mom had found him when Tina was a teenager. Ron was a great therapist; he never took credit for what he did. She wasn't even sure *what* he did, but she realized now she hadn't appreciated it enough. She regretted that pride and shame had kept her from going back to see him when things became dangerous during her marriage to Jimmy. Tina never shared the worst things—not with *anyone*—the things she feared would get someone in trouble. Then Ron was gone, and Jimmy was gone, but then there was John.

Tina yearned for one more chance to feel the way she did when she was with John. The therapist she saw after he died called John her "knowing witness." He was also the closest thing her older children, Carson and Cathy, had to a real dad. Penny was four when her daddy died. She repeated stories like she remembered them vividly and spent a lot of time looking at the photo album they made after the accident. Tina wondered how Penny could remember that much or if she was just pretending. She was so young. She could only assume the partial memories must be confusing for Penny. She believed that had to be the cause of Penny's emotional outbursts.

After six years, Tina still ached with loneliness and she doubted it would ever get any easier. She thought maybe this was her lot: being alone and feeling lost. Her mom was right. There isn't a wand. Tina was happy her mom found peace when she and Tina's dad moved down to the coast after he retired. It was well-deserved after all the chaos. Tina knew it was wrong, but she still felt abandoned.

Tina's younger critical voice made sure she remembered every single horrible mistake she ever made. That voice kept Tina in her place. It reminded her of her guilt and shame about her older sister's accident. Years later there was the possible damage to Carson and Catherine from the abuse during her first marriage to Jimmy. Most days it seemed easiest to simply go through the motions and put the children first. She made sure their needs were met and stayed busy doing whatever was expected of a widow times two and single mother of three. It didn't matter how depressed or overwhelmed she felt.

"But that was then," she mused, "so many things have happened since *then*. And this is now. Time to get up and get busy cooking that meatloaf before Carson and Cathy get home. Mom would tell me Jesus is waiting for me to let go of my will, to give my troubles to Him. Why would He have time for me?"

5

Carson

Carson McKenzie straddled the bench of the leg press and wiped sweat from his face and neck with a towel. This was his favorite time of day at the gym. He had few distractions, not too many people had come in yet after work, and the pulsing beat of the music kept him focused. He had barely gotten warmed up when he saw the face of his phone light up. He groaned when he looked down and read the text from his mom, "Please pick up Cathy at 4:30." He wondered what happened to Cathy's ride. A quick look at his watch and he hung the towel around his neck while he fumbled through his bag for the car key.

Anyone new to the gym would assume Carson worked there since he made an effort to help others train. He fit in like a model on the cover of a bodybuilding magazine, lean and muscular with a ruddy complexion, square jaw, and deep-set green eyes. On his way out of the brightly lit gym, he pulled the hair tie from the tight ponytail on the crown of his head and shook his ginger-blonde hair loose.

He drove toward the swim club where Cathy was practicing after school with her team and felt his usual mixed feelings about being sixteen. Driving anywhere without running an errand or giving rides to one or both of his sisters was a rare event. At least Mom let him have the car most days to go to and from school, work, and the gym. It was fair enough, but he missed hanging out with his friends. Something had flipped the switch on Carson's birthday. He had waited with a demanding sense of urgency, and now he was finally in the position to start planning his future. That drive for accomplishment was growing in him, and he found ways to tackle obstacles whether they were financial or physical. He knew his initiative would pay off eventually if he didn't quit. His strength and determination came from the example his dad set for him about faith and responsibility. His friends laughed at his seriousness.

Carson felt differently about freedom than most of his friends. When he was younger, bullies took advantage of him being smaller than other boys his age. They called him a girl when they heard his middle name was Carroll. Dad got him started in gymnastics when he was eight and he had a knack for it. He was sure if he competed he would get some respect and that would stop the teasing about his size. It never mattered that he was good at it though. He had a bad fall and a serious back injury when he was twelve. His recovery required several months of rehab and pain medication. The result was major depression. Back then he felt like the world was against him. He desperately wanted to understand why his life was so messed up. He missed his dad.

Once he was stronger, Carson didn't want to feel that helplessness ever again; not like after his fall, not like that small frightened boy in elementary school, and never like his earliest memories. Now he stayed focused on his faith, his education, his strength training, and his music.

Carson searched the radio in the old Subaru as he drove along Beech Street. Too much silence was dangerous for him. He swung into the gravel parking lot of the swim club and looked around for Cathy, hoping she was ready and waiting.

"Not here *as* usual," he said under his breath and checked his watch, "4:35," he growled, wondering how he would make it back to the gym by 5:15 to train with his buddy, Jay. Jay was training for a ninja competition. Carson thought that would be an interesting thing to try, but he had to be a little older.

He spotted Cathy on the side of the clubhouse with several other team members. Carson tapped the horn and waved through the open window yelling, "Hey, Cathy, *come on.* You're gonna make me late again."

His thirteen-year-old sister ran her fingers from her forehead to the back of her head to push her wet, blonde hair from her face. The water ran down her torso, catching the afternoon sun and forming a golden outline along her slender silhouette. She turned and looked at Carson with her usual *Oh, I didn't know you were there* expression, held up one finger, and disappeared around the side of the building in the direction of the lockers. She reminded him of a cartoon superhero with her towel flapping from her shoulders, impervious to the cool air on her wet skin.

Carson looked at his watch again. "You knew I was comin' you little brat," he hissed under his breath, "this is so *typical.*" He laid his hand down on the horn and gave it a long blast. As several people turned to stare, he sank down a little into the seat, embarrassed by his own explosive impatience. He punched the steering wheel. "I can't keep doing that. *Jesus!* I need you to help me control my temper."

Cathy emerged from the side of the building and made silly faces at Carson as she bounded across the parking lot toward the car. She pulled her jacket on as she ran and dragged her waterlogged towel behind her through the gravel. As she ran, a shoe flipped off her foot. She hopped along the gravel and tried to grab it, but then dropped her bag and backpack and the contents scattered across the ground. Finally, after she gathered her belongings, she climbed into the car in a heap, rolled her eyes, and pinched up her lips. "*Oop*sie."

"*Cathy!* You are such a clown. Do you realize what a show you put on?"

"*I'm* the clown? You're the one putting on the show, *Carson*, out here blowing the horn like a crazy man, um, *boy*." Cathy returned her brother's look of disgust and flipped him a bird.

With that gesture, Carson whispered, "How mature," then shot a discreet one back at her when he reached over to turn up the music with his middle finger. He threw the car into reverse and proceeded to back out of his parking space, then pulled out of the lot with a spray of gravel. Carson thought about his reaction, "Man, why do I let her get to me? I'm an idiot. That was stupid. I should apologize."

The drive from the swim club usually took almost fifteen minutes but felt like an hour on days he and Cathy locked horns. "A Taurus and a Capricorn", he thought, "stupid astrology." Carson scowled as he wondered why his parents bought a house out on the edge of town. At least the house was close enough to things like the gym and the swim club. As he navigated the curvy hills, he checked his gas gauge to make sure his mom could make it to the clinic for work without having to stop. Pulling into the driveway on Franklin Court, he almost hit the small budding dogwood tree that, as far as he was concerned, was planted much too close to the edge of the drive—stupid tree. He felt the familiar scrape of the tailpipe on the street as he turned in. He wondered how something so annoying could still be comforting.

Cathy climbed out, barely getting her things from the floor before the car was in reverse. He stopped short and called to her, "Hey Cathy, take these to Penny for me, okay?"

Cathy leaned down and looked through the window as Carson held out a plastic zipper bag of pennies.

"There were some really old ones in the drawer at work today. . . and Cath, I'm sorry."

Cathy rolled her eyes as she reached in and snatched the bag from him, then cocked her head a little as the corners of her mouth gave an okay. He backed out to go back to the gym as she went up the walk toward the front door.

Carson relied on music to stay grounded. He chose lyrics with positive messages to help transform his old fear, sadness, and disappointment into optimism and determination. While on camping trips, John had taught him to play chords on his guitar. He'd gotten rather good over the years by practicing every day. He was serious about almost everything. He didn't want to end up like his real dad in a dead-end life or like his mom. As he saw it, she was sad, lonely, and shackled by children. He worked three afternoons a week at the music store, The Beat. It didn't pay much, but it got him out of school early and counted as his business class the last period of the day. His boss gave him great discounts and he felt appreciated there.

The emotions Carson felt were in many ways a mystery to him. He kept the fears locked away in a hidden cache protected from his conscious mind. They had grown big, and if he wasn't paying attention, they could get loose, grab him mid-stream, and yank him into a dark place. He recognized them as the colors of bruises, the sound of weeping, the smell of bourbon, and the humiliation of being teased. He could feel them when they were close to the surface. He had to stay vigilant. He had to look normal and he had to be strong. It wasn't easy. He kept all that to himself concealing his fears with a big smile and quick wit.

Carson's friends believed he'd give up his big plans and end up a stand-up comedian; they said he reminded them of Robin Williams. He didn't see that as a compliment. He saw it rather as something to avoid. What he had heard about Williams' tragic life felt too close to home. Others thought he was more like Jim Carrey. It wasn't so much what he said, but more *how* he said things and used his facial expressions to be funny. Carson knew he was a complicated young man. Comedy kept the dark shadows away.

It was important to Carson to remember Jesus was always with him. If his dad had not come into his life, he wasn't sure what it would be like. Somehow, Dad made it all make sense and he was there long enough for it to stick.

Before he got his license, Carson found time to ride around with his best friends, Kenny and Jerry Branson, who were twins and six months older than him. He shook his head when he thought about his friends and the BMW convertible their dad had given them to share for their sixteenth birthday.

Mr. Branson was an attorney with high-profile cases, often out of town. Their mom was a consultant of some kind, always either gone somewhere or on her phone or her laptop. The twins had plenty of money and unbridled freedom, yet they seemed unhappy and ungrateful, and they were always bickering.

Carson was sure they cared about each other; they were brothers, after all. They weren't so critical about little things or so quick to put each other down when they were in middle school. The winds of their teenage years had blown, and something had changed.

6
Cathy

Cathy pushed open the heavy front door and dragged the soggy towel behind her over the threshold. Her bag and backpack landed on the floor with a thud as she tossed the bag of pennies onto the table by the door.

"Hold it, Cathy! Don't go upstairs yet. I need to talk to you." Tina called as she headed from the kitchen hoping to catch Cathy before she got up to her room. "And where's Carson?" she asked as she approached the entry. She gasped when she saw the mess that had come through the door. "What in the world . . ."

"Carson went back to the gym to train with that guy. It's *Monday*, Mom." Catherine McKenzie stood in the entry. Her sweatpants and jacket hung on her wiry frame. Short, half-dried chlorine-bleached hair stuck out in every direction like straw out of a scarecrow.

Tina couldn't help but smile when she saw her middle child, even though she was a mess and sporting an attitude. This daughter of hers hadn't yet developed the ability to keep her opinions to herself, at least not the ones she felt moved to share. People who knew Cathy well were aware of her secretive side. She had a bad habit of saying things before she considered their effect, but it wasn't normally malicious. Tina knew she had a heart of gold, she was usually the first one to champion the underdog, and her determination was enviable. The things Cathy told Penny were hurtful and unacceptable, though.

"So? *What?* I'm wet and cold, Mom. Can't I go up and change and come back down in a few minutes?"

"You hold on . . . Penny's having a rough day, and I want to know what possessed you to tell her I gave her a funny name because she was a funny looking baby. *Really?* You *know* she believes things you say to her. What's wrong with you, Catherine?"

Cathy threw her head back and rolled her eyes, letting out a half-laugh, half-growl. "Give me a *break*, Mom. I was *teasing*, and besides, that little drama queen deserved it. When is she *not* having a rough time? She gets her way all the time by playing you, Mom. She's a good actress and she knows how to manipulate people to feel sorry for her and give her attention. *And* of course, you don't know what *she* did to *me*, do you? She got Bill Redding's number from my phone when I let her play a game on it, *for the last time.* She *called* him, Mom! She told him I have a crush on him *and* that I write his *name* on everything. Now he bugs me all the time at school. That is *not* okay. So maybe I'm not having such a great day either. Oh, and there's a bag of pennies on the table by the door for her from Carson."

Assuming her answer had taken care of the problem, Cathy reached down and grabbed her bag and backpack. She turned to climb the stairs and mumbled under her breath, "*whiny little brat.*" About halfway up the steps she heard a door quickly close and a click of a lock. If looks could have set that door on fire, it would have been in flames.

"I don't think I said you could go yet. You listen to me, Catherine. You're acting a bit too high and mighty. You be ready for dinner by 6:30 so we can eat as soon as Carson gets home. I want a family meeting and I want it to happen before I go to work tonight. Get your shower now so you can get your homework done before you go to bed, and don't say you don't have any. I know your exams are right around the corner."

Cathy went on up the stairs wagging her head from side to side while she silently moved her lips to mimic Tina. She wished her mother would stop reading books about how to raise children. "You sound like your *mother*, Mom," she said, loud enough to make sure Tina could hear her.

Tina's back stiffened and she felt her jaw tighten. The words "what possessed you, what's wrong with you, and high and mighty" reverberated in her mind and she thought back to the six months she and the children stayed with Carol and Jack before she and John married. It had left an indelible mark on Tina even though she was sure the children couldn't remember. If they did remember, their memories would be of how wonderful Gramma and Pop were. She thought, "Well, I guess they're right, eventually you'll turn into your mother."

When Cathy passed Penny's room, she made sure her bag banged hard against the door since she assumed her little sister had her ear to it trying to hear what was being said. She went into her room, threw her things into a heap, and stripped out of her wet clothes. Flopping onto her bed, she rolled over and examined how the late afternoon sun came through the blinds and made stripes across the contour of her body and onto the wall. She thought about taking her shower, but she decided to write in her diary first. She could hear Sheba scratching at her door, so she let her in the room when she went to get her robe and the key to unlock her diary. Sheba demanded some rubbing and scratching before she would let Cathy write. The big cat pushed the pen away, knocking it out of her hand and flipped her thick, fluffy tail in Cathy's face.

Cathy and a friend found Sheba behind the big Rhododendron on the side of the house when Cathy was six. She was tiny, white, and fuzzy. Mom said she couldn't keep her and told them to look for the owner. Cathy didn't look awfully hard, and Daddy gave in and said okay, so Mom got outvoted. They couldn't tell when she was a kitten, but she turned out to be a beautiful white Persian cat with an orange face. The closest pictures they found online said Flame Point, so that's what Cathy told people she was.

"You silly cat. What's going on, Sheba-doo? Nobody lovin' on you today, huh?" Cathy was rewarded with a roaring purr as she lovingly cuddled and scratched Sheba, finally getting her to back off so she could write to her journal she had named Jennifer. Cathy was inspired by Anne Frank and got her idea for talking to Jennifer in her diary like Anne talked to Kitty.

Dear Jennifer,

Today was SO stupid. I got in trouble at school and I didn't even do anything. Tiffany Harrison put a candy wrapper on my desk and I picked it up right when Mrs. Whitehead looked up so I got written up for it. I couldn't tell on Tiffany because she's already in trouble and I owe her for covering for me last week. Then I found out they finally scheduled the next swim meet for the second weekend of May. That screws up the plans for my birthday party but then it's a good thing too because I only need this win for district and it will be in time to qualify. Then I got home and mom jumped on me for teaching Penny the brat a lesson. I'm never letting pencil face use my phone again. I still can't believe she called

Bill Redding! This is SO MESSED UP! OMG! He is
so cute and he's wearing himself out trying to get
me to go out with him and I can't do that to Kelly
since she's liked him for so long. Maybe one day she
won't like him anymore, but I can't be the reason.
No worries though because I don't have time for
a boyfriend anyway.

I'm SO tired of getting the blame for things other
people do. I'll tell you, Jen, once I win district I'll
qualify for the Junior Olympics and I'll show them
all, and that could happen this year since I don't
have to move up after this birthday. I just have
to get my endurance up and I'll do whatever I have
to do. I know I can do it! I'm practicing like crazy
and when I'm famous people won't mess with me
anymore. I'll get more attention than Carson the
Great.

Yours Truly,

Mary Catherine the GREATEST!

After Cathy locked her diary, she admired it for a
moment. She loved the crazy cover. It was the face of a
purple monster with wild yellow eyes, jagged teeth in a red
mouth, and green letters that read "TOUCH ME AND DIE
A TERRIBLE DEATH." She flashed it at Sheba and got
no reaction, then put the key back in its hiding place under
the bottom lining of an old purse hanging in the back of
the closet. She made sure Sheba went out and headed down
the hall to take her shower. Cathy stopped for a minute
and studied herself in the bathroom mirror. She reached
up and smoothed her hair, stood up a little straighter and
tilted her chin upward with a big smile, then shrugged her
shoulders and turned on the shower. Coach Benning told
the team to see themselves on the Olympic podium every
time they looked in a mirror if they wanted to make their

dreams come true. She was supposed to practice making the future feel as though it was now.

The concept was nothing new to Cathy. She wasn't sure why she was different from her brother and sister, but she knew she was. She didn't need to depend on anyone. She didn't believe she *could* because few people could be trusted. She was determined not to set herself up for disappointment. As far as she knew, she had always felt that way. It didn't matter to her that she didn't know why. It seemed like any time someone told her they had her back they ended up breaking the deal. She knew it was stupid, but that was how it had always been. Even Mom would get tired or busy and not be able to do something she had promised to do. As much as they fought, the one person who always kept his word was Carson. No matter what, she could depend on him. He was so honest, though. She worried about sharing some things with him because she respected him and didn't want to put him in a position to have to keep her secrets. She kept a lot to herself. She planned and schemed, and if she wanted it, she usually found a way to get it on her own no matter what *it* was. She had a lot of friends, but very few of them were inside her trust circle.

When it came to swimming, Cathy's goals helped her stay excited. Once she set her sights on something, every part of her did whatever it took to get past each obstacle. Sometimes it felt like she could step out of her body and draw energy from the earth like hooking up to an electric cord to get a charge. When she jumped back into her skin, everything was different. It was like she had a laser beam pointed at whatever it was she wanted. She knew it was in her imagination, but it kept her head full of things that made her feel powerful, like the motivational videos she found on YouTube that ran constantly through her mind.

Now it was the Junior Olympics. Once she got there, she'd be looking for support to go for the Olympics.

"Well, Girl," she said, "You are going to have to step it up."

7

Penny

Penny stood at her dresser and looked at herself in the mirror. After Cathy bashed her bag against the door and went into her room, Penny ran down the stairs and grabbed her pennies. She tossed them onto her bed and returned to her mirror. The red was almost gone from her face now, and she inspected the puffiness of her eyes hoping to think of a way to keep them puffy enough for her misery to be obvious at the family meeting. She thought maybe some hot water could help. But that was over an hour away, and by then she was afraid she'd look like her usual boring self. Cathy and Carson would sit there and say, "Yes, Ma'am" to their mom and Cathy would say, "*Sorry Penny*" to her, and then things would go right back to the way they were before the meeting.

Being the baby of the family was hard. Everybody listened to Carson's music and admired his muscles and they would say, "Isn't he *great*? So *talented* and *smart*, and good-looking, too." Then they would say, "You should see Cathy swim—like a *fish!* Bet she's headed for the Olympics."

And then they would say, "Look how *cute* Penny is—so *tiny.*" She was sick of being *cute.*

Penny stuck her tongue out at herself. She sat on her stool with a handful of her thick hair pulled up to the top of her head. Turning from side to side, she covered her nose with her right hand. She imagined what she would look like when she was older, after she had gotten her new and improved nose. She would have grown by then. She could wear make-up to cover her freckles. She had already started saving all the money from birthdays, Christmases, and her lemonade stand. As soon as she was old enough, she would start a baby-sitting business and save all that, too. One day she would have enough, and she'd disappear for a week. When she got back everyone would be shocked. They would say, "Wow, look at Penny! S*he's* turned out to be the star of the McKenzie family."

She dropped her hair and turned away from the mirror, then spun around and cocked her head back, thinking her boring dishwater hair, as Cathy called it, would be much better with some color in it. Speaking in a low, soft, southern drawl, she said, "Pe-*ne*-lo-pe *Es*-ther Ma-*Ken*-zie," then she made an awful face like she had bitten into a lemon. "*Mel*-a-nie Ma-*Ken*-zie," she pinched up her lips and gagged. Then she smiled, leaned her head back, and pursed her lips as though she was throwing a kiss, "*Kris*-ten Ma-*Ken*-zie . . . Hi there, I'm Kristen," she winked a little at the mirror. When something banged hard against her door she almost fell off her stool.

"Hey, *Pencil*-face, who you talking to in there? You have some new invisible friends?" Cathy taunted from the hall.

"Go away, Cathy. Leave me alone. Stop calling me pencil-face, *fish*-face."

"*Gladly*, I can come up with something better if you really want me to, but for now Mom said to tell you to come downstairs to finish your homework so she can check it."

Penny let out a deflating exhale. She looked around her little room. Maybe that was something else she should change. Her bedroom was a home office when Mom and Daddy bought the house, but they made it into the nursery when she was born. She had a small dresser on one side of the window and her bed was along the opposite wall with her closet in the corner. Once she started school, Mom added a desk on the other side of the window and a big net up along the wall that held all her extra stuffed animals. Lots of framed things were hung on the walls. Her favorite was the one from the Bible that said "Be Still, And Know That I Am GOD," from Psalm 46. She had good stuff in her room. She decided it was probably best to keep some things the way they were. Sometimes when Penny was in bed, she pretended her glow-in-the-dark stars on the ceiling were real. She liked to think her stuffed animals in the net planned to have a party as soon as she fell asleep. She enjoyed reading books about magical toys and people, but she pretended she had outgrown all that to avoid Cathy's teasing. Penny thought it would be nice to have that magic wand Gramma said she wanted. She'd use it on Cathy.

Penny's teacher this year, Mrs. Jenkins, was also a writer. She encouraged her fifth-grade class to write at home in their free time after they finished their classwork to earn extra-credit for their Language Arts grade. There were rules, though. To get points, the story had to have good grammar and spelling with lots of adjectives so the characters and settings would come alive. Mrs. Jenkins put a big poster in the front of the classroom that said *STAR WRITERS*. Once a student's name was on the poster, they'd get a star for every complete story she accepted. When Penny got her first star, Mom put the stars on the ceiling above Penny's bed. She had seven stars on the poster now, more than anyone else. She dreamed of seeing her name as the author of a book, or at least of having some of her stories included in a book Mrs. Jenkins wanted to have published. She called it *Stories for Children by Children.*

There was also a *STAR READERS* poster, and Penny had the most stars there, too. Her favorite books were by G.M. Plessy who wrote about the adventures of a girl named Kristen Hargrove. Mom said they reminded her of books she had read that belonged to Gramma about a girl named Nancy Drew, who solved all kinds of mysteries. Penny read one of those books she found in the library, but it was too old-fashioned. She liked the books about Kristen Hargrove better.

Penny picked up her math workbook and her pencil then unlocked her door, opening it carefully in case Cathy was lurking outside. She wanted to hurry and get her home-work finished so she could look at her pennies and work on her new story. She had peeked in the bag to see that Carson had found good ones. She headed downstairs with her fingers crossed behind her back the meeting wouldn't last too long. After all, Mom had to go to work.

She was right, it was like every other meeting and Mom left thinking everything was fine. Penny resolved it was time for some changes. She knew she couldn't change her family, but she *could* change herself. She had been thinking about the things Mom said earlier. Maybe Mom was right about Bobby. If he really thought he was winning when she got upset, she was going to have to teach him a lesson. It was time to come up with a new plan.

Penny was stretched out in the sleeping bag she kept on top of her bed with her curtains closed and her light off. It wasn't very late and she was wide awake. Her mind was full of too many things that included Cathy teasing her about the bedwetting again.

After Mom left for work, Carson told Cathy to stop being a bully. He promised to come wake Penny and walk her to the bathroom before he went to bed so she wouldn't have an accident. She always slept better when someone did that for her. The accidents almost never happened anymore, but it still made it impossible for her to feel safe spending the night with friends. It was too embarrassing. She could come up with all kinds of excuses when there were slumber parties. She usually blamed allergies. Every night in her prayers she asked God to let her finally outgrow her problem like her doctor said she would.

Penny was sure Carson would find a nice wife and he would be a good dad. She didn't think he meant it when he said he didn't want to have any kids, at least she hoped he didn't. That hurt her feelings. She worried about what would happen to Cathy's children, if *she* had any.

A crack of dim light slid under her door from the hall, like a creepy fog crawling along the ground, but it was still dark enough for her to study the stars on her ceiling. Except for the faint chattering of Cathy on her phone in the next room, it was as still and quiet as a night on the mountain. She decided to pretend she was in Africa and her sister's chirping voice was a trouble-making monkey swinging in the trees.

Camping trips on weekends when her daddy didn't have to work were the memories she prayed she would have forever. Daddy knew all about the stars, about cooking on a fire, and about keeping the family safe from bears and snakes. He pretty much knew about everything. He told good stories and he sang sweet songs when he played the guitar by the campfire. More than anything, she felt safe when he said prayers with her at bedtime. Penny knew all this was true, but she couldn't quite remember things like they were real. Thinking about Daddy was more like magic. She reached up and took a framed poem from the shelf by her bed and shined her flashlight on it. It had been in her room all her life and it was written with beautiful, fancy writing. She thought for a while about how Daddy loved the stars. She imagined he was the one who put that poem in her room. It was enough to believe that.

It said:

Silently, one by one,
in the infinite meadows of Heaven,
Blossomed the Lovely Stars,
The Forget-Me-Nots of the Angels.

Henry Wadsworth Longfellow

Usually, whenever they could, they camped in Alabama up around a mountain they called Foggy Crest. One time they went to a forest in North Carolina when she was four years old. She remembered it was cold at night. Daddy put her sleeping bag right next to his with his big arm wrapped around her. He told her about the constellation Leo. It was an exciting story about a lion that terrorized the people and a strong man killed the lion with his bare hands.

When they got home, Daddy gave her a drawing that told about Leo. That drawing was one of the things she wanted for her Daddy box, but she must have been careless because it was lost, and then he was gone. She looked up Leo in the school library to learn the name of the star, Regulus. It was getting harder to remember Daddy.

The Daddy box was Penny's most valuable treasure. She got up, turned on the closet light, and tugged at the trunk in the corner. Opening it, she lifted the smaller metal box of pennies and set it aside. She picked up the worn box that once held a pair of his boots and took it to her bed.

Penny sat for a moment and stared at the box. Then she opened it to examine all her treasures with her flashlight.

There were the pictures of the wedding day with Mom and Daddy and Carson and Cathy, and the one with the judge when Daddy adopted them. She moved the one of Daddy holding her when she was born to touch her favorite picture. It was taken on Easter Sunday when she was three. She thought she must have felt like a princess wearing her new shiny white shoes with socks that had lace on them. Her dress was all pink and white ruffles. Daddy was standing behind her. Her giant stuffed troublemaking rabbit, Flop, was in her arms.

There were so many special things in the box. There was the pair of shiny gold cufflinks Mom had given him for their wedding, waiting to be worn to church with his favorite tie. She lifted his big fireman glove and held it to her face. She took a deep breath imagining it smelled like him, trying to remember. Penny memorized it as what feeling safe smelled like. Under his big glove was the folded paper he had kept in his wallet that had been his grandfather's. She took it out of the plastic bag to read it:

SIX STEPS TO MAKING A NEW START

1. Re-Discover your Genius "I can do all things through Christ which strengtheneth me."   Philippians 4:13
    a. Know What you Want
    b. Find Yourself
    c. Get Motivated

2. Understand Success "Thou wilt show me the path of life."   Psalm 16:11
    a. Do Your Best
    b. Create Positive Images
    c. Commit Yourself to God

3. Seek Opportunities "But seek ye first the kingdom of God, and His Righteousness. And all these things shall be added unto you."   Matthew 6:33
   a. Open Your Mind
   b. Develop Your Personality
   c. Discipline Yourself

4. Forget, Forgive, and Live ". . . forgetting those things which are behind, and reaching forth unto those things which are before, I press toward the mark . . ."   Philippians 3:13-14
   a. Forget the Past
   b. Forgive Yourself and Others
   c. Live TODAY

5. Cultivate Optimism "O give thanks unto the Lord; for He is good."   Psalm 136:1
   a. Don't Limit Yourself
   b. Get Outside Yourself
   c. Think HEALTH

6. Tap Into The Power of Prayer "What things soever ye desire, when ye pray, believe that ye receive them, and ye shall have them."   Mark 11:24
   a. Talk, Visualize, then Listen
   b. Remove all Barriers
   c. Believe in Miracles

She could tell it was old. It had been folded until it was about to come apart, so she was careful with it. Daddy loved to talk about Jesus. She believed she could remember him singing songs about Jesus with her. He loved his grandfather and called him Papa. He had grown up in his Papa's house.

One night last summer, when she was visiting Gramma and Pop at the beach, Gramma told her that as long as people who died were remembered, they would be with the people who loved them. This stuff Gramma said was not even close to things her Daddy had told her about going to Heaven. It didn't feel right at all. It made Penny worry about what would happen if she couldn't remember because she was too little. Would Daddy go away thinking she didn't love him? Would Daddy know her if she saw him in Heaven? Carson used to play a song about a man wanting to know if someone would know him if he saw him in Heaven. It sounded sad and it made Penny cry. Mom said crying was okay because it's your heart overflowing, and Penny shouldn't be ashamed to cry. Still, she didn't like to cry when she couldn't control it. It made her feel stupid and weak. It was so embarrassing.

When his grandfather died, Daddy thanked God for taking his Papa home so he wouldn't be sick and in pain anymore. Penny didn't remember it because she never met Daddy's Papa except when she was a baby. Carson remembered it. He would tell Penny about it if she asked. She was feeling confused. She loved and trusted Daddy *and* Gramma. Either one of them didn't know what they were talking about or one of them wasn't telling the truth. Penny couldn't imagine Daddy not telling the truth. She hoped Gramma was wrong.

There were so many things Penny didn't understand, but then there were also things she knew. People would look at her and say, "You are too little to know about that" or "You wouldn't understand." Why did people think she was stupid because she was small? It was awful to be curious and to ask questions only to be ignored. It was even worse to be called pretentious because she was *not* a show-off. At least she didn't mean to be. Penny had been called precocious, too. She didn't mind that once she looked it up and understood people thought she was smart.

Penny wished she knew what she needed to do to make people take her seriously. She thought again about the meeting after supper. As usual, everybody said they were sorry and they promised to be nicer to each other. Mom smiled and told them how much she loved them and that she was proud of them. Penny thought Mom looked sad, and she could tell she had been crying. The smile didn't match. Things needed to match. Carson took over because he had to let Mom know when he needed to have the car and it was time for an oil change. Now that he could drive, he was a car expert. Cathy butted in to complain about all the terrible and unfair things that had happened to her all day long, and of course, what she wanted to do for her 14th birthday party. All her big plans had to change because there was going to be an important swim meet that weekend.

Penny had wanted to tell Mom about the new story she was working on, but she saw it was time for Mom to go to work. She quietly turned and headed up to her room instead. No one seemed to notice. Penny hoped there would be time for her tomorrow. Mom's job at the all-night walk-in clinic seemed cool last fall, but there was nothing cool about it anymore. Summer was almost here. There were only six weeks of school left, counting this one, and she wondered how they would be able to be quiet enough for Mom to sleep all day.

Penny reached under her bed and felt around for her notebook and pencil. She pulled them up onto her lap and sat up, ready to add a few more paragraphs to her story in the beam of her flashlight. It had been a yucky day and sometimes that helped her come up with new things to write about. At least being miserable could be worth *something*. She was glad she had gotten Daddy's Papa's paper out to read. She wasn't sure what all of it meant, but it seemed to be important and she planned to study it.

Before she started writing, she inspected the ten pennies Carson brought for her. Her eyes lit up when she saw there were eight wheats and two Indian heads. She set the bag aside to be put in the penny box. Mom had promised to get her a good magnifying glass for her pennies. She had looked up pennies on the computer. There were some old ones worth a lot of money. Now that the weather was getting warm, she looked forward to going out with Daddy's metal detector. She had taken it with her to Gramma's last summer and they had found a ring on the beach about a foot down in the sand. Penny thought digging up treasure might just be more fun than writing.

At 5:15 Tuesday morning, Tina crept up the stairs avoiding the squeaky spots. When she eased Penny's door open, she smiled at the faint glow under the bed and tiptoed into the room. Penny had fallen asleep using her flashlight again and the batteries were almost dead. Tina turned it off and gently closed the notebook that had fallen to the floor. Once her eyes adjusted to the dark room, she saw John's old boot box on the foot of Penny's bed. A tightness gripped her chest. She stood frozen for several minutes while she picked at her cuticles and watched Penny sleep. Tina wondered how hard it must be for her.

After Tina slipped out the door, Penny smiled and snuggled deeper into her sleeping bag. Those last two hours of sleep were always better once she knew Mom was home.

8

North of Town April 23, 2018

The old man emerged gracefully through a hedge of blooming Rhododendron, surrounded by an other-worldly aura of peaceful clarity. His gnarled hands removed dying blossoms from the massive flowering bushes and tucked them into his frayed, baggy pockets with a deliberately gentle movement. Deep creases in the leathery skin of his face mirrored decades of exposure to the elements, yet his eyes were as clear as those of a young child. Mostly bald, with a scraggly beard hanging from his chin, his lean body appeared tall and strong, yet lost in his well-worn overalls, threadbare at the knees.

As he eased across the clearing, he stopped for a moment to study the sky. With closed eyes he lifted his face, taking in the afternoon air like a different man might inhale the bouquet of a fine wine. There was no sound beyond those where he found comfort: a few birds, the breeze whipping the tops of the trees, and the distant rush of the creek as it brought melted snow down from the northeast Alabama mountains. He opened his eyes, viewed the rolling clouds, and shook his head with a barely audible hum, then turned and silently ducked back through the hedge leaving no trace of having been there. Just before he disappeared, he looked up and whispered with a smile, "Me again Lord, Moses here, checking in—hoping maybe today you'll tell me."

9
Haywire

Step one of Penny's new plan was in effect. The paper in the Daddy box said "know what you want." For almost a week Penny had insisted on being called Kristen. Even though they thought it was silly, most everyone cooperated, except Cathy, who stubbornly *forgot* and called her Penelope instead. For pay back, Penny called Cathy Mrs. Redding. Penny spent the first few days trying out ideas. She convinced her classmates to call her Kristen by telling them the hospital had mixed up papers for two babies, and the other girl had been forced to go by Kristen when she was the real Penny. Penny didn't care if they believed her. She knew they probably didn't, but this was all part of the plan. The goal was to be interesting. Penny told her closest friends she was doing research for a book she planned to write about a baby stolen from a hospital years ago. They thought it sounded exciting. Penny found that when she said she was researching something, she felt more confident that she was respected for being smart.

She had finally turned in her new story the previous Friday with the name Kristen McKenzie as the author. Mrs. Jenkins tolerated the new name half-heartedly but called Penny's mom and openly expressed being annoyed. The weekend had dragged by. Penny hoped the papers would already be graded. This new story was different from her old ones. She was sure it would get Mrs. Jenkins' attention since it was a more mature story than her other elementary school writing. Penny was more advanced in Language Arts with a big vocabulary, and she would be moving on to Middle School in the fall. It was time for her to make a new name for herself, and not only her actual name. The idea was thrilling. She told her friends to get ready because big changes were coming.

They had obviously noticed a difference since last Monday when Bobby had won, as Mom called it. Penny went to school on Tuesday a different and more determined girl. If no one wanted to listen to her, she planned to make sure they would have to anyway. Bobby started to mess with her on Wednesday at lunch. She told him his rude games were too immature for her, so he'd better change the way he talked to her if he knew what was good for him. Then she gave him her new *I'll ruin you if you mess with me* look. She noticed a few of her girlfriends looking at each other with shocked expressions and giggling, so it must have packed a punch like she planned. She practiced the look for about an hour and tried it out on Cathy before school that morning. It wasn't a total success, but Cathy didn't laugh at Penny the way she normally did. All she said was, "Well, okay then . . ."

Of all days for Mrs. Jenkins to decide to do things differently. Moving Language to the end of the day didn't make sense to Penny at all. She tried to tell herself it wasn't a big deal—it would be okay. No matter what she said to herself, it felt like things were going terribly wrong. She hated that routine mattered so much to her. She wasn't sure how or why, but it seemed her plan was getting messed up and it made her feel crazy. This was what Gramma referred to as going haywire.

Penny asked Mrs. Jenkins about the story, but her teacher acted like she didn't see her standing there and talked to someone right over her head. Yet another disadvantage to being vertically challenged. That was her friend's polite way of calling Penny short. Penny figured Britney had read it in a joke book. Brit said one day Penny would be glad she was petite because girls get their height earlier than boys and boys like to date girls who are shorter than them. Right?

That one really cracked Penny up. What a ridiculous idea. Why would a boy care if a girl was tall? Their biggest challenge, as far as she was concerned, was being nice enough to attract any girl at all. Well, any girl with half a brain anyway. None of that mattered to Penny because having a boyfriend was on the bottom of her list. "Once I have a boyfriend, he'd better appreciate me and treat me with respect." Penny chuckled to herself when she thought about all the things she learned watching Lifetime movies to get ideas for her stories even though she wasn't supposed to watch them.

Mrs. Jenkins picked up the stack of papers on her desk that she had graded over the weekend. "Something is wrong with Mrs. Jenkins! She's doing something *else* at a different time? We don't get our papers until we have Language Arts. Why now? Why before recess?" Penny's mind was racing with confusion and she was getting one of those feelings that always seemed to come before something bad happened. She had no idea why things were being changed up, but she was relieved at the same time. "At least I won't have to wait until the end of the day to get my star."

First, Mrs. Jenkins handed out some random things that had been done for make-up work. Then a few people had turned in late assignments and she had graded those, too. Penny watched, shivering with anticipation, as her teacher started moving around the room to three or four other students who had written stories, giving smiles and nods to each one. As she came to Penny's desk, she stood very still looking down at her with a serious expression, holding the last of the papers up against her.

Penny felt a chill run up her back and neck that lit a fire in the back of her head when her story was laid face down on her desk. She stared apprehensively at the paper.

"Kristen, I'd like to have a word with you while the others are outside at recess, please."

Penny nodded, looking down. Her stomach was doing flip-flops. With trembling fingers she turned her paper over. There was no grade. No star. She turned the page. *Nothing!* Not a mark on it at all. She wasn't sure what to think. She felt her face getting hot. She tried to pretend no big deal by turning the paper back over and reaching into her desk for her writing notebook. Maybe it would look like a planned meeting. Mrs. Jenkins was telling the class to go on out without her and join Mrs. Crabtree's class for recess. Penny wasn't sure where it was coming from, but this all felt horribly familiar and she was starting to feel sick. Then, as the last student was out the door, Mrs. Jenkins turned to her.

"I didn't look at your story until about 8:00 last night. I wasn't sure of your mother's schedule and I didn't want to upset her at work or keep her from sleeping. I decided to speak with you first."

Someone tapped on the door. Mrs. Jenkins opened it and greeted a man Penny had never seen before.

"Kristen, I've asked Mr. Quintana to join us. He came over a week ago from Riverside Middle to work at Culver and will stay for the next five weeks until the end of the year. He's the Guidance Counselor for sixth graders at Riverside and he wants to get to know some of the fifth graders who will be there next year. He's only here today so you will know who he is. He's the person available for any students who may need to speak with someone."

Tears filled Penny's eyes. What had she done? Why did they think she needed help? She couldn't speak. She was so embarrassed, and angry, and totally confused. She felt like she might throw up. She covered her face with her hands, not wanting to see their faces or for them to see how unable she was to control her tears.

Muffled by her hands, she quietly asked, "What did I do wrong? I don't understand. I'm not failing. Do you think I'm crazy?"

With that question Mrs. Jenkins' expression softened. She put her hand on Penny's shoulder and squatted down to be eye-level with her. "No, sweetheart, your grades are great, and you aren't crazy. You haven't done anything wrong. Why, you are one of my best students. But this story you turned in is quite different from your usual work, and it's, well . . . very dark. I've noticed changes in your behavior lately, and the name change thing . . . um, it's getting a bit out of hand." Mrs. Jenkins struggled to find the right words.

"I also know you are growing up with a single mother who works at night, and your father has been gone six years now. Don't you remember? Your brother was in my class when I taught fourth grade. These are the things I've shared with Mr. Quintana. I want you to know you don't have to go through things alone. He's an excellent guidance counselor. I've known him for a long time, and I'm thrilled he'll be there for you at Riverside."

Penny looked at Mr. Quintana. He seemed okay, but there was no way she was going to tell him anything about how she felt. No way at all! He was a stranger. He sat there and listened. He did look like he was interested, but she didn't know him. She couldn't imagine how he and Mrs. Jenkins were friends. He wasn't nearly as old as her. The name Quintana confused Penny, too. It sounded Hispanic. She thought Hispanic people had dark hair like Maria in her class, but he had light hair and blue eyes. That was just one more thing that didn't make sense.

Penny was embarrassed and ashamed for thinking her story was good. Maybe Mrs. Jenkins was upset because she had arranged for her sister to die in the story, but it was totally accidental; or maybe because it looked like her brother had been set up to be arrested for murder. What was so wrong with that? It was fiction, after all.

Then it dawned on her that Mrs. Jenkins would want to talk to her mom. Mom would never understand, and she was already stressed out and upset about too many other things. Penny was afraid she would end up being sent back to talk to that terrible counselor lady she had to go see after her daddy died.

Penny's thoughts were getting jumbled and there was still another hour and a half before she could leave. This was supposed to be her new and improved life? Maybe Cathy was right. Maybe she was too stupid to go to middle school. This was all one big disaster. She realized Mr. Quintana was politely telling her it was nice to meet her, and he was going back to his office, but if there was anything . . . blah blah . . . just to talk . . . blah blah . . . come by . . . She was still trying to sort out what had happened when she heard her classmates lining up to come inside.

The humiliation was banging in her head from a memory that was emerging from the fog. There it was. It was how she had felt when she wet her pants in first grade when she had waited too long. She had tried with all her might to hold it, but it had started to seep out. Her pee had filled her pants and her seat. It had flowed down her legs and into her socks and shoes. It had gone down the legs of her desk and had formed a puddle under it. Kids had whispered to each other, and Gary had said, "Hey Penny, I think something in your desk spilled." Then, when he realized what it was, he had turned bright red. The rest of the class had to go out while Miss Spencer called her mom to bring clothes. They had to get the janitor with his bucket to come mop up the mess. The memory was so vivid it was like she could smell the urine, and then the Lysol in the bucket.

There were kids in her class *now* who were in her class then. Bobby had teased her and had called her Pee-pee-penny, pretending to be stuttering. If new rumors started now, it would be enough to destroy anyone thinking she could *ever* be taken seriously or become an important professional writer.

Her confidence was zapped in forty-five minutes while she sat at her desk and relived one of the worst days of her whole life. She grabbed her book and started reading. She hoped her classmates would believe she stayed in because she hadn't been feeling well. She didn't know which upset her most: being kept inside because of her story or remembering first grade.

She realized she needed a different plan since this had all gone totally wrong. She couldn't stop worrying about the possibility of gossip. She wouldn't be surprised if Bobby was to start it. They could tell she had been crying. She had to sit there and wait. And when it was time to go, she would head straight out to her bike. Thank goodness she rode her bike today.

Penny felt her face burning and she knew it was red. She gripped the straps of her backpack and gagged the scream she held inside as the pressure moved up her neck, through her throat, and into her forehead. It took every bit of her strength to hold back her tears. Eighteen pairs of eyes penetrated her. It was torture. She imagined them looking at each other with puzzled expressions. Why had she been kept inside? What had she done for Mrs. Jenkins to think she needed help? How could her teacher have done this to her? It rivaled the shame and humiliation she had felt when she was six.

She stared at the clock in the front of the classroom. Every tick of the second hand made a thud in her brain. The wait was excruciating. A fuse had been lit. If she didn't get out fast enough her head was going to explode. She looked at the door and pictured the flood of students into the hall. She couldn't bear the thought of having to talk to anyone. She needed to be the first one out of the room—the first one to get to the bikes. She needed time to make sense of everything she was feeling. Beyond getting on her bike, she had no plan; just go, go fast, fast and far.

The bell rang and Penny was already moving toward the door. She dashed out and took off running, thankful her classroom was near the end of the hall. She was so focused on the grey and white linoleum squares of the hallway floor she almost ran head-first into the door of the next room as it opened in front of her. She shoved her way past other kids, out the double doors and down the brick steps. Her teacher's voice echoed in her head as she fumbled with her lock and pulled the chain from the frame of her bike.

"Penny, wait!"

She heard Brit calling to her, but there was *no* way she was going to hang around and talk to her. Not today. Brit wouldn't understand. *She* didn't understand, so how could she expect anyone else to? They would think she was being stupid, and maybe she was, but that wouldn't stop the tears that were already pouring down her cheeks. It was one of those times she couldn't tell herself anything. That part of her brain wouldn't listen when she was this upset. She needed to go where she could think.

As she looked up at the blurry sky, she saw the clouds were dark and rolling. The air felt heavy. She reached to grab her jacket, but in her mind's eye she saw it on the back of the chair at her desk where she had left it. "Perfect," she whispered to herself, "just perfect." She wasn't sure where she was headed, but it *wasn't* home. She threw her backpack into her basket and yanked her bike out of the rack.

"Penny! Stop!" Brit was right behind her.

"Get out of my way, Brit, I can't talk now!" She pushed her way past, stepping through and onto the pedal.

"But Penny . . ."

She rode away.

10

Missing

At 3:45, Tina looked up the number for Carver Elementary School. It wasn't like Penny to be this late getting home. When she rode her bike, she was usually home by 3:15, and it looked like it was going to rain soon. The bus had just come by. She checked with a few children who rode the bus, but they only knew she went out to her bike. The office said Mrs. Jenkins had already left for the day. Tina called her number and left a message.

A gnawing fear was growing in Tina. It was one of those unexplainable feelings that something was wrong. She looked at her watch again, but it had only been a few minutes. "It isn't that late. She's gotten sidetracked. Typical Penny. She was probably daydreaming, planning another story. She'll come through the door any minute now."

Still, Tina couldn't shake the worry. A horrible old feeling was taking over as her mind raced and nothing felt real. It had been a long time since she felt this way. No matter how desperately she tried, she couldn't rationalize

THE SCENT OF SAFETY

the situation. She was getting chills and felt numb. Her head was spinning . . . it was hard to get a deep breath.

"I know what this is. It's only panic. Why now? This is crazy. Is this different?" She noticed pain in her chest and her jaw, down her left arm. "Surely I'm not having a heart attack," her mind reeled. It was hard to tell what was real. She went to the couch and stretched out flat, then attempted to focus on her breathing. She had to stop hyperventilating. "I'm not letting this happen. This makes no sense. What could have triggered this? I can handle this. I have to breathe." It felt like the couch was moving under her.

As she took slow, deep breaths, Tina tried to remember how she was taught to manage panic attacks. It had worked for her panic after the fire, but would it work for this? She wasn't sure, but there was no reason why it wouldn't. It had been several years since she had a bad one. The woman who had taught her to manage them told her she could do this alone if she had to. She needed to get back in control. "Lord, I need you to help me remember. I need you to help me handle this . . . think, Tina, think."

She remembered she was supposed to speak out loud—to get her bearings—and she needed to tap on the side of her hand. There were other places she should tap but she couldn't focus enough to remember. The side of her hand would have to do. "I'm thirty-four years old. This is 2018. I'm at my house, on my couch, breathing. Oh, that's right, breathe in, hold, and take longer to breathe out and count in my mind . . . in 2-3-4-5-hold-2-3-4-out-2-3-4-5-6-7-8 okay . . . that feels right." Tina noticed as she tapped on her hand and focused on her breathing, she began to feel calmer. Maybe this was all she needed to do.

She stayed still with her eyes closed, breathing. Things were popping into her mind. "I don't want to think about this stuff. Damn! I don't want to remember this, but I can see what was happening. It isn't happening now. It looks like it is, but that's just an image from my memory. I don't want to remember this . . . why can't I stop it? Tell myself! I'm safe here now. It's only a memory. Breathe, Tina!" It was like she was standing outside the window looking in. She could see herself at twenty-two. "Jimmy is drunk, and he is hurting me . . . no, I'm here, he's hurting *her, the younger me!*" she pushed her fingernails into her palms, trying to stay separate from the memory that was feeling all too real. "I'm not there. I'm only watching. I can freeze the action and go inside. She's terrified and she doesn't understand. I can talk to my younger self. I can tell her I am her, but I'm thirty-four, and she needs to know she did her best . . . even if her best wasn't enough then . . . '*you did the best you could.*' She needs to know that was the last time. The children are fine. They don't have to hide in the closet anymore. Show her the children, sixteen and almost fourteen, and they are *fine*. Thank her . . . 'thank you for always warning me, but you don't have to anymore. I'm taking care of the babies.' Let her see the police come. Let her see the paramedic."

The therapist had explained how the brain gets confused about memories and real time. If the memories are vivid, they show up on the visual cortex like they are happening, and things like smells that are imprinted from the event can easily trigger it. The smells go straight to that part of the brain that scans for danger. That's why she bought the lotion she liked to use. Whatever it was, it left her feeling calm and safe.

Tina kept on with what she remembered. These were things she and her therapist tackled before she quit going to see her. The woman she had seen was known as a bit of a renegade back then and wasn't around anymore. Tina knew she needed to find someone else. She sat up slowly, kept her distance from the scene, and felt grateful she could be present and think about what had happened twelve years ago. She wanted to see if she could look at it from a fresh perspective adding all she had learned over the years. Miraculously, the sense of desperation and panic had lessened. She wanted to release even more, but now wasn't the time. She was hungry for freedom from it. She looked at her watch. It felt like she had spent hours, but it had only been minutes.

Tina froze for a moment when there was a knock at the door. It was a knock like the one that dreadful night. Even though panic was right there, she had made her way successfully back to today and she refused to give it power. She ran to the door and jerked it open, still foggy. It was her next-door neighbor, Sheila, Jeremy's mom.

"Jeremy heard you were looking for Penny. He told me Penny looked really upset about something when she ran out to her bike. When she left the school she went up toward Jackson Road instead of heading home. What's going on? Is there anything I can do?"

"Jackson Road? Why in the world? Thank you, Sheila. That's got to be important. I'll let you know. It's not so late yet. I need to get Carson to bring the car home. Thank you. I'll call if the situation changes. Thank Jeremy for me, okay?"

Tina had to think. She needed her car, but she didn't want to leave the house. She grabbed the phone to call the gym. She knew Carson wouldn't want to answer. She told herself to hold it together. Pacing in the kitchen, she asked the girl at the desk to tell Carson he needed to come home right away. She went out on the deck and looked at the sky. She was grateful there had been no thunder and the rain that was starting to fall was light. She told herself Penny stopped to get out of the rain. Hopefully, she had her poncho in the basket of her bike. Penny had been acting strange for the past week. Tina had no idea what was going on with her lately.

The phone rang.

"Hello?"

"Tina, this is Rita Jenkins. I just listened to your message. I saw Penny getting her bike, but I wasn't watching when she left. I talked with her during recess about the Kristen thing and about her recent behavior, and her most recent story that was . . . well, let's just say it was *different*. There's no question she was upset, but I thought she had calmed down before she left. What's happened?"

"It's not like her to be this late getting home, especially when the weather's bad. She's been upset so often lately. Is there anyone you can think of she might have talked to?"

"I can't think of anyone, except maybe Natalie Cross, the new girl who sits next to her."

"Well, Penny's never mentioned her. I hope she's just gotten sidetracked. Thanks for calling back."

As she was looking for the class directory and debating calling the police, the front door burst open.

"What's wrong, Mom? Why didn't you call me instead of the gym?"

Cathy had just been dropped off about the same time Carson parked the car. As she followed Carson through the door she exclaimed with confusion in her voice, "Why are you home, Carson? What the heck is going on? You could have picked me up!"

"Penny is missing." Tina said flatly.

"Missing?" they asked in unison.

"How could she be missing? *Really* Mom? Get a grip. It's only 4:15." Carson gave Cathy a sharp look for her remark.

"She rode her bike to school, she was upset when she left there at 3:00, she went the opposite direction instead of heading home, it's raining, and it'll be dark in a few hours. That's all I've been able to find out," Tina's voice was robotic. Her brain was mush and she wasn't sure what to do next. She knew she should call the police.

"Here we go! She knows I'm planning my party and she's starting drama to ruin it."

"Cathy! How dare you be so *selfish*." Tina was fed up with the feud between Cathy and Penny. It amazed Tina how, with all her talent and confidence, there was that side of Cathy that saw herself as the victim when something had nothing to do with her. "This is your little sister we're talking about. *Really?* How ridiculous! Your party is almost two weeks away. You can act like part of this family or you can go pout in your room, but you will *not* complain about being inconvenienced when we don't know where she is or if she's okay. It's not all about you."

"Right! Drama Queen strikes again. Let's all freak out and buy into her chaos."

"That's enough! Go upstairs. I can't even look at you right now."

Cathy waved her hands in the air and stomped up the stairs. "Damn, Mom, she's probably hiding somewhere so she'll get special attention."

"You watch your mouth, Mary Catherine."

Tina felt fear and rage crowding into the emptiness that was there only moments ago, and there was that shaking again. She had to stay focused. She was here, now. She wasn't waiting for Jimmy to come home. "Oh, God it's been a long time since I've been thrown back there," she thought. She wasn't waiting to hear from John after the fire, either. She was needing help to find her ten-year-old baby. She looked around and realized Carson had disappeared. She stared at the phone. "This time it's different," she said, convincing herself, "this time *I'm* calling them."

11

Galaxy Drive

Penny loved to ride her bike. She was grateful she got such a good one for Christmas; one with enough speeds to go up steep hills. She could go so fast coasting down Jackson Road that she could pretend she was flying, which always made her feel happy inside. It was exactly what she needed today; so that's where she headed. The wind whipped her hair and made it spin behind her head. The cool air felt good on her face. It helped take away the sting her tears had left on her cheeks. For a moment, today hadn't happened. She turned in the opposite direction from the way home, pumped the pedals hard and gripped her handlebars as she took some hilly and curvy roads on the edge of town in the direction of the mountains.

Galaxy Drive—where no one would think to look for her. Penny made a quick left turn. She had seen it one day last summer when Kenny gave Carson and her a ride to somewhere. It sounded like a wonderful place. Finally, she found it again one Saturday while she was out exploring on her bike when her mom thought she was riding around the neighborhood. She claimed it that day as her thinking spot. Only one person had been invited to go there with her and it was for a special occasion.

Sally Greene had been her best friend for as long as she could remember. Sally's dad had gotten a job in Washington and she had to move away. A few days before they left last August, Penny took Sally there for a farewell picnic. They still wrote letters even though everyone else used phones to text. Mom said Penny wasn't old enough to have her own phone yet. They wrote about Penny's visits to the *other galaxy*, and about what it was like to live in Washington.

Galaxy Drive was a curvy road that looked like it was ready for houses except for the overgrown bushes and weeds. There were driveways and curbs, and in some places there were even sidewalks; but no one lived there to walk on them. You could tell there were markers where other streets turned off with little curbs and sidewalks but no street names. To Penny it felt like a magical place. Penny pretended the houses were there but they belonged to another galaxy so earth people couldn't see them. She wondered at first if maybe she was the only one who could see this place since she never saw anyone else there; but Sally could see it. It was odd to Penny that she never felt alone. She believed the aliens must like her because twice there had been a fresh apple where she usually sat, like a gift letting her know she was welcome and expected. Either they could see her, or they knew when she was going to be there.

Penny pulled her bike into a clearing behind a large clump of bushes and ran to her thinking spot. After sitting for several minutes, she decided it wasn't enough for today's problem. She stood at the top of the steep hill and looked down through the woods. The thick clouds made it dark and scary under the trees even though there were nearly three hours of daylight left. It was nothing like the first bright July morning when she had been exploring. It didn't matter. She felt like she needed to go to the vine house again and hope for an idea to fix her messed up plan. The idea for her first story came to her there. It wasn't that far, and she knew the way. There would be time to get back to her bike and ride home. It felt like a reasonable plan at the time.

Once she got to the vine house, Penny believed she would be able to make her mind slow down, stop feeling crazy, and think of a solution. It wasn't really a house, but it looked like maybe it was a long time ago. Vines had climbed all over it and it was more like an odd-shaped room with living walls. When she went behind the wall the ground was level like a floor. There were open spaces in the wall that looked like they might have been windows at one time. It was so beautiful and magical, and there were even flowers growing there that smelled nice. She imagined it was like a hidden fairy tale cottage in the woods, but the witch was gone and instead of being scary it was calming.

A light rain was beginning to fall, but she couldn't let that stop her. There hadn't been any thunder and it wasn't blowing like it was about to storm. She scrambled through the bushes sliding a little on the slippery clay. She worked her way down the hill looking for the first apple tree. Once she found it, she would have to face the creek down below her and turn to the right until she came to the second apple tree. Where she needed to cross the creek was straight down from there, then back up the hill to the vine house.

12
Looking for Clues

Tina was waiting for someone to come from the police department. The dispatcher said it would only be a few minutes. She heard an argument starting upstairs and it sounded like it was coming from Penny's room.

"Hey, what's going on? What are y'all doing up there?" Tina saw a flash that looked like Cathy storming out headed toward her room as Sheba shot down the stairs.

"Maybe you should ask Carson the Great. He's digging through Penny's writing stuff like there's some great mystery to solve."

Tina had decided to stay home by the phone and wait to speak with the police and to have Carson drive around the area. She called up the stairs to Carson and asked him to come down. He emerged from the doorway with a pile of papers and letters in his hands and loped down the steps.

"Carson, I need you to go drive anywhere you can think of and call if you see her or her bike or anything, okay? I'll be here in case she calls or gets home. The police will be looking. I've called. They're on the way."

"But Mom, look at all this. I think there might be somethin' important in all this, and the letters from Sally are here."

"Leave it. I'll look through her writing. I need your eyes out there. It's getting dark soon."

"It's gonna be okay, Mom, we'll find her. Pray and ask Jesus to keep her safe and to take your fear so you can stay calm," Carson sounded like he was trying to convince her, but Tina could hear the fear in his voice. He was calling Jerry as he left. He hadn't been gone five minutes when there was a knock at the door.

Tina had managed to get focused and was prepared for the police. This was going to be okay. She had gathered things of Penny's in case they had a dog. She had pictures that weren't too old, but most of them were in her phone and they could be shared.

The officers were nice; but she felt like they really weren't as worried about a missing child as they should be. "Officers, aren't the first few hours the most important?" Tina asked.

They smiled and looked quickly at each other. "Yes, Ma'am. This is Detective Robbins, and I'm Sgt. Davis. Of course, Ma'am, every minute is important when we're looking for a missing person, especially a child. I think you've heard about the first hours when there's been a kidnapping. Have you received any kind of a call? Anything going on you didn't tell the dispatcher, or is it possible someone else, like her father or some other family member or friend, may have picked her up?"

"Oh! No, no calls. Her father is deceased. There are no shady characters in our life wanting to steal her from me, not that we *know* anyway, if that's what you're asking. She's got a big imagination and she daydreams, but she *always* comes home. She would never accept a ride with anyone unless she knew I sent them. We have a word we use to let each other know."

"I'm sorry Mrs. McKenzie. Your husband was John McKenzie?"

Tina nodded.

"We don't mean any disrespect; these are things we have to ask so we can rule them out. I knew John. He was a fine man. Such a tragedy. We already issued a BOLO." The detective must have seen Tina's confused look. He added, "That alert means be on the lookout and it goes to all patrol cars. We need photos and a description of her bike. I see you have those ready for us. We need to know what she was wearing when she left for school, and anything else you can tell us about her habits so we can find her."

Tina described Penny's emoji backpack and the clothes she had worn that morning. She told them what Jeremy said about her heading toward Jackson Road and shared the photos. She even had one of Penny on the blue bike she had gotten for Christmas. The officers sent the pictures from her phone to the station and the other patrol cars. Tina stood alone in the doorway after they left with her arms wrapped around herself. She felt alone on a raft in a sea of black ink. No word from Carson. It was almost dark.

Her mind went back again to that early morning twelve years before. That memory had startled her. She wanted to be able to think about it and really put it to rest. What she had managed to handle today was amazing, but she knew there was more. She knew she needed the right kind of help to do it for good. Tina made a resolution that when this was over, when Penny was home, Tina would do what she should have done a long time ago and find a good therapist. She stared at the phone.

She thought about Carson, the big brother, out there looking for Penny. She saw him at just four in his footie pajamas, putting the big pillow out for Cathy, his baby sister, and lowering the side of her crib so she could climb out. On that horrible night she had finally gotten them calmed down by letting Cathy sleep in with him. He had his arms around her whispering to her it was okay. Tina had made her way back to the recliner that dreadful night, had waited and dozed, unable to really sleep, until the knock at the door at 4:00 a.m.

As she remembered things she had locked away, she was relieved she was able to stay in the present, waiting to hear from the police. She jumped when she felt a hand touch her shoulder. She turned to see Cathy's red-rimmed eyes pleading for forgiveness.

"I have the perfect thing for you to do to help. First, go feed Sheba. I never fed her this afternoon. Then come help me look through all this stuff Carson brought down from Penny's room. Maybe we can figure out where she went." Cathy grabbed her mom and hugged her, then ran to the kitchen while Tina headed to the sofa to sort the papers until Cathy joined her.

"You start looking, Cathy, I have one more very important call I need to make."

Tina took a deep breath as she listened to the ringing phone, waiting for an answer.

"Hello?"

"Mom? I'm so sorry . . ." Immediately sobbing, Tina shared her fear with her mother, but it was much more than that. Filled with compassion, she needed her mother to know she was aware of what her parents had gone through when they lost Karen, Tina's older sister. Then years later, waiting for calls to know if Tina was safe. Finally, she realized how much her mother had suffered and how much her parents must love her. Now she was asking for prayers and emotional support. Then the phone beeped, and she had to hang up to answer the call.

"Hello?"

"Mom, have you heard anything?" Carson sounded frustrated.

"No, I was hoping you had. I was talking to Gramma."

"Nothing. No sign of her. I really don't know where to look. I haven't been able to get in touch with Kenny and Jerry and I'm sort of at a loss. It's almost dark. Penny really doesn't have anywhere she hangs out. I mean, she's in elementary school, after all. I'm just drivin' around wastin' gas."

"Come home. You're right. Driving around is like looking for a needle in a haystack. I've given all her information to the police. We'll go through these letters together and wait here to hear from them."

Tina went back to the couch to join Cathy wondering what else there was, if anything, she could do. She was doing her best to act as if she knew things would be fine.

13

Hope

Tina and Cathy were digging through Penny's papers they had spread out on the coffee table. Cathy was shaking her head about all the stories and ideas for stories that really had nothing to do with any place Penny may have gone. "Mom, do you have any idea where pencil-face keeps her diary?"

"Cathy! Do me a favor and drop the nickname! You're right though, her diary makes a lot more sense than these stories. I'm not sure where she keeps it. I don't remember seeing it for a while. You go look." Cathy apologized for the name calling, admitted it was a bad habit, and headed up the stairs to Penny's room.

Tina was trying to read Sally's writing when Carson came through the door.

He didn't have to ask any questions. He could tell from his mom's strained expression there was no news and he probably should stay quiet. He went over and gave Tina a little hug, then sat down and picked up a handful of letters. He looked at the postmarks and decided to sort them by date. Once he found the oldest one from the end of August, Carson opened it. The first thing that caught his eye was a number.

"Mom, it's Sally's phone number!"

"Thank God! I had it right after they moved, but that was before I had to replace my phone and lost all my contacts. I can't believe I didn't think to look for it in the letters!"

Tina picked up the phone, then hung up and grabbed her cell in case the police called. She entered the number. It was ringing.

"Hello?"

"Beverly? Oh, thank God! This is Tina McKenzie. Penny's missing and I'm hoping, if anyone in the world knows where she may have gone, it would be Sally. Is she home?"

"Oh my God, Tina! No, she's not here, she's with a friend. They've gone to the library to work on a project for school. I'm not even sure which library because she went with a friend. I'll find her. I'll be praying. Don't give up. I'll call you the minute I get her. Is this the best number?"

Tina thanked Beverly and gave her the house number. She hung up and quickly added Beverly Greene to her contact information.

"She has to go find her. She'll call as soon as she has her. Good Lord, Carson, I could never live somewhere so big that I didn't know which library my child had gone to."

"That's great, though, Mom. I think were gonna find out where she is. Sally will know. They're gonna find her. I just *know* it! I think there's still some chili in there, want me to heat it up?"

"I can't eat. You and Cathy have some."

Tina walked outside and stood on the deck, pulling her collar up around her neck. It had stopped raining and things were beginning to dry up. Even though she was cold with worry, it really wasn't any cooler. She realized it must not have been a cold front. That made sense—no lightning and thunder. She felt a little better and laughed at herself for thinking about the causes of lightning. Seeing the stars peeking from behind the clouds comforted her. At least it wasn't the first night of a spring freeze. Tina was haunted with questions about what could have made Penny run away, if that was what had happened. She wondered if it was something she had said or done. "Where are you, Penny? What was so terrible that you wouldn't come home? Or has someone taken you . . ."

Whenever Tina was on the deck she thought about John. Building the deck had made her feel useful and capable. Those were feelings she hadn't felt since middle school when her sister died. John was always telling her she was special, but it was hard to believe that could be true after making so many mistakes. There was another barrage of memories; this time she was waiting for John to come home from the fire.

At her children's urging, she came back inside and sat in the recliner, with Sheba giving her gentle comforting nudges. Tina wondered why it was taking so long for Beverly to find Sally. When the detective called to tell Tina they had organized a group of volunteers to start a search, she filled him in on hopefully getting information from Penny's friend. Now they could only hope, pray, and wait.

14
The Creek

Penny picked her way down to the bottom of the hill through the slippery, clay-coated rocks and bushes, searching for her best route. She looked for a good place to cross. She knew she was in the right area because she had found both apple trees. Now to cross and go uphill to the vine house. There was so much more water in the creek than there had been last summer or in the fall when she'd come to sit and write. She loved the leaves falling around her; they made a comfortable, natural blanket on the hillside.

She knew the creek wasn't very deep, but it was wider than she remembered. The water looked dark and it was moving much faster than she had ever seen it flow. Right where the creek was narrowest, she spotted a good size rock, nice and flat. It was just above the surface of the stream and only about two feet from the bank; then there was another one not too far from it. She thought she should be able to jump easily from the second one to the bank on the other side. It looked like the perfect place.

Penny counted to three, then held her breath and jumped onto the first flat rock. Right away she felt it start to lean. She shifted her weight to try to get it to stay flat, then looked back at the spot on the bank she had left. In a moment of panic she thought she should try to go back. The darkness made it impossible to see the hole that had been dug out by the flowing water in front of the rock. It was wobblier and much slipperier than she had imagined, and she waved her arms around like a tight-rope walker at the circus.

Before she could ready herself to jump to the second rock, the one she was balancing on tilted over. Down she slid, straight into the cold, rushing water. Grasping for something to hold onto, she reached for the big rock to pull herself up. Instead, it gave way and dropped the rest of the way down onto her foot.

Penny shrieked as she felt the crushing blow to her ankle. No matter how she tried, she couldn't move the rock. She was trapped. It was way too heavy. She was facing upstream with the water to her chest and she didn't dare let go. Her hands slid on the rock and she fell back too far. The water rushed onto her face. She grabbed again for the rock and got her grip. She lifted her head up, gasping and coughing. The rain was falling steadily now. The clouds were thick. Dusk was quickly looking like night and the woods had gotten darker. Penny tried to see, but everything was a blur. She was wet and freezing and in terrible pain. She wanted to lean back to take pressure off her foot, but she didn't dare. That rock was the only thing keeping her from drowning. No matter how bad it hurt her foot, she had to hold on. She wasn't sure how long she could keep it up. Her fingers were numb and burning.

Penny screamed for what felt like forever, but it was pointless—she was alone in the woods. She had never been so afraid. By now her mom would be looking for her, but how would they ever find her? Shame washed over her. She felt so stupid for thinking how cool it was to have a secret place to go. She had been careful to make sure no one knew about it, and now she could see how dangerous secrets could be.

No matter how much she hated crying, one unnoticeable tear after another seeped from her eyes and blended with the rain that continued to fall on her face. Nothing mattered anymore. If they never found her, she would die there. If they did, everybody would know the truth about her. Either way, this was proof she wasn't who she wanted people to think she was. She needed a miracle. She closed her eyes and could see Daddy's Papa's paper. "Tap into the power of prayer . . . believe in miracles."

She looked up sobbing and shaking, and whispered to herself, her teeth chattering, "I know you're looking down on me Daddy. Please get somebody to come, Daddy, I'm so cold. I don't want to die!" Her body was shaking as she prayed to God, to the angels, and to Jesus for someone to find her. "Jesus, please send someone to help me, I promise I'll never do anything this stupid again."

15
The Flash

Moses had made his way over about a square mile of his territory in the morning hours. It felt good to work in the early spring warmth after a long cold winter. He made himself a lunch of jerky and berries with some bread and cheese he had brought up from his shed and stored in the natural cooler dug into the side of one of his many cave-like shelters. After thanking the Lord, he ate and stretched out in his hammock to read for a while by the light of the old window he had built into the overhang behind the bushes.

Heavy clouds were building and there wasn't quite enough light for reading without lighting a lantern. He was feeling a little sleepy, and since he never took the chance of falling asleep with any kind of fire burning, he decided a walk would wake him up. He thought maybe it was about time to head down to Red's and play a game of checkers with Hank. Just before he went to step outside, he heard the sudden spatter of rain falling on the window. "Waited too long I guess," he said. "Maybe I'll lie here and rest my eyes a bit 'til it blows over and see who comes walking through my mind." These were the times he waited for. The rain and the smell of the ozone lifted his mood, made the air feel and smell clean and fresh, and opened his mind as though it was anticipating an unknown guest. "Maybe today," he hummed, "maybe today." Then he smiled as he closed his eyes, allowed himself to let go and fell into a deep sleep.

In his dream he was floating, drifting like he was on a boat, or maybe a raft. Then, he was lifted onto a limb near the top of a tree looking down over a glorious garden of fruit and flowers. The smell of it was vaguely familiar. He searched his memory for the smell. It was a calm scent, and it was loving and safe. Yes, it smelled very safe. And it was a smooth, soft, lavender blue. He drifted as though he was being carried inside a blue light. He felt peaceful, but at the same time, excited. He watched from above, safe inside the bubble, and saw himself walking down a steep path. Then he was in a long hallway with tall shelves on either side.

At first, he thought it was a library, but the shelves held pictures instead of books. It was more like a gallery. He had been shown this place before. The pictures on the lower shelves were of people and places he knew. As he peered at each one, they grew deep, like doors opening for him to go through them into another world. When he looked up, he couldn't quite make out the images on the higher shelves, but it was urgent for him to see them. There was a ladder a long way down the hall and he felt himself being pulled toward it. No matter how he tried to reach it, it didn't get closer. He kept going until he was going downward, and cold rushing water had come up from underneath, lifting him. The blue light surrounding him was bobbing in a current, moving slowly toward his goal. When he finally got to the ladder, he found himself in cold water to his neck. He felt a crushing pain in his foot and his hands felt like they were on fire. The rain was coming down in torrents. There was a low rumble followed by a blinding flash of lightning. All the pictures were either floating away or they were blurry—all except one that was clear and bright in the light of the flash.

He grabbed for the portrait with all his might and yelled, "Leah! Here! It's me . . . it's Moses!" Then he got a closer look. Those eyes and the freckles . . . he realized it wasn't Leah. Leah was gone.

Moses awoke in a panic. The image flooded his mind and he was confused and startled by his tears. He tried to shake himself from the dream as his senses searched to identify the smell that was suddenly strong. He recognized it to be that of lilacs and he wondered why he didn't know that right away. His mama loved lilacs. When he built his first little hidden place, he planted lilacs for her, and he took her there once before she died. Long after the structure was devoured by Kudzu, the lilacs persisted, determined to keep her memory. Even the ones he planted down by the creek where Leah loved to play when they picnicked continued to bloom.

When the development started near there, he abandoned the place and moved farther up into the hills. He hated having to do that because it was once Mr. Bradley's land and it remained a sacred place for Moses. That was the closest he ever came to being one of them. The little place he built was just up the hill from where the Bradleys went for picnics near the creek. He had been allowed to go a few times, and sometimes he and David went on adventures there. His mama could see how attached he was getting to Leah, and Leah to her son. Etta Mae put a stop to him going. She said it wasn't appropriate. She said a little white girl could end up in trouble being so friendly with Moses, or some well-meaning person might think she needed to be protected from him. He was heartbroken, even though he understood. Still, it was wrong.

Moses went out from his cave through the rhododendron into a misting shower. He wasn't sure how long he had laid there, but it was getting dark. He could tell by the rivulets of water running downhill there had been a good soaking rain while he slept. He felt a growing urgency. The thrill felt like a jolt of electricity tingling through his body. He believed he had finally seen the flash for which he had waited all these decades. He knew where he had to go, but first he ran back into the cave for some things he knew he would need.

16
Answers to Prayers

At 7:55 the phone rang. Tina recognized Beverly's number.

"Hello, Sally?"

"Ms. McKenzie, Momma said Penny is missing. Have you found her? What happened?"

"Oh, Sally! Penny was upset after school and went somewhere on her bike. She hasn't come home, and it's been raining. The police are looking for her, but they have no idea where to start. Do you know of anywhere special? Somewhere she might have liked to go to write her stories. We found one place where she said something about her thinking spot, but no one knows where it is."

"Oh, I know! I know! She took me there for my good-bye picnic. It's in a different galaxy, that's what *she* calls it. It's out past school and up some hills then down Jackson Road and then you turn up a couple of curvy roads. I don't know what it's called, but there are sidewalks for people who aren't there. Really. I know that sounds weird, and it *is* weird. I bet the police will know if you tell them that.

It's like somebody got ready to build houses and then just stopped. I wish I could remember what it was called."

"Sally that's perfect. Thank you! I'll call back when we have her home safe, okay? Tell your mom thank you, Sweetie."

Tina quickly hung up and called the detective to tell him what Sally had said. Within a few minutes there was a knock at the door.

"I was only a block away," said the detective. "Would you like to follow me? I know exactly where the place is. I've radioed the K-9 handler to meet me there."

Tina turned to find Carson already standing behind her holding the keys out for her, "Go Mom, we'll be fine, just call and let us know."

"There's no way you could ever understand how much I love you. ALL of you." Tina grabbed Carson and hugged him and threw a kiss to Cathy. As she started backing out of the drive she took a deep breath and said a quick prayer before pulling out behind the patrol car.

Tina followed Detective Robbins onto Galaxy Drive. "*Galaxy* Drive, who knew? If I'd known this place existed, I would have known exactly where to look. Thank you, God, for stopping the rain."

The handler had pulled over into a cul-de-sac and was getting the dog out when they arrived. Tina started to open her door but the Detective came over and asked her to wait in her car. Shocked, Tina blinked away the tears that were filling her eyes. She wanted to convince herself this didn't mean they thought the worst.

"With all the rain it's muddy and slippery out here. Let's let our dog tell us where she went, if this is where she is. And if she's gone down that hill, we don't need to have to carry you up the hill too, okay?" Tina nodded wishing otherwise. The detective patted her hand that was in the open window. "You wait here while we go find your little girl, Mrs. McKenzie."

Tina watched as the dog was shown the sweater she had given them earlier. He immediately had his nose in the air, then on the ground. He jerked and circled on the sidewalk, whining, then headed into the road and zig zagged to the next driveway. He whined and barked, then moved quickly toward the bushes. His handler followed closely with a big light that cast a wide beam. Once he went behind the bushes, he shouted to the detective that the bike with the backpack was there. Tina jumped out of her car and ran to where he was. The detective held up his hand to stop her. "She's not with her bike. We will let the dog look for her. Until we find her, we can't touch or move the bike. It could provide information as to where she is."

"You'd have to lock me up if you think I'm gonna stay inside my car. You shouldn't have asked me to come along if you thought that. And don't worry, I won't touch anything or go down the hill." Tina headed back beside her car to wait, pacing.

The handler brought the dog back out from behind the bushes. Tina stayed back and watched how the dog moved; how he was so intent. She thanked God for sending him. He tugged toward the hill, whined, and carried on. The handler told Detective Robbins he was ready to go down and got a nod to go ahead. It was pitch black and the clouds concealed the moon with only a few small breaks that exposed the stars. Tina could see the bright light flashing as it moved. The detective followed down the path after the handler and the dog when he saw another patrol car pulling in. Tina caught herself holding her breath and had to remind herself to keep breathing. She picked at her cuticles, wrung her hands, and shifted her weight from side to side. She could hear the men calling Penny's name. Then the dog squealed and there was a change in the men's voices. They sounded like they were talking to someone, but she couldn't hear what they were saying. The minutes felt like hours. Then they yelled they had her.

"We're on our way up, Mrs. McKenzie, with a very cold little girl who tells us her name is Penny." shouted Detective Robbins. Tina ran to the edge of the ravine and watched the big lights move in swinging zig zags as the weight of the climbing men shifted from side to side. Finally, she could see the detective carrying a bundle in his arms. He radioed to the patrolman at the top of the hill to get an ambulance to the site. Tina shrieked "What? What's wrong?"

As he reached the top of the hill, the detective explained, "She needs to be checked out. She's very cold. We don't know how long she was in the water, and she has an injury to her ankle. She seems confused. I'm not a doctor . . . maybe hypothermia. We want to make sure she's examined and rule out any other injuries."

Tears of joy streamed down Tina's cheeks. She reached for Penny and held her sweet face in her trembling hands, kissing her forehead and her nose. Detective Robbins held her to keep her still until the ambulance got there, but he sat down where Tina could get closer to her. Penny was crying and whispering, too hoarse to speak. Tina was look-ing curiously at the blanket and the big poncho that was wrapped around her daughter. She looked at the detective. He shook his head a little and pinched his mouth up with raised eyebrows and a wrinkled forehead. Tina fought back fears of a potential nightmare of what could have happened to her baby, then smiled and quietly reassured Penny that she was safe now. Everything was going to be okay.

"Let's call home to let them know you've been found," Tina said as Penny nodded, staring at her mother.

"They found her. She's okay, a hurt ankle, and she's wet and very cold, so there's an ambulance coming, but she'll be fine. Call your grandparents!" Tina was breathless. She held the phone so Penny could hear them cheering. "Could you call Rita Jenkins, too? Penny's teacher. Her number is on the tablet by the phone. Oh My God! I never called work."

Carson laughed a little, "No worries, Mom, I called the clinic when you left with the detective. No matter how things went I knew you'd be wiped out. They said to tell you to take as much time as you need. They're happy to cover for you."

"Oh my, they're all so kind. Carson, thank you for thinking about that for me. My brain has been all over the map today, and you're right. I'm totally exhausted. Please call them and tell them Penny's safe, okay? Oh, dear, two more calls. Let Sheila next door know and call sweet little Sally back and tell her she saved Penny's life. Okay, I'm going to stay with her until they take her to the hospital, then I'll follow the ambulance there. I'll call if there's anything important. Y'all try to get some sleep, alright?"

"Okay, Mom, I can tell you're worn out. By the way, it's only 8:45. Slow down and take a deep breath. Everything's fine. We love you, Mom."

"Wow, it feels like midnight. Well, there're some leftovers in the fridge. Y'all find something to eat if you haven't already. I love you both so much! I'll talk to you later."

Tina had been holding Penny's hand the whole time and watching her face while she talked. Penny was looking at her with such intensity, like she wanted to talk, but she could barely whisper. Finally, the ambulance turned onto Galaxy Drive.

Once Penny was able to nod and shake her head to answer a few questions, the bike was put in the back of the Rodeo. Tina kissed Penny and told her she'd meet them at the hospital. The paramedics got Penny settled, checked her vitals, and reported to the ER before they left. Detective Robbins said he'd see Tina there after Penny had been examined. He was required to take the dog back down and track the scent of the poncho before he could leave. For a moment, Tina sat in the driver's seat of her car and simply breathed. There was no more shaking. She finally completely knew where she was; but she couldn't wrap her head around everything she had been through in less than six hours. She had become aware of so many things and re-lived too much. She didn't know how it was possible. She started her car and pulled out of Galaxy Drive behind an incredibly beautiful ambulance.

17

More Questions Than Answers

The lights felt harsh outside the emergency entrance after coming from the darkness of Galaxy Drive. Tina parked on the other side of the street and crossed to enter through the doors for walk-in patients. She could see where the ambulance had pulled into their bay, and she watched the attendants at the back of it as they moved the stretcher into the building. She let them know at the reception desk she was the parent of the child who was just brought in by ambulance and filled out all the paperwork. Then she went into the restroom before sitting down to wait where she saw herself in the mirror for the first time in hours. "Oh, Lord, I look like death warmed over!"

Penny was terrified. She wanted her mom. Mom said she would be there. There were so many people talking to each other and saying things she didn't understand. Then they would say something nice to her like, "It's okay, Honey" or, "You're safe, Sweetie."

They looked at parts of her they didn't have any reason to see—her private places. Mom taught her that; but Mom also told her doctors were allowed. She knew she had to let them, but she didn't like it at all, and she couldn't stop her tears. She tried to ask for her mom. Only a whisper came. Nobody heard her. At least she was finally getting warmer. They had taken her wet clothes off and put a dry gown on her. The bed was nice and warm.

A nurse came and put a needle in her hand that had a tube hooked to it. It went to a bag hanging on a shiny hook beside the bed like in the movies. They brought a big thing they told her was a special camera that took pictures of her ankle where the rock had smashed it. She knew it was an x-ray machine, but if they wanted to call it a camera she didn't care. She was used to being treated like she was either stupid or a baby.

It was easier if her eyes were closed, and she felt safer that way. Besides, she was trying hard to keep the picture in her mind of God. She didn't think many people got the chance to meet Him in person while they were alive like she did. She couldn't imagine why she was so important that He would come to save her in person. She was quite sure that was the only reason she didn't drown.

Looking through the doors when they opened and closed sent a chill down Tina's spine. It was getting hard to slow down the progression of memories now that so much had surfaced. The old emotions were raw. Her life had been a nightmare for over four years after she defied her parents and ran off to marry Jimmy after she graduated. Her brain had been swimming in sewage that night. The weight of the debris that had fallen around her had crushed her spirit. The officer who had come to tell her about Jimmy had called for a Paramedic when he saw her bruised and swollen face. That was the call that had changed the course of her life and the lives of her children. It was one of those things people refer to as a blessing in disguise. That was the last thing anyone could have convinced her was true at the time.

Tina fought thoughts of failure and shame as she remembered looking into the calm, steady eyes of the man who had watched her closely and had checked her vitals. He had repeatedly asked her questions—her name, where she was, what she could hear and see, what her children's names were, and how old they were. He was so kind and attentive.

While she sat there floating through time, flipping through pages of a home improvement magazine, and watching the door to the ER, someone came up behind her and touched her shoulder. She jumped up and almost fell as she spun around.

"I said your name, but I guess you were too deep in thought to hear me. I'm sorry I startled you. Has anyone told you anything yet?" There was a compassionate expression on Detective Robbins' face.

"No, nothing. I'm really having a hard time sitting here. I can't imagine why I can't be back there. Do you know anything I need to know?"

"Not exactly. We hoped to find out where the blanket and poncho came from. The *really* crazy thing? The dog couldn't track them. I've never known him to go cold like that. We took him back down where she was. We went up and down on both sides of the creek. Nothing. Whoever was there vanished into thin air. When we found her up on the bank, her hair was wet. When we asked her if she could walk, she shook her head and pointed at her foot. We're careful never to ask leading questions. That's left to the experts who come in and talk to her here. The next step is to see what the doctors find. Now we stay focused on being grateful she's alive and in a safe place, getting the care she needs."

"So, you thought . . .," Tina began to feel a wave of nausea as she realized what he was saying. The thought of the possible meaning of Penny being wrapped in a mysterious blanket on the bank overwhelmed Tina. She had allowed that thought for a moment earlier, so she wasn't sure why it surprised her, but she had blocked the possibility and overridden it with joy.

"Oh my God . . ." The color drained from her face.

"Whoa, hold on, we don't know anything. Your little girl's tears were tears of relief. I've seen enough to know that much. There wasn't a mark on her face, arms, or her legs other than the ankle. There was no sign of any kind of struggle. She shook her head when I asked if anyone had made her go down the hill or if anyone had hurt her. Otherwise, I never would have allowed the bike to be moved. She didn't seem to be at all afraid of us. I hope I'm not overstepping, or giving false hope, but that's not usually the case if a child has been hurt by a man. They tend to generalize the fear, if you know what I mean."

Tina was shaken and it must have been obvious because as the Detective spoke, she didn't appear to be hearing him. He took her by the elbow and guided her back down to her seat, then sat down beside her. "Mrs. McKenzie, it's Tina, isn't it? From now on how about you call me Greg. Is that okay? And for a minute I want you to look at me and tell me where we are and what you can see."

Tina looked at his face. His eyes were kind. She could feel his hand on hers and there was a strangely comforting familiarity to what he was asking. Clarity washed over her. "We are in the waiting room at the ER, I'm waiting to be told I can go hold my daughter, who I was afraid I had lost. But she is alive. And God is good. Thank you, Greg, for being here. John McKenzie once asked me those same questions. He was on duty the night my first husband died, and he was the one who brought me here. I hate admitting it, though you've probably already figured it out . . . this isn't my first tragedy rodeo, and I have a few too many t-shirts to prove it."

Greg smiled and patted her hand. "Well, you wear them well."

The door to the E.R. swung open. A smiling nurse in scrubs with her mask hanging under her chin appeared. "Mrs. McKenzie?" Tina nodded and stood. "There's a little cutie pie in here who would be much happier if her mama was with her."

Tina grabbed her bag and practically leaped to the doorway. She turned to gesture half-heartedly to Greg to come with her, then thought differently. Anxious to hold Penny, she didn't want to be in the middle of a conversation about a possible investigation in front of her daughter. She hoped the smile on the face of the nurse was a sign they didn't find anything other than the injured ankle.

Penny's face lit up when she saw Tina. She was propped up and smiling with her arms wrapped around a pink teddy bear. Maneuvering around the injured ankle and the IV, they awkwardly managed kisses and hugs.

"How bad is her ankle?"

"The doctor will be over here soon to give you all the details, but the detective is first in line. That should only take a few minutes." The nurse smiled and nodded, then gestured toward the doctor as she spoke.

Tina returned the reassuring smile and breathed a sigh of relief. When she leaned close to give Penny an Eskimo kiss, Penny whispered, "I love you Mom. I'm sorry I was so stupid. I promise I'll never do anything like that again."

"Shhhh", Tina touched her finger to Penny's lips. "Enough of that. All that matters now is that you'll be home in your sleeping bag and writing stories before you know it. How about we call home and let Carson and Cathy know I'm back here with you so they can tell you goodnight. Would that be okay? I bet they're waiting up to hear from us." Tina gave Penny a wink.

Penny nodded eagerly and Tina pulled out her phone to call home.

"Hello?"

"Oh dear, Mom! I was calling home. I guess I tapped your name by accident. While I have you on the phone, I'll let you say hi to Penny. She can only whisper, but she can hear you just fine."

"That's fine, Honey, but you didn't call a wrong number. I left home ten minutes after you called. I got here a little while ago. Hand the phone to Penny."

"Oh Mom, thank you. I'm so happy you're here! Here's Penny."

"Hi Gramma, are you gonna sleep in my room? My sheets under the sleeping bag are clean." Penny's hoarse whisper was barely audible.

"Well now, Sweetheart, that sounds like a plan. Don't try to talk anymore right now. You need to give your throat some rest. I wanted you to know I love you and I'm here to help y'all as long as you need me. I'm thanking God right now for keeping you safe."

"But Gramma, I met Him, and I got to thank Him myself. I can't wait to tell you about it."

"Okay Honey, you do what the doctors say, and I'll see you soon. Someone else is waiting to say hi to you."

Carol shook her head with a startled look on her face when she handed the phone to Carson, who told Penny how happy they were she was safe. Cathy promised to be nicer to her. As Carol told Tina goodnight, they made plans for her to go up to the hospital in the morning.

Tina turned off her phone and looked at Penny with a long questioning stare. "Who did you tell Gramma you met, Penny?"

"I met *God*, Mom. I called to Jesus for help. I asked Him to send someone, and I asked for a miracle like the paper from Daddy's wallet said. I was having a hard time holding onto the rock. I was screaming, but I knew nobody could hear me except Jesus. I was sure if I let go I would fall backward. I thought I was going to die. Then, all of a sudden, there He was! God was behind me! Right there in the creek, right where He needed to be. He said His quote from my room. He said, 'Be Still!' Then He said, 'Don't be afraid, I'm here to help you.'"

"Penny, that sounds like the beginning of a great new story for you to write. But right now, I need you to be quiet and rest your throat."

"But, Mom, *He was real!* Don't you believe me? Mom, please . . ." Tears were filling her eyes. Tina didn't know what to think, or even how to respond, she just wanted Penny to be calm and quiet.

"Of *course* I do, Sweetheart. But it's time to rest. You can tell me more about it later, once we are in a room and your throat has rested, okay?"

After Penny was moved to a room in the early morning hours, Tina camped out in the glow of the monitors on a chair that opened into a single bed. They continued to watch Penny's temperature. Her ankle was stabilized until the orthopedist could make rounds in the morning. Greg had left after talking with the doctor in the ER. Tina remembered his quick wink and smile of reassurance as he gestured he'd see her tomorrow.

Although depleted in every way possible, Tina's mind was racing as she tried to sleep. How could so much have gone on in such a short amount of time? What in the world really happened? The mysterious blanket and poncho, Penny on the bank, and *God?* Who moved Penny from the creek? Why was she in the creek to begin with? It wasn't the kind of place someone would be out for an evening walk in the woods. None of it made sense. Penny going there after school and in the rain didn't make sense either. Tina couldn't fathom what had been so important or so terrible that Penny would take off like that. Tina wasn't sure they would ever know exactly what happened. She wasn't sure she had it in her to try to find the answers. She resigned herself to being satisfied with knowing Penny was safe.

Tina finally gave in to her exhaustion. She had no idea how long she had slept when she became aware of a sound like a bird squawking. She opened her eyes and saw the alarm was sounding on the IV monitor because the bag was empty. The door opened and a nurse came in with her cart. Dazed, Tina could see it was still dark out and Penny was fast asleep. Flashes of what she had been dreaming lingered in her mind. She was in dark water. She needed to rescue what she thought was Penny but ended up being pulled from the water by her own hair. Whatever had her hair lifted her out of the blackness. She looked up to see what was pulling her. Penny was above her, desperately clinging to Tina's hair while dangling from a cliff, with Carson and Cathy holding Penny by her legs. All she could think was that the day had taken its toll on her. Her confused brain was using crazy dreams to make sense of it all.

"Can I get anything for you?" the nurse asked before she left when she realized Tina was awake. Tina shook her head and grunted. "Well, there's coffee right across the hall in the waiting area. Breakfast will be coming around in about two hours. They'll have a tray for you. Doctors will be making rounds all morning. We're right down the hall. All you need to do is push the call button if you need anything at all."

Tina thanked her and closed her eyes, hoping not to fall asleep again.

18
Gramma!

Tuesday morning Carson and Cathy awoke to the smell of coffee and bacon. Carson found Carol busily digging around in the kitchen, making a list of what she could pick up at the store. She told him she had called the hospital early to find out the room number but didn't want to wake Tina in case she was able to get some sleep. Carol was wondering what she could do to help when her phone buzzed.

Carol smiled, "Hello, Tina, you must have read my mind. I was making plans and I didn't want to wake you."

"Well, I've been thinking, if you could bring Carson and Cathy up here to get the car, they can head on to school and you can come up to the room and visit for a while. Penny wants her writing notebook and she's going to need some clothes if she's discharged today. Either Cathy or Carson can get those for you. I'm not going anywhere until the doctor comes. I know we need some groceries, so maybe you could grab a few things while we're waiting? Then when we're ready, you can come back by and get us."

"That's exactly what I was thinking. I'm fixing them some breakfast and making a list. I'll see you in a bit."

"Perfect! Thanks Mom."

Carson was already in the kitchen when Cathy joined them. When they were little, Gramma always brought presents. It had been years since that tradition had faded. This visit was unplanned, so she was surprised to see a bag of gifts. She grinned at her grandmother.

Carol was cooking and wiping the counter and pouring juice while she talked a mile a minute. "Like old times, huh? I've planned to bring these up for almost three months. Remember that trip Pop and I took to Chile right after Christmas? We found this amazing little bookstore. Not sure *what* drew us in there. It wasn't the kind of place you go for souvenirs, but it confirmed my belief there are *no* coincidences. They had the nicest calligraphy quotes that were obviously meant for each of you. They still need to be framed, but I couldn't resist bringing them. I was tired of the bag sitting in the closet. Y'all eat your breakfast. I'll get them out to show you. As soon as you're ready, I'm taking you to the hospital to get the car. There won't be time to go in for a visit, but your mom thinks Penny will be home tonight. If not, you can see her up there later. I need someone to get Penny's notebook for me to take up to the hospital when we go, so don't let me forget it. And whether she's home tonight or not, Carson, I expect to hear you playing your guitar, okay?"

Carson and Cathy grinned at each other as if to say *she's ba-ack* while they got plates out for their bacon and scrambled eggs. Not just anyone could talk that fast and still have that southern accent. It had been a while since the old Gramma they knew and loved had been for a visit, and they were both happy about it.

"Mom's eggs are good, Gramma, but there's something different about yours."

"Well, Carson, it's partly a trick that comes with age and partly science. I talk to the food while I cook it, and then it's more cooperative, like water when it's told it's loved. Remember that book I sent you by the Japanese man? Dr. Emoto, wasn't that his name? Then the trick—I stick my little finger in it, and voila!" Carol chuckled. "Here. Wipe your hands so you don't get grease on it. This is the quote I got for you, Carson. It had your name all over it. It's by a writer named Isabel Allende. I think she must be from Chile, I'm not sure, but if she isn't, they sure like her there." Carson smiled and took the folder with the tissue paper covered quote.

"I'm not sure when, but I've heard of her. 'Music is a wind that blows away the years, memories, and fear, that crouching animal I carry inside me.'" His face flushed when he read it.

"Wow. Gramma. I don't know what to say. You are the queen of finding cool stuff."

"Like I said, your name is all over it, Sweetheart. Creepy, huh? And Cathy's is quite different, but from the same author." She handed Cathy hers, and waited, hoping to get the same reaction from her granddaughter.

Cathy read hers to herself, and stared at it, blinking. Then she handed it to Carson and asked him to read it, so she could listen with her eyes closed.

"I strike the ground with the soles of my feet and life rises up my legs, spreads up my skeleton, takes possession of me, drives away distress and sweetens my memory. The world trembles." He grinned and looked at Cathy, who had a stunned look on her face. "Well? What's goin' on in that chlorine-blonde head? You need somebody to explain it?"

"Sometimes I could just punch you, Carson! You are such a jerk. What? You think I'm not smart enough to get that? It's awesome, Gramma, thank you. Really, it's amazing. I'm going up to brush my teeth so we can go. I'll bring Penny's notebook down Gramma." She disappeared around the corner.

"That wasn't very nice of you, Carson."

"Well, she's been pretty hard on Penny, and on Mom, too. It's been rough since Mom started this workin' at night gig. I'll apologize, Gramma, I'm sorry. These quotes you chose for us are dope. Um, I mean, really awesome."

"It's okay, I knew what you meant. Wait 'til you see the two I found for Penny. I want her to see them first. She can show them to you herself. This is going to be such a great week."

"Gramma, considerin' all the worry about Penny and your unplanned drive last night, you sure are cheerful. For the past couple years it's seemed like you were either sad or irritable. Has something happened? I mean, I'm sorry, I guess that was rude. I've missed the Gramma I knew when I was little. I'm glad to see you actin' so happy. Whatever it is, do you think maybe it could rub off on Mom?"

"I don't know, Carson, I'll see what I can do." She winked.

The ride to the hospital was quiet. Cathy was noticeably distracted by the clouds she pointed out looked like an exploded bag of cotton balls. Carol parked close to Tina's car and said goodbye to Carson and Cathy on her way into the hospital.

When she got up to room 319, Tina and Penny had finished their breakfast and were playing a game of Go Fish.

"Well, *hey* there Precious! You are a sight for sore eyes. Let me come and give my baby granddaughter a hug and a kiss. Here, I brought your notebook like your mom asked me to. I forgot your clothes, but I can get them later." Carol nuzzled Penny's ear and made her giggle. "So, tell me how that ankle is feeling. Has the doctor been up here yet?"

"No ma'am", Penny whispered, shaking her head, "they said he'd be here soon."

"Once he makes his rounds, we'll know how soon we can go home, Mom. I'm hoping they won't have any reason to keep her another night."

There was a tap at the door, and Greg peeked in. Tina motioned for him to come inside. "Good morning, Greg. Come on in and meet my mom." Tina waited a moment for Greg to come into the room. "Mom, this is Greg. He's the detective responsible for finding Penny and bringing her up from the creek."

"Well, hi there, Detective, I'm Carol. It's nice to meet you. We sure are grateful to you."

"It's nice to meet you, too, Ma'am. I know Tina's happy to see you. I wanted to check in and make sure things are fine, Tina. The doctor had no concerns about our questions. Not that the questions go away, but they don't have the same implications as they could have had. Well, I don't want to be in the way of family. I just wanted to reassure you. If you need anything at all, Tina, don't hesitate to call, okay?"

Tina stepped outside and thanked Greg as he left. When she came back in, Carol gave her a look with raised eyebrows.

"Mom. Stop it. He's genuinely concerned and that's *all.*"

"Hmmm. *Okaaay.* Looks to me like Prince Valliant's thinking he's found a damsel in distress to rescue. I'm sorry, but you're vulnerable, Honey. You've been alone a long time. I hope you can keep a clear head. He's probably a real nice guy, but the last thing you or your children need right now is to have a man swoop down and rescue you."

"Don't you think I know that, Mom? It would make life so much easier to have another income and to have the security of a relationship; but in the long run, it's the *last* thing I want. I need to find *me.* I don't need another obligation, and I *don't* need to have this conversation right now." Tina glanced over at Penny and noticed her look of curiosity as she listened to their conversation.

There was another tap and the door opened. A short, grey-haired, rosy-cheeked man wearing old-fashioned, round wire-rimmed glasses and a lab coat came in carrying a clipboard, followed by his nurse. He logged into the computer and reviewed the notes as he spoke to them. Tina imagined this must be what Santa looked like with no beard.

"Hello there, I'm Dr. Gould, here to take a look at Miss McKenzie's ankle." He extended his hand toward Tina. "You must be Mom." Tina returned his smile and nodded.

"Well, Miss Penny McKenzie, they said you have some laryngitis. Are you able to talk at all?"

"Yes sir," Penny whispered, it doesn't hurt, there's just not any sound. I think I screamed my voice away."

The doctor nodded and smiled, "Can you tell me how you hurt your ankle?"

"I was crossing the creek. The rock I jumped on was slippery, and I guess there was a hole under it because it fell over and I fell in. The water was coming at my face and I grabbed for the rock to pull myself up and the rock went straight down on my foot. I was stuck there, and it was freezing cold. I thought I was going to die and I prayed for Jesus to help me. God came in person and told me to be still and He held me against His legs and lifted the rock off me, then He put me on the bank and wrapped me in a blanket and put a poncho on me. Then He told me to rest and wait and someone would come to get me."

The four adults in the room were silent. Dr. Gould took a deep breath and smiled, shaking his head as he spoke. "The Lord moves in mysterious ways. I love hearing things like this. Sweetheart, the injury to your ankle could have been much worse, and indeed, you could have died in that creek. What a blessing; a miracle."

There were smiles and nods all around. No one knew what else to say, except Carol, who chimed in with an "Amen!"

The doctor was satisfied with the way Penny's ankle looked this morning and let them know there were no fractures. Still, there was considerable bruising, an upper ankle sprain, and some soft-tissue damage. He wanted Penny to wear a boot for about a month and start some physical therapy in two, possibly three, weeks. He felt that would be all she needed, but they would reassess when she started the therapy. Dr. Gould wrote the discharge orders and Penny would be ready to go home by early afternoon. She was to stay home the rest of the week and gradually increase time wearing the boot. No gym class for the month. He was already writing out a prescription for Tina to take to the medical supply to have the boot fitted.

"WooHoo! What great news." Gramma said, giving Penny a high-five. "How about I run and get a few things from the grocery store, drop them at the house and get the clothes I forgot. I'll come back here to get you and Mom when they finish the paperwork."

Once Penny was settled at home, Tina called the school and arranged to pick up Penny's work and to fill them in on the doctor's instructions.

Carol was in the kitchen cooking dinner. She called out to Carson when he got home to remind him he had promised to play his guitar for her. While the lasagna was in the oven, Carol took Penny's quotes to the living room where she was propped up on the sofa.

"Your brother and sister can show you theirs later, but these are especially for you. Pop and I found ourselves in an interesting bookstore in Chile. They had some beautiful calligraphy quotes by several famous people. They had a favorite writer named Isabel Allende. These quotes sounded like she was talking about *you*."

Carol handed a folder to Penny that had two heavy sheets of paper with writing on them covered with tissue paper. When she read the first one, she looked up at Carol with her big eyes. Carol told her to read it out loud so everyone could hear it.

"You can tell the deepest truths with the lies of fiction." Penny moved her fingers along the surface of the paper. She moved the first one to the back and stared at the second for a long time before she read it aloud. Carol reached over and held Tina's hand.

"When everything else fails, we communicate in the language of the stars." Carol heard Tina catch her breath. Penny looked shocked. "How would someone else know that? I thought Daddy and I were the only ones."

19
Truth Too Long Unspoken

The week had gone by too fast for Tina. Despite all the drama, it was nice to have a break from work. For the first time in a long while, she and Carol were able to enjoy each other's company doing everything from cooking to gardening together. The weather had cooperated, and they had kept the conversation light and pleasant. It looked like it would be a quiet weekend.

Penny would be going back to school on Monday morning. Arrangements had been made for her to go to Mr. Quintana's office during the time for her gym class, but Penny didn't want to do that. She was afraid she would have to talk about why she went to the creek. Penny thought maybe she should do her work at home for a few weeks. Because Tina was going back to work Monday night and needed to be able to sleep, Penny staying home all day wasn't an option.

It turned out that Natalie Cross, the new girl sitting next to Penny in Mrs. Jenkins' class, lived nearby. She had come over to visit once earlier in the week and today for the afternoon. They were upstairs in Penny's room playing cards. Sally had really been missed this year. It was wonderful hearing laughter coming from Penny's room again. Cathy went to a movie with some friends and was making plans for a low-key birthday party next Saturday afternoon. Carson was at work at The Beat, and then had plans to work out at the gym. He had played his guitar several times for Carol but told her he was working on a special song he had been learning just for her. He promised to play it before she left.

Tina sat in the living room quietly reflecting on her gratitude for the calm after the storm with Sheba curled up beside her. Carol came around the corner and asked if she'd like to join her on the deck for a while and have a glass of wine.

"Well, I'd love that Mom, but I doubt I have any. It's been ages. I've avoided falling into the habit of drinking alone."

"I brought a bottle. I want you to taste it. We had some on our trip and enjoyed it so much I found a package store that carries it. I had no idea Chile produced so much wine. I think I remember you liking a good Cabernet. I've already opened it. Come on out, it's a beautiful afternoon."

Tina followed Carol through the French doors onto the deck and immediately noticed the warm breeze. A hint of summer on the way. There was a wrapped box on the table beside the wine.

Carol smiled when Tina saw it. "Open it!" Carol sounded like a child on Christmas morning.

"Mom, what's with all this gift giving? It's April. My birthday isn't until June."

"Just *open* it!"

Tina took a sip of her wine, then pursed her lips and raised her eyebrows. "Wow, that *is* good! Don't give me much though, I won't be able to cook dinner."

She tore into the box. "Oh, my goodness! I've seen these advertised. I've wanted to get one, but I couldn't justify spending that much. Thank you, Mom." She lifted the wind chime out of the box and held it up. It was made to hold ashes in the part that moves with the wind. "Oh, my goodness, listen to that. The tone is absolutely *beautiful.* I haven't done anything with John's ashes. Six years and I still have them up in our room. This is the perfect solution. Now I'll be able to share afternoons out here with him."

"Exactly what *I* thought. Out here where you two worked so hard to build this deck. You both loved being out here. Every time you hear it, it'll be like him touching you. I hoped you would like the idea. I got one for Karen's, too. After twenty-three years I decided it was time to deal with it. I can't quite read Jack, though. I think he's okay with it, but it's hard to tell. He's been having a tough time lately."

"What's going on with Dad?"

"He's *finally* been seeing someone at the VA to help him deal with the flashbacks. I don't get why they're so behind on the therapies that are getting to be mainstream now. Our problem is that most of the things that look really promising aren't being done anywhere near us. He refuses to travel for therapy. It'll be okay. You don't need to be worried about it."

"Mom, I'm sorry Dad's having a rough time, but at least y'all have found somewhere to live that obviously works for *you*. I love you so much, Mom. I don't know what you've been doing, but there's something different. I can't put my finger on it, but you seem so much more relaxed."

"Well, maybe I am. Carson said the same thing while you were at the hospital. I found a church I like, and I read my daily devotional every morning to start the day. I started listing things I'm grateful for in a journal; it started with one thing and it's grown. It's helped me be more mindful and it all fits together. Now that I'm paying attention to little things, I realize how much I've taken for granted. I can't say any one thing has made more of a difference than anything else." Carol smiled as she spoke.

"I've been feeling crazy lately, Mom. I catch myself expecting things of people, and I don't like how I feel when I realize I'm doing it . . . that didn't come out right . . . " Tina thought for a moment about how she could express what she was feeling. "What I meant to say was that I anticipate people's reactions, not that I expect anything." Tina paused again. She wasn't exactly sure what she wanted to say. There was so much that had gone unsaid for too long. It was time.

"You know Mom, I meant it the other night when I called to say I was sorry. I hate that it took me thinking I could lose Penny to realize how I took you and Dad for granted when I was a teenager. I was shallow and selfish; totally self-centered. I've looked back at it all; the years of therapy and the never-ending help you and Dad gave me—*still* give me. I was so self-destructive; it almost cost me my life. No telling *what* kind of long-term problems I've caused the kids. I know it's been hard on you. I can't imagine what you must have gone through worrying about Karen, and how terrible your grief must have been. Then there was me and my willfulness. I was oblivious about how I was adding insult to injury."

"I'm going to stop you right there, Tina. You were a *child*. The things Karen went through . . . well, I didn't know how to deal with it all or how much was okay for you to know; how much you were ready to know or would even understand."

"I realize that *now*, Mom, and I realize I was filled with anger. I was angry at Karen, at you and Dad, and I was *furious* at God. It wasn't fair. My sister quit on life, and it sucked the life out of our family. I felt like I'd been left on the side of the road in the dirt. I've never known how to say all that without fear of hurting you and Dad. I didn't want you to feel guilty. I've held it in and it's bound me."

Tina stopped herself. She wondered how much of this was the wine talking. When she looked over at her mother's face, Tina could see Carol was listening with patience and compassion—more needed to be said. "I've never believed I deserved happiness, Mom. I've spent so many years feeling worthless and ashamed, prepared for punishment. Then John rode in on his white horse and swept me off my feet. Oh God, I feel so ungrateful saying anything negative about all that. John was an *angel*, he saved me *and* my children. But where is he now? Gone. Gone like Karen, and Jimmy, and for all it's worth, Dad. But I'm okay, I'm paddling along, sometimes floating, sometimes treading water. Sometimes I close my eyes and imagine I'm riding on the back of a huge bird, pretending to be fine, real fine, as John's Papa used to say." Tina fell back onto her chair, tears streaming down her face. Carol continued to listen quietly.

"I'm so sorry, Mom. I didn't mean for all that to pour out. No one needs to have someone spew like that, but I've needed to say it for so long. I don't know what to do, Mom. I'm lost. I'm so worried about my children, but I'm barely able to keep my own head above water."

"Tina! First of all, your dad is not *gone!* He struggles with his PTSD, but he's *fine*. He loves you more than you could ever imagine. Jack's fighting his *own* war. The same war he fought in Viet Nam. He couldn't save the children in that village, he couldn't save Karen, and he's lost confidence in his ability to make a difference. Now he only does what seems right day to day. He has no idea how to respond. All that does is complicate how he deals with my emotions. I've known for a long time how hard all the things our family came up against have been on you, Sweetheart. I've had my struggles, too. Nothing you've said is anything I haven't either felt myself or thought about. So no, you aren't hurting me. If anything, it hurts most knowing it has taken this long for you to finally voice it."

Carol looked at Tina. Tina could tell there was more she wanted to say, so she shifted into a different position and reached over and took her mom's hand. Carol took a deep breath and after a long exhale, continued.

"Karen's problems had nothing to do with us or with you, even though it devastated all of us, Tina. We believed she was doing better. There was so much more that none of us knew. Afterward, I didn't know how to deal with my grief, and I didn't know what to do about yours either, except to tell you I love you and send you to a therapist. Everything I saw reminded me of her. She was a joyful child. She took such a delight in you when you were born. I'd look at you, and I'd see *her*, and I had to find a way to keep you from taking that same route. I know I was hard on you, but I felt so desperate."

Carol looked off into the vacuum of her memories, then continued quietly, "Every happy memory twisted itself into a knot of anger in my heart. The rage built whenever I faced the fact there would be no more happy memories made. Even worse, memories I held as happy ones likely weren't that for Karen. I couldn't fix it. No matter how I tried. No matter what I did. *I* lost her. I lost her on *my* watch. God loaned her to me to raise, and my best failed her, failed Him. At least that's how I saw it then.

"It was your Aunt Jenny who stayed by my side and never gave up on me. She reminded me it wasn't my fault and that Jesus would never give up on me either. Even when she knew I wanted to tell her to shut up, she stayed beside me, praying for me. How can something so simple feel so impossible?" She poured a glass of wine and offered Tina more. Tina covered her glass with her hand.

Carol was quiet, staring across the yard, a wisp of grey moving in the breeze. She wiped tears from her face and turned to look directly at Tina, "That's the reality of it, you know. It *is* that simple, *and* easy, but not when you are the one who is mired in the anger. When I finally accepted God's promise, my faith grew; and with faith came Grace. I'm sorry it took me so long. I wasn't there for you like I needed to be when things were so bad with Jimmy. John was something different. Sometimes I think God sent him to save all of us." As Carol spoke, she watched Tina's face.

Tina got up and walked across the deck thinking about John and listening as well as she could. With the Rhododendron in bloom a deep inhale brought the memory of how safe she felt with John. Maybe that was one of the things that made the deck so important.

"If you've had enough, I'll stop," Carol continued, "but it feels like there are years' worth of things that we've both been unable to say. If we don't now, it might never happen."

"I know, Mom. I feel the same way. There's always a child listening, or somewhere to go, or it has to be a phone call . . ." Tina sat back down.

Carol turned to face her and reached again for her hand, then continued, "There's more I want to say about John. He stood by you. He reminded me you were fine. He encouraged me to spend some time taking better care of myself. I don't care about the gossip; I don't believe he would have gone back into that house if he had known the roof was going to give way. He loved you and the children with all his heart. He wanted more than anything for you to allow yourself the forgiveness God's word offers you.

"For years I lived with one foot on the path of faith, and the rest of me questioned how a love that great could be possible. Then, oh, maybe only in the past three or four years it dawned on me that I loved Karen *and* you *that much*. I started thinking about how, no matter *what*, even if I wasn't happy about things you *did*, it didn't alter how deep my love for you ran. Then it clicked—the word *unconditional* and God's promise to always be there with open arms. He never said He would give His children everything they want. Like I've always said, no is also an answer, especially when what we think we want isn't part of His plan, Tina. He gives us what we *need*. Sometimes what we need is a harsh lesson. When you open your heart to His will instead of demanding your own, things become simpler.

"The other key, as far as I'm concerned, and then I'll end my sermon," Carol winked at Tina, "is compassion. I couldn't know why you believed Jimmy would change, and I didn't know why Karen was acting the way she was. Once I understood how important it was for me to forgive and to pray instead of being in control, my entire life began to fall into place. Things are going to be fine, Tina. I believe that. I've come to the conclusion that life is far from perfect. It's full of *moments*; some good and some bad. In the middle of all the everyday stuff there are moments that feel simply *perfect*. When you experience the blessing of one of those, imprint it on your heart and keep it safe, because your soul registers every impression made on it. At least that's what *I* believe. Those things are permanent and they're powerful. Those perfect moments are God exposing His work and His plan for your life. So, cling to *them*. Keep those perfect moments close and be grateful to Him for them."

Carol had been holding Tina's hand and was beginning to squeeze a little too hard. Tina realized she was still crying, but the tears had taken on a different feel. She had begun to feel a sense of relief, at least until Carol said something about the gossip. It had been a long time since she had thought about the stories that had circulated after the fire. She didn't want it to ruin how she was feeling; but she could feel it sucking at her energy like a vacuum. She shoved it away and changed the subject in her mind.

"What do you say we go to church tomorrow while you're here, Mom. Penny has been asking to go. Except for Easter Sunrise Service, we haven't been going like we should. When we go, I usually insist on early service so I can sleep afterward, but since I'm not working tonight, we can sleep in and go to the 11:00 service."

"That sounds like a great way to be ready to get back into the weekly routine. *And* I think we might have to order pizza tonight instead of cooking. You have the number for a decent delivery place? My treat."

"You won't get any complaints from me. I'm getting cool—okay with you if we move this inside?" Tina was amazed at how many of the things she and her mom needed to say had finally been said. The opportunity came and went so quickly, she wondered if it even touched beyond the tip of the iceberg.

Natalie's mom came by with pajamas and clothes for church. The girls were upstairs watching a movie and eating popcorn, and Tina and Carol were relaxing in the living room when Carson got home. He grabbed a couple pieces of pizza, went up the stairs two at a time, then hurried back with his guitar. When he came back into the living room, he turned to Tina with an excited smile.

"You're not gonna believe what happened at the gym today! It's why I'm this late gettin' home, I had planned on comin' back early to have more time with Gram, but . . . oh *man*, this is crazy! You know the owner, right? Mr. Hyatt? He came over to me and said he has this friend who has a son about my age who was in a bad accident and pretty messed up, and he, Mr. Hyatt, knows all about my back and rehab and all that, so he thought I'd be a good partner to help this guy now that his doctors have cleared him to start doin' a normal workout. So, I said sure, I mean, why not? I felt honored. I'm good with helpin' people. When I asked him the guy's name, he said it was Luke Freeman!"

Tina's eyes popped. "No! You're *not* serious, *the* Luke Freeman?"

"Who's Luke Freeman? I never heard of him."

"You wouldn't have, Gram, he's the bully from first grade. Mrs. Solomon saw my middle name and asked me if I was named Carroll after you. Luke was the biggest, meanest . . . started callin' me *Carol*. He's the one who pulled my pants down in front of everybody on the playground to check to see if I was a boy. Oh *man*, I decided in elementary school I was gonna grow up and get big and strong and then make everybody who laughed at me pay. I listen to some of the a.. holes, 'scuse the language, guys at the gym—really *mean* guys—hopped up on steroids. They aren't there to take care of their body 'cause it's a gift from God. They're there to get big to be able to hurt people or to go show off like they're somethin' to worship. I don't want to be *any*thing like them. *Anyway*, let me get back to the story so I can sing this song. So, I told Mr. Hyatt I knew Luke from elementary school, but I thought he moved away. He said Luke *did* move away with his mom. It turns out bad stuff was goin' on when he was little, and he was just actin' out. Now he's been in *so* much trouble, and it sounds like so has his mom. She sent him back to stay with his dad to get him straightened out. I'm not sposed to know, but I heard him say she went to rehab. I don't know how I would've handled today, well, *any* day if it wasn't for Dad. I'm so grateful he came to us when he did. I wish he could've stayed, but I guess that wasn't the plan. I think we were his job in life, and I think he did a good job. What I learned from him changed my whole life."

Carson realized he was getting distracted and reeled himself back in, "So, there we are, standin' there talkin', and in walks this beat-up lookin' Luke. Whoa, I mean, we traded places and no way would I have known him. He *was* the big kid. Not anymore. You should've seen his face when Mr. Hyatt introduced us, and he realized who I was. I thought he was gonna fall down and cry. I guess he was afraid I was gonna beat him up or somethin'. His dad just stood there lookin' lost, had no idea."

Carson was having a hard time keeping a straight face, laughing a little as he related the events at the gym. "I reached out my hand and said it was good to see him after all these years. He must've thought I was gonna crush his hand 'cause he shook really quick and pulled it back. Mr. Hyatt walked away with Luke's dad, and he still looked like he was about to cry, that or wet his pants or somethin'. I told him not to worry. I think I said somethin' like, 'I don't hold any bad feelin's toward you Luke.' He looked really confused, so I suggested we pray before we started the workout. You'd have thought I was throwin' a vampire out in the daylight. I smiled at him and put my hand on his shoulder the way Dad used to, and I felt him relax a little. All I did was ask the Lord to bless our time together. Then things started to change, and it all turned out okay. Before we were through, he said he was sorry for all the mean stuff he did to me, and we ended up laughin' about it. I'm not sure if it sounds weird, but it was like I could feel Dad standin' there next to me today. It was like somethin' out of a book."

As Carson began to play, he was still excited and his face was flushed. He was beaming with joy. When she realized what he was playing, Carol reached over and gave Tina's hand a quick squeeze. "Oh my, I love hearing him, and I *love* this song!" she whispered. Carson sang as he played, watching his grandmother's reaction. Tina had heard the song playing upstairs, but she hadn't really listened to it until now. When he finished, they realized Penny and

Natalie had followed Carson downstairs to listen, and they heard the whole story about Luke.

"The name of the song is 'Just Be Held,' Mom, it's from a CD Gramma sent me by Casting Crowns. She told me it's her favorite, so I decided to learn it. It sure does have a powerful message, don't you think?"

"That was beautiful! What was that line? The part about when your world is falling apart?"

"That's my favorite part, too, 'it's falling into place.' Tina, I think you need to listen to that CD. With all that's been going on, it would do you good to listen to some praise music. It never hurts to be reminded that sometimes we need to be still and let God hold us."

"Be still! That's what He said! That's what God told me when He came to pull me out of the creek." Penny chimed in, beaming.

"I know, Honey, the great mystery of our lifetime. I doubt we will ever have any definitive explanation for that," Tina said as she and Carol looked at each other. Suddenly the room was awkwardly quiet, but Penny wasn't the least bit phased. She didn't have a single doubt about what had happened; and since last Monday she felt confident knowing God was right there, ready to take care of her.

20
Falling into Place

Sunday turned out to be a pivotal day. The service was one of those when you know the Lord has something for you to hear, and He makes sure you feel like every word is being spoken directly to you. The sermon was on Giftedness, and how the gifts we get from God are to be used for the good of others. The Pastor said some people don't understand the concept of being gifted. For some their gifts have gone cold, but for others, their gifts are burning like a fire that draws others closer to God. During the service, Tina looked at Carson and thought about how his fire was burning bright. It was a perfect time for reflection, especially about Carson's experience with Luke on Saturday afternoon. She was touched by her son's expression of gratitude for John.

The Pastor asked the congregation to think about who their igniter had been and how they could pass the flame of faith to others. The part that touched the family the most was the analogy of the campfire—rekindling the flame when it had gone cold. He said they needed to step out in faith greater than their fear and lean on the power of the Holy Spirit. It was the perfect message for Tina. Even Penny, who usually doodled on the bulletin, seemed to be listening.

After church, Tina took a long nap to get back into her daytime sleep schedule. She was grateful to have her mother there for another day. If only her break from work could last another week; but she knew the longer she put off going back the harder it would be. Fortunately, things were settling down. Cathy was making an obvious effort to be nicer to both her and Penny. Thank goodness she settled on going bowling with some of her friends for her birthday instead of having a big party at the house. Overall, Tina was feeling relieved and closer to being ready to make some changes for the better. She wondered how long it would take to get a degree to increase her income. That was an idea she had kept to herself, set aside like most of her dreams.

Instead of going to the gym, Carson spent the afternoon working in their yard and did some clean-up next door for their elderly neighbor, Mrs. Miller. He had learned the hard way the grass could get away from him quickly this time of year. Everything was starting to turn green and flowers were finally blooming. There were still too many sticks and branches he had to pick up before he could mow. Since he knew how much his mom loved to be out on the deck, he pressure-washed out there while she was asleep to surprise her.

Carson couldn't get his friends off his mind. His invitation to the twins to come over for the afternoon had gone unanswered. He wasn't sure what was going on with them. After he came in and showered, he went up to his room to work on a song he had been writing. He checked his phone again—still no reply.

Natalie went home after church. Penny was dealing with some anticipation anxiety, so she practiced walking in her boot and imagined conversations with her friends. She knew they would ask lots of questions. She didn't want to be too dramatic and she didn't want to get too much attention about it. Mom told her Mrs. Jenkins said she had already explained to the class it would be inappropriate for them to bombard her with their curiosity. Penny wondered what she would learn about Mr. Quintana. She had acted like she didn't want to go to his office; but to be honest, she was looking forward to finding out more about him. As usual, Penny had some ideas in the back of her mind.

Tina was delighted when she got up and saw what Carson had done. She and Carol had one more late night to talk, but they were still drained from Saturday. They looked through the old movies and had a good laugh watching *9 to 5*. Afterward, Carol went on to bed. Tina stayed up reading with Sheba curled up next to her on the recliner. Returning to work Monday night was going to be a challenge.

21
Mr. Quintana

Monday morning was relatively uneventful with the typical arguing over bathroom time and smart-alecky comebacks. It was life as usual as everyone grabbed breakfast and readied themselves to get back into the school day routine; only four more weeks until school would be out for summer.

Tina borrowed her neighbor's car. She wanted to take Penny to school on her first day back without worrying about getting their car back to Carson. As they walked into the classroom, Tina was pleased to see how welcoming Penny's classmates were. She had no problem leaving Penny there since she would be spending the time for gym in the guidance office. Penny wanted Tina to stay long enough to meet Mr. Quintana. Mrs. Jenkins thought that was a good idea and suggested they walk down to his office for a few minutes; it was fine for Penny to come back to class a little late.

As Tina and Penny approached his door, the blinds on the window were open and they could see Mr. Quintana in his office. He was walking in their direction, about to open the door for another student to leave. Tina wondered why Penny hadn't said much about Mr. Quintana, as he was quite good-looking. He greeted them with a welcoming smile.

"Hi there, it's good to see you back at school today. Is this your mother?"

"Yes sir, this is my mom, Tina McKenzie. I wanted her to meet you. Mom, this is Mr. Quintana. He's going to be the Guidance Counselor at Riverside for sixth grade next year."

"Well now, thank you for that very polite introduction, Kristen."

Penny giggled and blushed, "My name change was only an experiment. I'm back to using Penny, the real name my parents chose for me."

Mr. Quintana looked up in time to see Tina's raised eyebrows and look of surprised relief. They shared a moment of eye contact, then Tina quickly said she thought she needed to get back home since Penny's grandmother was only there for one more day. After Tina thanked him for making time to spend with Penny they turned and headed back to the classroom.

As they walked down the hall Tina said, "My goodness, Penny, you didn't say anything about how handsome Mr. Quintana is," and felt herself blush a little as she made the comment.

"Whoa, Mom, you are so weird," Penny said, shaking her head as she walked on ahead of Tina wearing a big grin.

When the bell rang to change classes and it was time for her class to go to gym, Penny made her way down to Mr. Quintana's office. She thought back to the day he had come to Mrs. Jenkins' classroom. Even though she was embarrassed about everything that had happened that day, things felt different. Penny had never been inside the guidance office, and she was curious about what it was like. Mr. Quintana seemed to be an interesting and kind man. Even though she didn't say anything to her mom, she *did* think he was very handsome. He had left the door partially open so when Penny knocked, he motioned to her to come inside.

"Come on in, Penny, I'm glad you're here."

She wasn't sure why he was glad, but for whatever reason, *she* was glad, too. Penny walked in and looked around for the best place to sit. As she scanned the room she stopped and stared at a framed quote that grabbed her attention. It was the same as one of the ones Gramma gave her. She stood there with her mouth gaping open.

"You like that?"

"I have one exactly like it. Well almost, the lettering is a little different and mine isn't framed yet, but it's the same quote. Gramma brought two quotes to me from Chile. She gave them to me when I got home from the hospital. Do you know anything about the lady who said it?"

"Isabel Allende is a well-known author, especially in the Hispanic community. She is a prolific writer, with many books, and her quotes are about all sorts of things. She's a brilliant woman; and she's especially focused on human rights. In fact, she was given the Presidential Medal of Freedom several years ago by President Obama. I'm sure she lives in California now; but she is from South America. That would make sense that your grandmother found her quotes in Chile. I think that's where she used to live. You said *two* quotes. What else did she pick out for you?"

"Well, there's that one like yours, about the language of the stars, and the other one is so amazing because Gramma picked it out since it's about writing. You know I plan to be a writer, right?" Penny's eyes were beginning to glisten.

Mr. Quintana pushed a box of Kleenex to the edge of the desk and motioned to the chair. "It looks to me like these quotes, or maybe your grandmother, have special meaning for you."

Usually Penny would have said her allergies were bothering her, but something seemed different. She didn't feel like she had to explain herself. This was not something she was used to.

"Well, I guess it's true about both. My Gramma is really special, and she knows what kinds of things I like. The other quote says, 'You can tell the deepest truths with the lies of fiction,' I like it because I'm learning to write about things that are true, but I change them around. They're not the same, but I can make them mean the same thing. After I write about things I feel, I feel better." Mr. Quintana was quiet and staring at her. She wondered what he was thinking.

Then he smiled and said, "You seem quite different from one week ago. I expected a confused child to sit in my office with me, but today I think I'm meeting the *real* Penny."

Penny wasn't sure how to take that, but she took it as a compliment. She nodded, smiled, and reached for a tissue as she sat and looked at his desk. There were all sorts of things on it like she had never seen on a teacher's desk. He wasn't like other men teachers she knew, but then, she wasn't sure if he was a teacher at all. He had a name thing on his desk that said "Hugo Quintana." He had a plant on his desk and a computer that was turned toward him so you couldn't tell what was on it. She thought that was cool. He could get away with playing games and nobody would know. Then there was a wooden puzzle and one of those twisty metal things that was two things stuck together that you had to figure out how to take them apart. She looked around the room. When she looked behind her for the first time, there was a big poster of the constellation of the lion. Whoa! Why would he have that? She felt like this had to be some kind of trick.

"So where are you from? I've really been wondering. You don't look like people I know who are Hispanic; but your name is, and you don't talk with an accent. And are guidance counselors teachers, or something else altogether?"

Mr. Quintana rocked back in his office chair and smiled a big smile. "Such wonderful curiosity. Let's see . . . you'll have to give me a moment. I want to make sure I answer everything. I am from the region of Catalonia. It is in the northeast of Spain, where Barcelona is. If you've never heard of it, you can look it up in the library. It is an incredibly beautiful place. Unlike Hispanic people of South and Central America, there are many blonde Spaniards. We moved to America when I was seven after my mother died. My father was born in California and met my mother when he was hitchhiking in Spain. He went there to learn more about his heritage. That was also where his father, my grandfather, was born."

"I'm sorry if my questions are rude. My grandmother would probably say they are. My Daddy liked for me to ask questions. It's how to get smarter. Gramma said it is rude to ask something personal or inappropriate. I'm not always sure about what is inappropriate. Even if I'm not sure, I ask anyway and then I find out. That's the only way to learn. But I do have one more question that might be rude. How old are you?" Penny grinned and looked around a little more. Then she had to ask, "Oh! And why do you have the constellation Leo on your wall? Do you love stars or are you a Leo?"

He burst out laughing, "I'm sorry, I'm not laughing at you, Penny. It is a delight to have you ask these questions. I'm thirty-eight, and my birthday is August 15th which makes me a Leo, but I also love the heavens. So, I guess you got several yesses. I considered getting a degree in

Astronomy before I settled on Psychology. That was a difficult decision. I realized I could always study about the stars, about space, and about the universe, but careers in that field are more limited than in Psychology. Oh right, there was one more question. Guidance counselors usually have a degree in psychology and are seldom teachers, at least not in the school where they are counselors. Now a question for you. Where did you learn about Leo?"

"We camped when I was little. Daddy loved the stars and taught me about some of them, but it's hard to remember the things he told me. I look them up at the library or on the computer. Did you know my Daddy?" This was one of the first times Penny had talked to a grown-up like this about her father. It felt odd to her and she wasn't sure if it was okay. When she was little, after Daddy died, they made her go talk to a lady who acted like she thought something was wrong with Penny if she didn't cry. She felt like she might cry now; but she didn't want to think about Daddy and be sad because he was always so happy. That was what she thought she loved so much about him.

"No, I didn't know him, but meeting you I feel like I know him. I imagine he and I could have been great friends. It is obvious you loved your Daddy, and you know he loved you."

"Yes, sir. He still loves me from Heaven. I miss him, but it's hard to remember him. I can remember how he smelled when he came home from work and hugged me, and I can remember what it felt like for him to sing to me; but I can't remember what he sounded like unless we play one of our movies we made when we camped. Mom made a book with lots of pictures for us to always remember. Is it wrong that sometimes I forget that I miss him? Sometimes I'm having fun and I forget to say my prayers, or I forget to tell him goodnight, and then I feel like I'm bad. Now I'm wondering why I'm saying all this stuff to *you*, Mr. Quintana."

"No, Penny, you are not bad. All of that is normal and okay. I think sometimes when you have been holding things inside for a long time, you wait and wait until a situation comes along when your heart says, 'this needs to be said.' When your heart thinks it's a safe place to do it, there it is, it just comes pouring out. I was a young boy when my mother died, and I can tell you I recognize much of what you are saying to me. There was a priest who was a friend of my family who was easy to talk with. I didn't see him often, but when I did my heart felt safe and my thoughts and feelings would pour out. I guess he had a gift and I think sometimes I must also, because there are times kids find it easy to talk to me. I'm honored every time it happens. I thank God for putting me here where you can have a place to say these things."

Penny leaned back in the chair, closed her eyes, nodded her head, and pensively said, "I think you're right."

The bell for class change rang, and she got up to leave.

"Penny, do you like to play games?"

"Like what kind?"

"Oh, I don't know, Chess, cards, Backgammon . . ."

"I'd like to learn some games if that's okay. We have Sorry and Connect 4 at home. The only card game I know is Go Fish, and it's really boring."

"Well then, we will do something fun tomorrow."

"Okay. Thank you, bye."

"Bye, Penny."

22
Revelations

Tina had just gotten up from her nap and walked into the kitchen when her phone rang. She glanced quickly at her watch and breathed a sigh of relief. Since last Monday she had noticed feeling a little panicky from around 3:00 until Penny normally got home. Tina looked at the caller ID and didn't recognize the number. With all the craziness that had gone on in the past week she picked it up anyway, wondering who wanted a piece of her now.

"Hello?"

"Is this Tina?"

"It is. Who's calling?" Tina tapped speaker and put the phone down on the counter while she took several bags of frozen vegetables from the freezer to start some soup.

"Oh, I'm so glad I have the right number, Tina. This is Gwen Prichard, uh, Long. Gwen Long. I haven't seen you since high school. Do you remember me?"

"Of course I remember you Gwen. How in the world are you? Didn't you move away when you got married?" Tina dropped the bags into the sink and picked up the phone.

"I did after my first marriage. Then I moved a few more times. I've finally found a good guy. We're getting married this summer. But this isn't about me. Not really, anyway. I'm going to be in town the end of the week and I wondered if you might be able to meet me for coffee or something."

"Well, I work during the night and sleep while the kids are in school. I get up around now . . ."

"Oh *no!* I'm *so sorry!* Did I wake you? Wow, you work all night!"

Tina wasn't sure what to think. She vaguely remembered Gwen being rather dramatic and the tone of her incredulous response rang a bell. "No. Actually, I had already gotten up. I work the intake desk and do billing at the walk-in clinic. I don't go to work until 8 tonight. My problem would be transportation. Carson, my son, has an after-school job. He takes our car to school most days. I can check with my neighbor and see if I can borrow hers. It's a serious juggling act. If you want, you could come *here* and visit."

"My goodness! One of your children is already old enough to drive. What if I come by and pick you up? We can go to the new coffee place they opened over by the theater, umbrellas outside, nice and relaxing. I think they call it Java something."

"That sounds nice, Gwen, what day are you thinking?"

"How about Thursday afternoon? I'll be coming into town Wednesday night. Jen told me you and John bought on Franklin. That's so crazy. It's not even a quarter mile from my mom's house."

"Well, I think that sounds like a great change of pace for me. I'll have Penny go home from school with a friend. Thanks for getting in touch with me Gwen, I'm looking forward to catching up." Tina felt a pang of weirdness. She wondered who Jen was, and what prompted a conversation about where Tina and John had bought their home.

"Fantastic! That worked out easier than I thought it would. You have my number now. If anything comes up give me a call, okay?"

"I'll do that. I'm at 1212. Is 3:00 okay with you? That will give me thirty minutes to freshen up. I'll make sure the plan works for Penny. I'll let you know if there's a problem."

"Sounds perfect. See you then."

Tina couldn't imagine what could be going on that would make Gwen want to spend time catching up with *her*. They had been acquaintances in school, but not social friends. Definitely not outside of school. What she remembered most about Gwen was how horribly depressed she had been. Then, thinking back, she remembered it was Gwen who had been suicidal after she supposedly had an abortion. Gossip could be so cruel, gossip and assumptions. Tina had dealt with more than her share in middle school. By the time she was in high school she had learned to stay to herself and ignore the petty BS.

The phone rang again. Tina saw it was Carol and answered while she was feeding Sheba.

"Hey Honey, I just got our girl from Carver and we decided we deserve a reward. We're on the way to get a milkshake and thought we'd see if you'd like us to bring you one."

"Ooooh, that sounds awesome. Thanks for thinking of me. How about one with strawberries and dark chocolate."

"You got it. We'll see you in a little while. Need anything from anywhere else?"

"Can't imagine what it would be since you've filled my pantry *and* my refrigerator, Mom. Y'all just bring yourselves home safe so we have a little more time to visit before I go to work."

"Okay, see you soon."

Getting back to normal gave Tina a feeling of satisfaction. She had asked the kids to put their dirty clothes in their baskets and leave them by the washer. She gathered her own clothes and headed out to get things on track in the laundry room. "Oh my, I can't believe this. Did Mom do this, or did the children finally figure out I'm not a maid?" There were a couple of neatly folded towels, several things hanging to dry, and the room was neat and clean. Either no one brought their clothes down, or it had been done and put away. She headed upstairs and was flabbergasted when she went into the bedrooms. "My goodness, a cleaning fairy has invaded this house. Maybe Mom finally got that wand she's always wanted." Whoever had done it, Tina was thrilled. She was on her way back downstairs when Carol and Penny came through the front door.

"Okay Mom, you've been caught. You don't need to be cleaning our house and doing laundry for these children." Penny got an uh-oh look on her face and scooted past Tina up the stairs. Carol and Tina headed to the kitchen.

"I didn't do their laundry. They did it themselves. They finished it yesterday after church while you were napping. I've been after them all week. I think they finally realized letting it build up will cause hours of work. You've been doing too much for them, like I did too much for you and Karen. I finally learned where things went wrong with my sad attempts at parenting. I think I sent the message that you couldn't do it well enough. I'm sorry I didn't know any better. But I do now, so I'm sharing what I've learned with your kids."

"Fine Mom, but they do a good bit of their laundry and a lot of other housework, too. Especially Carson. Since he's gotten interested in nutrition he's been wanting to learn more about cooking. He's even been doing some of the grocery shopping now that he's driving. Carson's going to end up a real catch for some lucky girl," Tina laughed.

"And Cathy's such a neat freak, she goes crazy if the house is messy and says she's embarrassed to bring her friends over. She keeps us on our toes. I do appreciate you helping while things have been so chaotic. It's been a blessing having you here with us. Right now though, I want you to sit down and relax and spend your last night with us as our guest and not our housekeeper."

Sheba jumped up onto the counter. Tina hissed at her and clapped her hands to make her get down.

"I love you Sheba but *get down!* By the way, Mom, I got an unusual call today. Do you remember Gwen Long? She went to high school with me." Carol shook her head and shrugged her shoulders slightly, looking off trying to remember. "Apparently her mom lives near me. She said she's going to be in town in a few days and she wants me to go have coffee with her. She's coming to pick me up Thursday afternoon. It was odd, she was sort of vague about why she wants to talk with me. I'm sure it can't be important." Tina drew a sip of her milkshake through the straw. "Yummy." Sheba jumped right back up. "Cat, I think it's time for you to go outside for a while." She lifted Sheba from the counter, took her to the French doors, and put her out on the deck. "That's why I don't like cats in the house," Tina said, spraying the counter with antibacterial spray and wiping down the counter.

"Do you have a yearbook with her picture in it? The name isn't familiar, but it's been a long time. Maybe if I see a face."

"Sure, that sounds like fun. Let me stir the soup I got started while I was talking to her and we can look."

Tina grabbed the folding ladder and climbed up to reach her yearbooks at the top of the bookcase, then headed to the living room to look. "There she is. *Wow* . . . look at how young we were and look at that hair!"

"Hmmm . . . I really can't say I remember her. Did she come over to our house?"

"I doubt it, maybe for a party, not that I had many. And I doubt I would have ever talked to you about the gossip that went around about her. Subjects girls keep from their parents."

Carol looked at Tina with a wrinkled brow. "What, like booze, drugs or sex? As if we didn't know things were going on. After the way things went with Karen, I think we were afraid to push you to talk for fear you wouldn't come to us at all. But that didn't work either, did it?"

"I don't think it would have made any difference, Mom. I did the things I did, and I can't take them back. Now I have to do the best I can with the life I made for myself. Gwen, though? Her friends were all worried about her. She wasn't worried about hurt feelings. I think she was afraid of what her father would do to her. I don't know if the stories were true. I heard it all, but I never added to it or shared it. But then, I never asked her if she needed help, either." Tina felt a sliver of sadness and regret.

"Supposedly she had an abortion and regretted it. She was so depressed the girls closest to her thought she was going to commit suicide. I'm glad she didn't. She was one of the reasons I hid being pregnant with Carson so long. I didn't want to be talked into doing that. And look at that boy of mine. There's something incredibly special about him." Tina shook her head. "Who would have ever thought I'd have one as strait-laced as him? With a man as disturbed as Jimmy, and me as wild as I was."

Tina was far away in memories. Up and down, good and bad—life had been quite a ride. And most likely she wasn't even halfway through hers yet. It was hard to imagine so much could happen in one lifetime. She glanced over at her mom. Carol looked like she had been punched in the gut. She was pale and her face seemed slack, her eyes staring far away. For a moment Tina thought her mom might be having a stroke or something.

"Mom? What is it? Look at me! Are you okay?"

Carol looked quickly at Tina and took a deep breath. Then, looking down, she closed her eyes and whispered, "It's time you knew the whole story. Maybe it will help you understand why I had such a hard time." She was very still and kept her eyes closed. Tina could see the tears seeping out onto her lashes. She stayed quiet and waited. "Your sister. We didn't know until they examined her after the accident. When they gave us the full report, they told us she was pregnant." Carol sobbed for a few moments, then continued as well as she could. "A friend of hers came to us afterward and told us the truth. He had been with her that afternoon, trying to get her to come to us. He was in the car with her."

Tina could tell how hard it was for Carol to tell her this. She reached for her mother's hand. Carol wouldn't look at Tina as she spoke, "Do you remember the police saying a man was seen running from the accident? It was him. He told us she had planned to go up into the mountains and drive off on one of the turns. He had begged her to calm down and talk to someone. Karen had been taking things, refusing to eat, throwing up, thinking she could cause a miscarriage. She had told him she believed if she had an abortion she would be better off dead." Carol crossed the room for a tissue, then sat back down.

"Oh Tina, Karen was so horribly troubled. She wasn't thinking rationally. We never knew why. We never understood what might have happened when she was younger to cause it. We decided not to report him. He only wanted to help. It wouldn't have brought her back. Apparently, what she had taken was too strong and she either passed out or just let go when she went off the road. Thank God she didn't take him with her."

Carol looked up at Tina with so much pain in her expression, it gripped Tina's heart. She was speechless. What she was unable to tell her mother was that she had blamed herself for her sister's accident since she was eleven years old. What good would it do to add that pain to what her mom was already carrying? That afternoon twenty-three years ago, Tina wanted a soda, a candy bar, and some gum. Karen was doing nothing important, just zoned out watching some old rerun on tv. Tina had been bugging her to take her to the store. Karen told her repeatedly to go away and leave her alone. Finally, Karen got up, grabbed her bag and the car keys, and stormed out. Tina remembered yelling what she wanted from the doorway, thinking her sister was going to get the goodies. But Karen never came home, and selfish Tina stomped around the house all day, wanting to know where her stuff was. Then there was the call. And then there was the long painful goodbye and the apology that Karen would never hear as she lay attached to machines. The last thing her big sister heard from Tina was a selfish shout about what she'd better buy for her greedy brat of a little sister.

Tina pulled Carol close and held her for a long time. The two grieved silently and deeply on levels each would never know about the other.

As life will have it, there's little time in a home full of children to dredge through emotional sludge. Carol and Tina managed to shake off the excess weight of the afternoon. They carried on with cheerful masks until it was time for Tina to go to work. Carson had given Cathy a ride home from swim practice and returned to the gym before Tina needed the car. Carol watched in awe how the gears appeared to turn so efficiently in her daughter's home despite their challenges. Penny was eager to share her day over dinner and was pleasantly surprised when her whole family paid attention to what she said. She made a point of stressing how nice and fun Mr. Quintana had turned out to be, then teased her mom for saying how handsome he was. That got everyone to turn and look at Tina, who blushed a little. After dinner they all retreated to their personal spaces. As Tina was leaving, she told them each goodnight. Cathy looked tired and pale at dinner and had a slight cough. She claimed it was only a tickle in her throat. She insisted she was fine and planned to go to bed early. Carol found herself sitting in the recliner with the lights off—deep in thought and far away.

23
What Else??

Carol said her good-byes to her grandchildren as they left for school while Tina straightened the kitchen before getting ready for bed. With bags already in the car, mother and daughter stood facing each other holding hands. For a moment they were simply two women full of compassion, sharing their pain; each unable to feel with certainty what the other was experiencing. That had to be enough. No words were spoken as they walked together to the car, knowingly embraced, and then waved goodbye as Carol backed out of the driveway.

Tina went to her room and closed the blinds. She lay down on her bed and with no conscious thinking she began to sob, each lurch of her body followed by a stronger one. It was as though every emotion from her entire life had been held behind a massive dam that collapsed with an unforeseen force. The release was of a magnitude she never knew existed. It pushed and pulled her lungs and jerked her abdomen. It pressed on her spine and drew her into a fetal position. Her convulsive moans, at first sharp and spasmodic, gradually slowed to an undulating rhythm as her conscious awareness grew. Finally, she was able to slow and balance her breathing. She felt so tired, so weary of life. Her eyes were open, yet she stared at a void. She struggled to focus and rolled over, picked up her phone, and robotically pressed the numbers.

"Gina, I called to tell you I think I must have either eaten something bad or maybe I have a virus, but that's a lie. The truth is my mom left this morning. I guess I'm finally feeling the full effects of this past week. I wanted to make an excuse and say there's no way I could work tonight, but I can if there's no one who can work my shift. I'm so sorry, I know y'all must be sick of covering for me. At least I've stayed caught up on the billing."

Gina assured her there were several of them hoping to work extra hours, so no problem.

Tina thanked her, then rolled back over, closed her eyes, and drifted off into a much-needed deep sleep.

At 2:30 when her alarm went off, she forced herself to get up. She knew she couldn't let this thing that was grabbing her win. She sat for a while on the side of the bed. Feeling both physically and emotionally beat up, Tina wondered how much of this uninvited pain was necessary. She had no idea how much she had willingly held onto, but she was ready for it to be gone.

Tina realized she never checked with Natalie's mom to see if Penny could go over to her house on Thursday after school. She grabbed her phone to call, but before she could her phone rang; of all people, it was Natalie's mom.

"Hey Julie, I was about to tap your name to call you. Don't you love it when that happens? What's up?"

"Hi Tina. Yes, I do! I just saw an ad where G.M. Plessy is doing a book signing on June 20th in Birmingham. I thought maybe, if it's okay with you, I could take the girls over there. Isn't Penny's birthday in June? Natalie's is on the 18ᵗʰ and I think I remember the girls telling me Penny's is a few days later."

"Oh wow, yes, Penny's is the 21ˢᵗ. That's great! Do you want to tell them ahead of time, or do you want it to be a surprise?"

"I was thinking I could pretend I have to pick something up at the mall. I can say if there's time we can go to the zoo. That should get them to be willing to go with me. They both love Plessy's books. This is the release of her new one."

"That sounds perfect. I'll put it on the calendar in my phone where she won't see it. We can work out details later. I was about to call you to see if Penny can go home with Natalie on Thursday afternoon. I have a chance to visit with a friend from high school I haven't seen in years."

"Oh sure, that's fine. Send a note to the bus driver for Penny to get off at our stop. She's welcome over here any time at all."

"The same is true for Natalie. I hope you know that. I'll talk to you soon. I'll have Carson pick her up before supper. Thanks again for thinking of doing that for the girls."

Tina looked around the room. Nothing was different, but something felt a little lighter. She couldn't quite tell what it was, but now that her focus had shifted, she felt more like getting up and getting some things done. The purging that had taken place earlier came out of the blue, and except for feeling a little drained, it hadn't left the mark she thought it would. For about a minute she felt guilty for calling out.

While she was in the kitchen getting things together for dinner, she heard the bus out on the street. Panic whooshed through her chest and her neck tightened. She ran to the window and could see Penny getting off the bus right in front of the house. "That sweet man, I know he isn't supposed to stop twice on the same street." Smiling, she went back to the kitchen, feeling the muscles in her neck and shoulders release the tension that was there a moment before.

"Mom? Hey, I'm home."

"I see you are Sweetie. You want a snack? I've got apples and grapes. How was your day?"

"Grapes, please, and do we have some lemonade? My day was good. Aren't you going to ask how Mr. Quin*tana* is?" Penny's voice was suddenly a little sing-songish. "I have something for you to sign, and *please* say yes." Tina gave her a *really, Penny?* look as she dug into her backpack for a letter from the school and handed it to her mom.

Tina read aloud, "End of the Year Dance for Fifth Grade," and scanned down to the space provided for name and contact information, then said, "Chaperone Needed . . . you want me to do this?"

"Yes Ma'am, *please* Mom. You'll already be there for graduation and you don't go to work until later. It's right after the lunch for the families for a couple of hours. *Please?*"

"Well, I don't see any reason why I shouldn't. It sounds like fun. Thanks for asking me, Sweetie. Graduating from fifth grade's a big deal. Now, do you have homework tonight?"

"One sheet of math. But I want to tell you about Mr. Quintana. He's teaching me to play Blackgannon, and it is so cool. It's with dice and we need to buy one so I can teach you."

Tina smiled. She and John had played a lot of Backgammon in the last few months of her pregnancy. She was told to rest and just lying around made her stir-crazy. "It's *Back*-ga*mmo*n, and I *love* that game. Your Daddy and I used to play. I think I might have ours up on the shelf in our closet. I'll look later. For now, you go get that math done so I can check it before dinner. Here, let me go ahead and sign the letter so you can take it back tomorrow."

"Thanks Mom. I can't tell you about it yet, but I have a great idea I think is going to turn out to be perfect." Penny put the signed letter in her backpack and headed up to her room.

Tina thought to herself, smiling and shaking her head, "A great *idea?* . . . Penny?"

Tina was in the kitchen getting things out to start dinner when the phone rang again. "This place feels like Grand Central Station today."

"Hello?"

"Hi Tina, this is Greg Robbins. How are things going?"

Tina felt a little shiver run down her spine. "Things are fine, Greg. It's sweet of you to check on us." It had been six years since John's death and she suddenly realized it had been six years since a man other than her dad had called her phone. She wasn't sure how to respond.

"Did Penny make it back to school?"

"She *did.* She's had a good couple of days. She's spending her gym hour in the guidance office and seems to be enjoying it. Mom left this morning, so this is my first night to start getting back to normal, if there *is* any such thing. How about you? I hope you've had a good week."

"Pretty much the same as most weeks. Um, Tina, I'm not much for phone chit chat. I called to see if you'd like to go to dinner with me one night. I realize you work at night, but we could make it an early evening."

"Well Greg, that's so nice of you. I'd enjoy that. When were you thinking?"

"I wasn't sure what works for you with the children. I've been moved to the desk starting next week, so I'm free after five starting on Monday. I know you understand there could be cases I have to take that could interfere, but it's looking like this is where they need me for a while, or at least where they want me after no resolution about the vanishing rescuer at the creek."

Tina swallowed. It sounded a little like he was blaming Penny for being stuck at the desk. "Okay. Yes, I'm familiar with emergency calls. How about Tuesday, a week from today. If we go around 5:30 I can make sure Carson comes home by then. I'll need to be home by about 7:30 so I can tell them goodnight before I go to work."

"That sounds fine. Put this number in your phone in case anything comes up, alright? I'm looking forward to it."

"I'm looking forward to it too, Greg. See you Tuesday . . ."

"Mom, who is Greg?" Startled, Tina turned to see Penny standing in the doorway listening to her end of the conversation with her arms crossed and an odd expression on her face. "Where are you going on Tuesday?"

"Oh Penny, I didn't realize you were standing there. You know who Greg is, Honey. Detective Robbins. He's the nice man who carried you up the hill from the creek. He came to check on you at the hospital, remember? He invited me to go out to dinner. Isn't that nice?"

"I don't want you to go with him. Gramma said that wasn't a good idea." Penny turned and left abruptly.

Tina wasn't quite sure how to take that. She wondered why Penny would have a problem with it. If they aren't doing something that puts the child in harm's way, children don't need to dictate to parents. Whatever Penny's problem was, Tina was sure she would hear about it at some point. Then she remembered her mom's comment in the hospital room.

The phone rang again. "Damn, I just can't catch a break . . .," she whispered under her breath.

"Hello?"

"Tina, this is Beth Benning. I think you may need to take Cathy to see her doctor. She came to practice with a little cough yesterday. Not a problem, not *then* anyway. But this afternoon she sounds terrible. I haven't tried to find a thermometer because it's obvious she's running a fever.

I hate that it's so close to the meet but practicing while she's sick isn't going to do anyone any good. I can't have her spreading something that could get others sick, too. She knows I'm calling you and she's upset about it. She told me Carson's picking her up after practice. Is there any way he could come get her now?"

"Oh Beth, thank you for calling." Tina glanced at the clock. "Carson has about fifteen minutes left on his shift. I'll call there now and ask him to head that way as soon as they can do without him. Sometimes he's the only one there for a little while. Have her sit tight, okay? Thanks again for calling."

"What else?" Tina was wondering how she could go for months in a boring existence, then suddenly it was one thing right after another. She called The Beat and Carson answered. He was receptive to being needed and sounded concerned about Cathy. His replacement had just walked through the door so he would head over to the club right away. Tina looked at the phone after he hung up wondering if she had entered the twilight zone. The oven was preheating so she got the potatoes ready to go in and finished snapping the green beans. The chicken breasts wouldn't take long. It was too late to call Cathy's doctor. Tina wanted to look at Cathy before rushing to their office. She told herself everything would be fine. It turned out to be a good thing she wasn't working tonight. Worst-case scenario they could go to the clinic. She decided that might be the best plan anyway.

Tina took one look at Cathy when she and Carson came through the door and knew her daughter was sick. Cathy didn't look like herself. She was limp, the muscles in her face were slack, and her complexion was pale and flat. Tina could hear her rapid, shallow breathing. Her cough wasn't loud, but it sounded wet and her eyes were bloodshot. One touch to her forehead and Tina didn't need a thermometer either. She sent Cathy up to her room to lie down and called the clinic to see how busy they were. "We'll go as soon as I tell Carson what to do with the chicken. On second thought . . ." She threw the chicken back into the refrigerator, turned off the oven, and told Carson to heat up the vegetable soup and make a couple of grilled cheese sandwiches for Penny and himself. She grabbed the keys and her purse and called to Cathy to come back down, but Cathy was on the stairs. She hadn't had the strength to go all the way up.

24
Life as a Pinball

Tina and Cathy headed into the clinic. There was only one person waiting to go back to the exam rooms. Tina had never come to work this early, so she was unsure what to expect in the afternoon. They only had to wait a few minutes before they were called for triage. Cathy had not felt well for several days. She hadn't told anyone because she wanted to practice for the upcoming swim meet and her birthday plans were for this coming weekend. The cough started with a tickle yesterday; it wasn't painful until today. It hurt worse to breathe. No, she hadn't been out of the country; yes, they had a cat in the house; no, she wasn't a smoker. Her blood pressure was elevated, and her temperature was 102 degrees. She and Tina went back to the exam room where they waited for the doctor on duty.

Dr. Harmon, one of the doctors whose billing Tina processed, looked in and greeted them, letting them know he'd only be a few minutes. Tina was grateful she was able to take Cathy somewhere she felt safe and where she was confident they would find out quickly what was wrong.

When he returned, he asked most of the same questions, but he added a few more, like whether Cathy had been using any energy supplements or if she had tried vaping. As Tina started to shake her head, Cathy nodded and began to cry.

Cathy was terrified. She had been drinking energy shots before swimming for the past week because she was so tired. When one of her friends had an electronic cigarette thing, she and several of her crowd had tried it. Mixed feelings flooded Tina. She was shocked Cathy had been trying things they had discussed on many occasions, but she was grateful Cathy was honest about what she had done. There were those pleading eyes again, asking for forgiveness. Tina put her arm around Cathy and tenderly smoothed her hair back from her face while the doctor got more details.

After he had asked about her activities, he had questions about the chlorine levels in the pool and what time of day chemicals were added to the water. These were questions Tina hadn't thought about. Cathy told him last week the new guy doing maintenance had forgotten to put the chemicals in the night before. When they got there for practice it was crazy strong because he had just added the chlorine. After he listened to her breathing he sent her for an x-ray. Cathy cried while they waited for him to come back in with the results.

Dr. Harmon came back and opened the envelope with the films. He pulled one out and put it up on the light board.

"Alright. What I'm seeing here is pretty much what I expected. See these white areas?" He pointed to the film of Cathy's lungs. "This is a build-up of fluid in the pleural space—right here—the area between the layers of your lung tissue and the lining of your lungs. It's called pulmonary effusion."

"Where in the world would she have gotten that? There's treatment for it? I mean . . . I'm sorry. I didn't mean to interrupt you, I . . .," Tina was beginning to crumble.

"You know what all we've been going through. I'm overwhelmed. Tell me what we need to do."

"Tina, I can't say for sure until we have some tests run. Most likely, we're dealing with pneumonia, and the fact that she has a fever is a good sign that's what it is and not anything more serious. Not that pneumonia isn't serious, but other underlying problems could be worse and need to be ruled out. It would be wrong for me to assume without checking. I'd like to have her admitted overnight, get some IV fluids in her, and run some tests first thing in the morning. She'll be able to rest, and we'll be able to determine what treatment will be best."

Tina was numb. She saw herself inside a pinball machine, being batted and bounced in every direction. She wondered how much more she was going to have to handle. Last week it was Penny in the hospital. Now Cathy? She wished her mom hadn't left.

It must have been obvious to Dr. Harmon she was going to need some direction. He carefully addressed Tina and Cathy with clear instructions.

"Tina, I'm going to get the paperwork done for her admission. Cathy, don't eat anything before you go. They'll give you IV fluids with nutrition so you won't be hungry. You can't have anything in your stomach before the tests. Digestion takes energy your body needs to devote to healing anyway, and the IV will give you everything you need. Tina, how much time do you think you need to get a few things together and take her up there?"

"Well how long are we talking? You really think she needs to be there tonight? You don't think we could wait and go in tomorrow morning for the tests?"

"No, Tina, look at me. I honestly believe the best thing is for her to get the IV fluids and let us monitor her breathing and her blood pressure. The sooner we rule out a few things, the sooner we'll have her back competing in the pool. All I can say at this point is that this most likely is what I've already said. The tests will likely be conclusive tomorrow and the odds are this will resolve treating the pneumonia. When there's an outside chance something more serious is going on, the sooner we know, the better."

"Okay," Tina said. Her thoughts were spinning. She picked at her cuticles, making a mental checklist, then responded, "I need time to go home and arrange for Penny to stay with a neighbor and get Cathy's personal things. I can have Carson take us to the hospital, then he'll have the car for school tomorrow. This will be alright." Tina looked at Cathy as she spoke, as she checked things off her mental list and reassured herself as well, then reached over and squeezed Cathy's hand as they shared an apprehensive look.

When Tina and Cathy walked into the house it was dark, but not too dark to see Carson getting up from the recliner and heading to meet them.

"Mom, I've gotten some bad news . . ."

"Julie, I know it's last minute, but Cathy's being admitted to the hospital with pneumonia and Carson's friend is there in ICU. I can't explain everything. I can't even think right now. I'm grabbing some things for Penny and I need to leave her with you if that's possible. Hopefully it's only for one night. She's already had dinner." Tina was trembling. Julie could hear it in her voice.

"You stay right there and do what you need to do to get ready to go. I'll be there in less than five minutes to pick Penny up. No problem. Natalie will be thrilled. I just need to tell Bill I'm leaving. Praying for you, Tina."

The drive to the hospital was strained. All Carson knew to tell Tina was that Kenny was in the ICU. He flipped the Beemer and landed upside down in a ravine. Jerry had called, but he was hysterical.

"Carson, I know you're upset, but I want to remind you of what you have said to me when I've felt like I couldn't handle anything else. You're only sixteen, but I'm beyond blessed to have you around to remind me of things I've known all my life. I haven't been the best example of walking the walk. Shoot, I don't even talk the talk, and I'm not proud of that. I keep hearing you singing that song to Mom the other night about things falling into place. I can't for the life of me imagine what good is falling into place with all *this*, but I do believe our Lord can hold us if we'll let him. *And* I believe if we wait and listen, He will tell us what He wants us to do."

"I know, Mom, I know. Maybe this is His way of givin' us a wake-up call. I don't think He makes bad things happen. We bring bad things on ourselves. No matter what, He's still there to care for us. I believe He puts us where He wants us when there's somebody who needs us to witness to 'em. I've been driftin' away from Kenny and Jerry. There's been somethin' goin' on and I've gone on with my life. At least I can be there for 'em now. That's what friends are for."

"I hope he's okay," Cathy added, "I'm too sick to be around people in ICU, but tell them I'm praying too, okay?"

"I will Cath, you need to do whatever the Doc says and get well. I know you think I'm a jerk, and I don't say things I should very often, but I do love you, Cathy, and I'll be prayin' for him to heal you. We need you to keep us on our toes at home." That got a smile from Cathy. Tina rubbed something from her eye.

When they got to the hospital Tina handed the keys to Carson and told him to go to the registration desk to see which room Cathy was in before going home. Carson carried Cathy's bag for her as the three went into the brightly lit admissions lobby.

25
Finding Missing Pieces

While Tina and Cathy were checking in, Carson found his way to the ICU nurses' station and asked them to let Jerry know he was in the waiting room. Too antsy to sit, he was standing and looking at an outdoor sports magazine when Jerry came to find him. The two young men embraced as Jerry began to cry. Carson wasn't sure what to think.

"Hey man, it's gonna be okay, Jere . . . how is he? What's happening? Is there any chance they'll let me go back there? It said somethin' about family only on the sign."

"He hasn't waked up, but the doctor said he will, he said he'll be fine in time. It *looks* bad, oh *man*, *really* bad, but he's alive. Thank you so much for comin' I was goin' crazy back there by myself. I'm gonna tell them you're our cousin and I need you back there with me 'cause I need to be back there when he wakes up. I don't want him to freak with all the tubes and shit stuck in him. Come on, let's just go back there, there's not a lot of people in there. I don't think they'll mess with you and I gotta be with him."

Carson could tell Jerry was terrified; his face was pale and his eyes were darting around. It would be bad enough for it to be just a brother, but this was his identical *twin*, and he was sure that made things different. The two walked back past the desk. Jerry spoke to one of the nurses and told her Carson was his cousin who had come to sit with him. She nodded and kept looking at her computer screen. Carson couldn't help but wonder where their parents were, but he was afraid to ask. He decided to let things unfold by asking an open question.

"What happened, Jere?"

"Oh *man* it's a long story, but I'll try to make sense. You know, I'm not feelin' like it makes any sense 'cause this has been buildin' over the past couple months." Jerry turned to face Carson directly and leaned close, slightly squinting his eyes, speaking with pressure through his teeth, "Our dad is movin' to Boston where he will be a big important lawyer in a big important firm and he's not takin' us with him. He assumed Mom would be happy for us to stay with *her*, but Mom is not only *her* anymore 'cause she has some dude like ten years younger than her keepin' her over at his place most of the time." Then whispering, "trashy whore." Jerry's voice fluctuated in volume and speed, startling Carson. "Our *mom?* Some mom. Never there. Obsessed with lookin' young like a street walker and even had some work done on her face—probably has new tits." He was visibly shaking and the expression on his face shifting back and forth between extreme grief and rage. Now Carson understood why he had felt his friends pulling away. He wished he had asked what was going on, although he doubted there was anything he could have done. It sounded like Jerry was feeling unimportant; maybe abandoned.

Carson was unaware of an entire element in the mix of problems. These twins were identical, but that stopped at their genetics. They both lived under the delusion that the other had identical feelings. What neither understood was that beliefs about self and the world are developed early in life. Our beliefs are based on individual perceptions of experiences, many from so early in life there is no conscious memory. To assume that beliefs and expectations about life will be the same for *any* two people, even twins, is ludicrous.

The two fetuses grow together, but usually, one slightly ahead of the other, at least in size and position. They are entwined and are connected to one another physically, to their own heartbeats, and to their mother's body rhythms. Then one leaves. Does the other feel left? Is there a deep, misunderstood sense of abandonment? Is it possible that the first feels pushed away? The newborn can't know it is the mother's body sending them out one at a time. And then the newborns are likely placed in separate incubators. These verbal explanations are only applied after the fact to sensations which occur preverbally, as many other early childhood events do. Beliefs begin to develop from different perspectives, and no feeling is ever identical again. They need each other. God glued them together so they are meant to be one force, but they can't be treated identically.

"Ken was upset this mornin' when Mom came in about the time we were leavin' for school. He got in her face. She basically said she'd already done her share of raisin' us and we were fine takin' care of ourselves since we'll be seventeen in June. She said Dad would send enough money and we could live in the house until we go to college. I mean, *what?* Just walkin' away and decidin' money takes the place of a family? I don't know why this feels like a spoiler alert, because that's been our life for a long time. But then, *you* know that don't you?" Carson winced and nodded. He hoped this was doing Jerry some good.

"So anyway, we went to school this mornin' and Ken was drivin'. He parked, and then when I got out he started the car back up and took off, leavin' me in the dust. I called him and he didn't answer. I went on into class and kept tryin' to get him to answer. At about 2:00 he sent me a text and said come to the side door by the gym and he'd pick me up. We had somethin' we needed to do. That's how we know about the dick Mom is shackin' up with. Ken went back to the street before our house and he sat and watched. Mom came out and took off. He followed her to a house on Second Court. When she pulled into the driveway, he pulled in behind her. The guy was standin' in the doorway. Ken asked her why. She told him he wouldn't understand until he was an adult. Then she told him if he knew what was good for him, he'd go back to school.

That's when he came and got me and drove me by to show me her car. He had a bottle of Jack Daniel's from Dad's bar in the car with him, chuggin' it straight." Jerry was sitting beside Ken's bed, staring at the floor, then at his brother. "Why? Why Dad's liquor? Why would he think that would help or that anything would change Mom? It doesn't make any sense. I would never have had that reaction to the things that were goin' on."

It dawned on Carson this had been an issue for a long time. Kenny tended to overreact and think he had to do things to make sure he was acceptable and everybody was happy. It was like he thought if he was perfect, they would do what they were supposed to do. He had way more emotional struggles than Jerry. That concept baffled Jerry because he could see the problems each of their parents had. It never occurred to him it was his responsibility to fix his parents' problems. And it didn't make sense to him that his brother seemed to think that way. Now though, there was a new opportunity, and it was a matter of time. Jerry and his brother would have a chance to figure it out, and if Carson could help, he'd be there for his friends.

Carson sat through the night with Jerry, praying for them and for their parents.

26
Filling in the Blanks

Early Wednesday morning Cathy and Tina were waiting for the tests to be done. Dr. Harmon made a special trip earlier than his usual rounds to discuss his concerns and to make sure things had been scheduled as early as possible. He expected to have at least a preliminary report by mid-afternoon and hoped he would be able to discharge Cathy. Tina was relieved and grateful for her job that gave her a connection to some good doctors.

Carson went up to Cathy's hospital room and asked Tina to call the school for him. He stayed down there with Jerry all night and hadn't slept. Kenny had come to around 2:00 a.m., but he was in pain and agitated. They put something in his IV to help him rest. Carson had wondered why their mom hadn't been to the hospital until Jerry told him they only gave their dad's name to admissions. He was afraid if Ken woke up and she was there it would be a bad scene. Mr. Branson's plane would be landing soon. Jerry wanted to be with their dad alone to tell him what had happened. Carson made him promise to call if he changed his mind and wanted him there, but for now he was going home to shower and see if he could get a little sleep.

Penny had no problem going to school with Natalie. School was okay, but she looked forward to her time with Mr. Quintana more than anything else. Today she had the signed paper from her mom saying she would chaperone the fifth-grade end of year dance. She didn't tell her mom Mr. Quintana was the faculty advisor for the dance. Now Mom had gone and made a date to go out with that detective. What could she do to keep her mom moving in the right direction? Mr. Quintana would be the perfect man to help Mom deal with Daddy being gone. He loved the stars and he was just the right age. It helped that he was handsome, and Mom had already noticed that. Penny told Natalie about her hopes and made her swear she would never tell anyone.

The bell rang and time for gym had finally come. Penny could hardly wait.

Mr. Quintana was waiting with a smile. Penny was thrilled when he smiled at her like that. She felt important. She went on into his office and settled into the chair at the side of his desk, expecting to play a game of Backgammon.

"Hi, Penny, how are you today?"

"Well, I spent the night at my friend Natalie's house. I'm good, but my sister's in the hospital having tests and my mom's there with her. My brother was there last night, too. One of his friends was in a car accident and is in the intensive care. We have a lot happening in our family."

"You are a brave girl, Penny."

Penny liked hearing Mr. Quintana say that about her, even if she didn't understand it. She didn't feel all that brave. Mostly she felt scared. She didn't understand yet that facing the fear was being brave.

"I brought the paper for the dance. My mom signed it before she left. And she likes to play *Backgammon*, did I say it right that time? She thinks she has her old one in the closet. She was going to get it out last night, but then Cathy came home sick." Penny was sure that Mom liking Backgammon the same as Mr. Quintana would be a bonus.

"I'll pray things turn out well with your sister. We can talk about that if you want. And yes, you said it right. How's your writing going? Have you written anything new?"

"I've been working on a new story, but I think I might want to write a book. I've been looking up some articles about how to make my characters seem real, and I'm learning about different points of view. Most of my stories have been in first person so far. I don't really understand some of them. Did you ever write stories?"

"No, I never wrote stories. I did write some song lyrics though. I guess that's actually more like writing poetry."

"My brother, Carson, writes songs. He works at The Beat. He plays the guitar. Daddy taught him."

"Carson at The Beat is your brother? He works at the gym too, doesn't he?"

Penny squinted at Hugo Quintana. "No-o, he works *out* at the gym, but he doesn't *work* there. How would you know about my brother?"

Mr. Quintana smiled. "I go into The Beat for strings for my violin and wax for the bow. And I go to the gym as often as I can after school. I've seen him there helping people. I assumed he worked both places."

"You play the violin? That sounds cool. Did you play it when you were a kid?"

"No, I took lessons when I was in college. My girlfriend was a music major and *she* played. She wanted me to be able to play along with her. I had always wanted to play an instrument, and once I started to learn, I sort of got hooked. I've thought about learning the cello, but I haven't done anything about it yet."

Oh, no. Penny wasn't feeling good about the direction this was going. She wanted to ask about the girlfriend, but she was pretty sure that would be one of those questions that's inappropriate. He didn't have on a wedding ring. Then she thought about him and his violin. She imagined him on a stage in a tuxedo with his hair slicked back like on tv. She hoped he broke up with the girlfriend, but then it occurred to her he could be gay. There were no family pictures anywhere in his office. Her imagination was running wild. She had watched too many Lifetime movies. Hoping she was wrong, she decided to nod and wait to see what else she could find out later. She changed the subject.

"So, are we going to play a game of Backgammon?"

"I guess we have time for a game. Let's see how well you remember the set up."

"I think you'll have to remind me, but I'll try."

Lunchtime had come and gone. Cathy was able to eat now that the tests were done, but then did nothing but complain about the food. Dr. Harmon had been right about the diagnosis. Cathy had pneumonia, and there was nothing going on involving her heart or her kidneys. Those were the two main things that could have been a possible cause of pulmonary effusion. The discharge papers were being signed on the condition Tina would be in touch with the clinic, bring Cathy in for breathing treatments, and maintain strict bedrest for the first week. He concluded Cathy had been stressed about Penny around the same time the chlorine gas was so strong at the pool, and that had been too much for her immune system to manage. He sent a letter to Cathy's coach explaining the importance of the chlorine having time to off-gas.

Cathy was devastated when he told her she shouldn't swim for at least a month. If Tina could bring her in for him to check her breathing in three weeks, he might change his mind since she was otherwise in excellent health. It still wouldn't be in time for the meet, and it would be another year before she had the same opportunity. Tina tried to get Cathy to understand there must be more to it. If she was meant to swim in the Junior Olympics it would have to be when the time was right. Cathy's attitude was terrible, and Tina was feeling grateful she was scheduled to work.

They called Carson to come pick them up and got Cathy's things together while they waited for him. He told Tina he decided to stay and check on Kenny and handed her the keys. Tina wasn't sure how things felt so smooth and organized. Whoever was playing the pinball game must have run out of quarters. Regardless, it all timed out exactly right. For a moment she forgot how insane the last 24 hours had been and she smiled at her feeling of confidence.

Carson got down to the ICU in time to see two security guards go around the corner and he could hear yelling coming from inside. When he moved to one side, he could see a red-faced Mr. Branson standing with his arms tightly folded across his broad chest. The woman he could hear yelling lunged forward into Carson's view, swiping at Mr. Branson's face while one of the guards grabbed her other arm. It was Mrs. Branson. Someone must have told her about Kenny. It looked like the guards were trying to remove her from the ICU. She was screaming that she had every right to be there, that it was her son, and they couldn't make her leave.

He wanted to go try to help, but Carson didn't think she would be receptive to him being involved. He chose to stay back out of sight and listen. He heard Jerry telling her it was her fault Kenny was in the wreck to begin with. She said that was ridiculous, but Jerry shouted that she was too busy with her boyfriend to be a mother. Then he heard Jerry ask his dad to please get her out of there because it was upsetting Kenny. Carson saw Mr. Branson nodding his head as he put his right hand on Jerry's shoulder and leaned close to him. Carson couldn't make out the barely audible message, but the cluster of people had been slowly inching out the doorway of the ICU and into the hall. Before Mrs. Branson realized it, the glass door slid shut, and the nurse pulled the curtain to block the view the unit.

Carson realized Jerry's dad had been easing him out of the way of the door a few steps at a time. Carson stepped a little farther back but not quickly enough. When Jerry spotted him, he ran to Carson and hugged him, leaning close. He whispered so no one else could hear, "My dad has the police on the way. I don't know everythin' that's happened 'cause Dad got here and I went to get somethin' to eat. I came back and *she* was here and goin' nuts. I think she must've threatened him or somethin'. She's stupid to mess with him."

A police officer came around the corner. Mrs. Branson jerked her arm away from the security guard, turned toward Mr. Branson, and gave him a glaring look and a barely audible growl of not to be repeated words. Jerry pulled Carson by the arm. The two boys went around behind where Jerry's dad was standing and tapped on the glass door. The nurse pulled the curtain back enough to see it was Jerry and opened the door so they could go inside. They went in to where Kenny was. He looked terrible but he was wide awake. When he saw Jerry, he appeared to be relieved and he smiled a bit at Carson. Carson wasn't used to seeing the expression on Kenny's face. He still wasn't talking much, but Jerry had told him Carson had come and had stayed all night and Jerry had told Carson everything.

"You know, Ken, you gave us a scare, man. It looks like your parents have some problems they're gonna have to work out, and you're gonna have to take good care of yourself to get healthy and back to hangin' out with me, 'cause I've been missin' you, man, both of you. Past several times I've called I've gotten voicemail and you guys haven't called me back. I stayed home Sunday afternoon and pressure washed the deck for Mom and did some other stuff in the yard. My Gramma was here. She hoped she'd see y'all while she was here. She said to tell you she'd see you next visit." He was hoping if he sounded matter of fact and sort of dismissed all the drama it would help Kenny feel better.

Kenny didn't need anyone pointing out what he did was stupid. Carson was sure he'd already had that thought on his own. And he didn't need to be told he should be ashamed of what he had done. His shame was obvious. What Kenny needed was unconditional friendship and to be told everything was going to be fine. More than anything else he needed to be reminded that his Father in Heaven thought he was perfect the way he was. He was about to say a prayer when Mr. Branson came in, and they turned to hear what had happened.

Mrs. Branson had left voluntarily in exchange for no police involvement. Mr. Branson told Carson that Tina didn't need to have to come pick him up. Now that Kenny was out of the woods, Mr. Branson or Jerry could give him a ride when he needed to go. Carson wanted to stay, but when Tina went to work it would leave Penny alone with Cathy, who was too sick to do much of anything. Carson also realized the boys needed time with their father. He was glad Jerry had told him the move to Boston had been postponed.

At about 7:00 p.m. Carson and Mr. Branson went out to his car. It had been an interesting couple of hours listening to his friends talk with their dad about how they had been feeling. Carson was impressed with how honest they were with him. At least Jerry was. Kenny mostly nodded or shrugged enough to express agreement. It seemed easier for Jerry to do all the talking. As Carson thought back, it had always been that way. Jerry talked for them both, but it seemed like they had a way of communicating silently. If they disagreed it was obvious, and they would end up having to discuss whatever it was. Now that he had imagined what it would be like for one to be gone, he could see how much a unit they were, not identical parts, but two individuals that made one whole.

27
Right Between the Eyes

On Thursday morning Tina got home from work to find all three of her children sleeping peacefully. She went into Cathy's room to check on her and breathed a sigh of relief when her forehead felt cool. The medication had obviously kicked in. She headed downstairs to the kitchen where she made coffee and began getting breakfast ready. When she opened the refrigerator, there was a note stuck on a jar with a heart drawn on it and the words "Best Mom Ever!" in Carson's handwriting. Tina smiled. "Now that gives new meaning to my day starting on a good note."

Penny left with her note for the bus driver that she would get off at Natalie's stop. Carson blew Tina a kiss and left for school, knowing he would need to go by after work and pick up Penny. Cathy would only be alone in the house for a few hours. If she needed anything she could call, and Gwen could bring Tina back home. Tina hoped she wasn't wasting her afternoon. It seemed like an awful lot of arrangements just to drink coffee with a girl she hardly remembered and wasn't even sure she liked. Tina wondered why she felt she needed to go. Before she lay down to sleep, she made sure Cathy had everything she needed and gave Carol a quick call to let her know things were fine. She set her alarm.

Tina woke easily, relieved she had no crazy dreams and no fear of impending doom. Still, she couldn't help wondering what was around the corner.

Gwen pulled into the driveway at 3:00 and Tina was ready and waiting. When Tina hopped into the car she reached across the console for a brief, awkward shoulder hug to greet this girl she hadn't seen in years and barely remembered.

"Wow, Gwen, you look great!"

"So do you, Tina. Looks like we're a couple of the lucky ones when it comes to ageing, but I'm not naming any names."

Tina smiled, but inside she cringed. There was one of those typical catty comments she hated. She hoped that wasn't an indication of what the afternoon was going to be like, thinking to herself, "I don't want to be sorry I agreed to do this."

"I've heard this little coffee place is nice, Tina, but I haven't been there. How about you? Is that still okay, or is there somewhere else you'd rather go?"

"Any place is fine with me. I hardly go out, especially lately. I almost had to cancel today. Cathy has pneumonia. We spent Tuesday night and most of yesterday in the hospital. She's already feeling better, though, and she'll only be home alone for a few hours. I'm keeping my phone on just in case."

Gwen had an exaggerated *Oh My* look on her face and Tina wanted to reach over and pop her under her chin to shut her gaping mouth. "Wow, *Ti*-na, and you're sure it's okay for you to go?"

"I'm fine, really, this is good for me." At least she hoped it was.

The conversation started off with the typical hometown questions, like "how's your mama?" and other benign comments about it turning into a nice spring. Polite. Avoiding anything too personal.

"Now let's see, Gwen, you said you're getting married this summer. How exciting! Tell me all about it."

"I'm one lucky girl. I've found the *nicest* guy. It's taken me a couple of big mistakes to learn, but this one is a keeper. His name is Jim Ross. He's a widower, and he has no kids. He's a CPA with his own firm in Huntsville and mostly does business taxes. That's about it. That's what's so good about him. It's hard to find someone without lots of baggage these days. I hope that didn't sound wrong. I mean . . . you know, you having three kids on your own and all. Okay, here we are." Gwen pulled into a parking space and they headed into the shop.

Tina wasn't sure what to think. She never thought of her children as *baggage*. She imagined after making the choice Gwen made in high school, having children wasn't something she felt alright about; or maybe she couldn't have any and saying she didn't want them kept people from asking. Tina thought about the Aesop's Fable about the fox who wanted the grapes and couldn't reach them, so he gave up and walked away saying he didn't want them anyway; they were probably sour. Maybe children were Gwen's sour grapes.

"Earth to Tina . . . hey girl, you're a million miles away. I think he's ready for our order."

"Oh, I was thinking about those pastries. But I'll just have a regular large black coffee. What do these places call it, an Americano? You have to remember my day is just getting started."

"And I don't know *how* you can do it. *I'd* go mad." Then Gwen ordered some version of latte Tina had never heard of, which left her feeling much like she did in middle school. Even though her curiosity was up, she was feeling more and more apprehensive.

When they got their order, they went outside to sit at one of the tables under a big umbrella. It was a nice afternoon and there was a fresh breeze. Gwen sat stirring her whatever it was and looked off into space for a moment as if she was trying to decide where to start.

"I guess you've been wondering why I called you after all these years, Tina."

"To be honest, I haven't been able to figure it out. We never were close. We didn't even have many mutual friends."

"Well, on that Monday when Penny was missing, and I'm *so* glad things worked out the way they did by the way, I was visiting my mother when her neighbor called. She's one of those women involved in community affairs and all the neighborhood watch stuff. She's a volunteer whenever something like *that* happens. She asked Mom if she could join the group gathering to start a search."

"Yes, the police told me one was being formed. It wasn't long after that when we finally heard from her friend who had an idea about where she was."

"Right. Well, when I heard the name McKenzie and realized it was your daughter, I got chills all over. Do you remember Ruthie Randolph? She graduated a few years ahead of us."

"No, but I kept to myself and my closest friends were girls I grew up with in church; at least until nobody wanted anything to do with me when I started dating Jimmy our junior year. He'd been out of school several years already. After that, I was only at school to graduate." The name

Randolph didn't mean anything, but still, Tina could feel the hair on her arms standing up.

"Oh, that's *right*, I remember hearing all about all those *horrible* things you and your little children went through . . . how you were abused and him *killing* himself and everything. He was an alcoholic, wasn't he?"

Tina felt like her head might explode. She told herself to take a deep breath, to stay calm, and to think before she opened her mouth. Nope. Let it rip. "Okay, *Gwen*, I'm not sure what your *deal* is, but whatever you *heard* would be in the category of *gossip*, because you didn't hear it from me. And *thank goodness*, it seems we have little in common. Frankly, I think I've had a blessed life. I have three *wonderful* children, who definitely aren't *baggage*, and I'm grateful for all of it. Now, would you like for me to share the gossip I heard about *you*? Because I never have shared it since it was exactly that, *gossip*. I didn't come here to listen to you throw sideways compliments at me and hint about how much better off you think you are than me. Let's cut to the chase. Exactly *why* did you bring me here?"

"Look Tina, I'm trying to do you a *favor*. *I* know things you *need* to know, so I'll tell you and then I'll take you home. Ruthie Randolph and I were friends since elementary school. We took dance together for years and our mothers were best friends, still are. She married Bob Kendrick."

Tina's mind began to race, and things were starting to click. Gwen could see recognition in Tina's eyes and that she wanted to interrupt. Gwen held up her hand as she continued, talking even faster as though she had rehearsed this.

"Bob took a job in Huntsville because their marriage was on the rocks. Ruthie met a guy she really fell for, but she lied to him. She told him she was divorced because he said he could never be involved with a married woman. She finally broke down and told him the truth after he asked her to marry him. He was devastated and he walked away like he said he would. She didn't think he really meant it. One week after they split her period was late. She panicked. She drove to Huntsville and seduced Bob. She told him she was sorry and wanted him to come home. They talked about it for about a month. Ruthie tried one more time to see if the guy she loved would change his mind, but he was seeing someone else. When she told Bob she was pregnant, they went to a counselor and worked through their problems. A few years later they had a second child, a boy. Their first, a little girl, was very fair like Ruthie. Bob's family is dark, and his parents urged him to have a paternity test. He refused. He had recommitted himself to the marriage and he loved his daughter. Bob truly was a good man. The little boy favored Bob's people." Again, Gwen shushed Tina when she tried to interrupt.

"Ruthie's father died when her children were small. Her mother lived near her and Bob and the grandchildren. *Now* her mother, Rhoda, lives in Atlanta, where she's raising the children. Phoebe is 11 and Robbie is 9. She's raising them because Ruthie and Bob died six years ago in a house fire."

"*Stop!* I don't want to hear any more of this!" Tina was hearing these names. These names at first only vaguely familiar, echoed in her mind. These names had been in the newspaper, but she had shut all that away. She buried it so deep she didn't think it could ever surface. Her head was in her hands, partially covering her ears and her eyes. This was crazy. Why was Gwen telling her all this about the people John died trying to save? About these children he *did* save, who so tragically became orphans . . . "*Please* Gwen, take me home."

"I'm not *finished*, Tina. The man Ruthie was in love with was John McKenzie, the same John McKenzie *you* married. If you'll look at a calendar, you'll see that Phoebe was born less than nine months after you started seeing John. The *gossip* was only that he had been involved with Ruthie at

one time. But the *truth?* The very important truth, *Tina,*
is that your daughter Penny has another sister.

Tina covered her ears, crying. Gwen reached over and
grabbed Tina's wrist, pulling her hand down and forcing
Tina to look at her.

"This is important, Tina. Penny's sister's grandmother
loves her desperately, but Rhoda is terribly ill, and that's
not the only problem. Bob's parents never liked Ruthie and
I think they see her in Phoebe. They weren't in the position to get Robbie after the fire, but they are now, and they
won't hesitate to ask for a paternity test so they can take
Robbie without Phoebe. They think Phoebe is old enough
to be sent to some other family member. Believe me, there
isn't one, at least not one where she would be cared for
properly. The only person on this earth she has left after
her grandmother dies is your daughter. Okay, I've said it
all, let's go. I'll take you home."

Gwen got up, put her bag on her shoulder, shoved her
chair up to the table, and turned to go out to her car, leaving her latte. Tina was stunned. She wasn't sure what to
think. Could this be true? She watched Gwen walk away.
She slowly got up, picked up Gwen's cup, threw it in the
trash with hers, and followed her out to the car.

The car was silent on the drive to Tina's house. When
they came to a stop in the driveway, Gwen turned to Tina,
who had been looking out the passenger window the whole
way with tears streaming down her face. She reached over
and took Tina's hand.

With a quiet sincerity Gwen said, "I'm sorry. This was
up there in the top two hardest things I've ever had to do.
I didn't do it to hurt you. It's not about you. I can't do it
for the one I denied, but I can for this one. If I wasn't sure,
and if I hadn't already found out as much about you as I
could, I would never have done this. I know people who
know you—who think you are an amazing person and an

outstanding mother. That's what Phoebe deserves." Gwen reached into her bag and handed Tina a photo of a girl who looked to be about Penny's age. "This is Phoebe Kendrick. She turned eleven on December 20th."

Tina took the photo, squeezed Gwen's hand, and got out of the car. Part of her felt so terribly angry, but she wasn't sure what the other feelings were that were mingling there with the anger. She went into the house and back to her room. Sitting on her bed, she stared at the photo of the lightly freckled face that was staring right back at her. She thought about calling her mother, but decided she needed some time to think about how she felt before she let other people's opinions dictate her decisions, as was typically her way.

She took out her phone and turned it on to look at the calendar. Starting with December 20th, she counted backward forty weeks, the length of a full-term pregnancy, and put her finger down on March 15th. She closed her eyes and went back to the night she met John for the first time; the night he took her by ambulance to the hospital in the wee hours of March 12th, twelve years ago. That was the morning Jimmy died. It was during the week after March 26th when she returned to work at the coffee shop that John McKenzie came in after a shift, looking like he'd lost his last friend. It hadn't occurred to her his sadness might have been personal, given his line of work and the kinds of tragedies he dealt with often. They talked for hours, on and off, and he'd asked for her number. Tina wasn't sure if she was happy to know why he was sad or hurt knowing she was the replacement for Ruthie.

She walked over to her dresser and stared at the photo she kept there of John. She took the photo of Phoebe and wedged it into the corner of the frame, then she headed upstairs to check on Cathy. On her way through the living room she spotted the yearbook she and Carol had flipped through to find the picture of Gwen. It was the one from her junior year. She needed to find the one from tenth grade. She got the step ladder and pulled the red and white Annual from the top shelf.

Randolph, Ruth. There she was, a very pretty blonde, and when Tina saw her, she was startled. Tina and John had gone out for lunch the day they had been to their official appointment with the OB/GYN the November after they had married. They were thrilled. While they were talking John kept looking past her, distracted, watching something or someone. Tina finally excused herself to go to the ladies' room so she could turn around to see what he was watching. When she did, the only person who stood out was a beautiful and *very* pregnant blonde. She asked John if he knew her because he had been staring. His complimentary excuse was that he was thinking about how beautiful Tina would look when she was that far along. Tina shook her head as she remembered how flattered she had felt. She kept hearing Gwen's words, "It's not about you." Tina wasn't sure how to stop the flood of painful questions that were hitting her right between the eyes.

Carson brought Penny home from Natalie's and went back to the hospital for an hour. He assured Tina he would be home in plenty of time for her to go to work, but he noticed an unusual look in her eyes. She was quiet and distant. He assumed she was tired from going back to work at night and was still adjusting, but something about her worried him. When he got home, Penny was playing with Sheba in the living room, Cathy was asleep, and their mom, according to Penny, hadn't come out of her room. He went to her door and tapped on it.

"I'm on my way out. Give me a minute."

Carson asked Penny if she had eaten after he looked around the kitchen and didn't see any sign of dinner. She had made herself a peanut butter and jelly sandwich. She didn't know if Cathy had eaten. Now Carson was concerned. There had to be something else wrong. This wasn't like Mom at all.

Tina came out of her room, gave Carson a quick kiss on the cheek as she took the keys, and ran out the door to go to work.

28
Sheba Won't You Please Come Home?

Friday came and went. Tina went through the motions of what felt to her like everyday life. For the rest of the family, there was an unspoken tension. Even Julie Cross, who called in the afternoon to check on Cathy, picked up on how distant Tina sounded. She called back to see if Penny could go to her house on Saturday morning, spend the night, and go to church with Natalie on Sunday. Tina welcomed the break.

Cathy's Saturday bowling party was cancelled, but she felt a little better, and complained to her friends about how miserable and bored she was. Susan, one of her teammates, called Tina to see if she and the other girls who had planned to go bowling could come over and surprise Cathy with a cake on Saturday night. They promised to keep it low and thought maybe they could watch a movie with her. They even offered to bring Chinese carry-out.

Tina agreed to the plan, but she asked Carson if he would mind being around so things wouldn't get out of hand. She wanted to make sure they left at a reasonable hour. Kenny was being discharged that morning, and Carson had planned to spend time at their house. He didn't want to see his mom any more stressed out than she already was, so he agreed to stay over at the Branson's all afternoon and be home by dinnertime. Tina made the mistake of telling Susan that Carson would be there. The girls didn't mind at all. A few of them were a bit moonstruck and hoped Carson would join them for the movie.

Unfortunately, one of the girls slipped and made a comment about being excited to see Carson and it was no longer a surprise. Cathy gagged at the thought. That would change the entire focus of the night. Now that she knew they were coming, and it was supposed to be an early birthday party for *her*, she really didn't want her brother there. But what was new? It was never about her. It was always either about *Carson* and how he had overcome being bullied, his *tragic* fall in gymnastics, and his *amazing* talent and looks; or it was about her poor little bratty, drama-queen sister and how *sad* it was she lost her daddy like that. Didn't people realize he was her dad, too?

Cathy had done a good job of setting herself up to have to do things for herself. She looked efficient, organized, and disciplined when she set goals and somehow achieved them. She was very capable of looking like the one who had it all together and didn't need help from anyone, but she was angry inside because she didn't know how to express what she needed, and she was jealous of those who could. If anyone had an idea of how hard she worked to make it look easy, they'd never believe it. The meet was coming up in one week. It wasn't fair. It had been taken away from her.

When those uncomfortable feelings came up, Cathy became frustrated and confused. She wished she knew why, but there was no way she could understand on her own. Hers were the reactions of a small child to events she couldn't understand. Cathy didn't learn to express her needs or her feelings because she hadn't acquired language when she experienced her father's violence. Instead, her brain recorded the sensations deep in her subconscious memory and made sure to warn her if something triggered it. She knew she wanted to feel better. She wanted to feel safe and in control. She believed working hard was the only way.

Tina slept away the day, grateful Cathy felt well enough to heat up some soup for herself. She didn't want to think. She didn't want to be worried about this girl whose face was tormenting her and staring into her with those eyes. They were John's eyes. She wanted to throw the photo away, but she couldn't make herself do it.

When she got up, she went to the kitchen to make sure Sheba had been fed. There was her bowl of food, but it didn't look like it had been touched. She called Sheba. No cat. She went upstairs and saw Penny's door was open and so was Carson's. She called Sheba again and tapped on Cathy's door.

"What's up, Mom?"

"Is Sheba in there with you? She hasn't touched her food. I'm making sure she isn't trapped in anyone's room."

"I put her out when I got my soup for lunch. It looked nice out and she was at the door."

"Okay, I'll go call her. I don't like her being out for hours. She wanders and comes in with stuff stuck in her fur. Next time you let her out, please call her in a bit and get her back inside, okay?" She could imagine Cathy's eyes rolling and couldn't resist rolling her own.

Tina went back downstairs. Passing through the living room, she saw the yearbook was still open to the Rs where she had looked up Ruthie Randolph's picture. She slammed it shut, climbed up the stepladder, shoved it onto the bookshelf, and then went out onto the deck. The wind chime brought tears to her eyes when she thought about John. Instead of feeling his arms around her, she could only picture his arms around Ruthie. She stood on a chair and reached up to take the chime down. Something caught her eye. Cathy was standing at the door watching her.

Cathy pushed the door open. "What's wrong, Mom?"

"You wouldn't understand."

"How about you try me? You don't give me much credit."

"It's not about *you*, Cathy. Please don't add more to it."

"You're right. It's never about me. Did you ever think it doesn't have to be about me for me to care?" Cathy turned and pulled the door shut behind her.

"Cathy *Wait!*" Tina got down from the chair and ran into the house, but Cathy had already disappeared up the stairs. She took a deep breath, exhaled her defeat, and went back out to call the cat. No cat. "Damn it, Sheba, not you, too. Come home, Sheba." She picked up the chime and took it inside to find the box it came in, then put it in the top of the hall closet.

Tina went back to her room and put the framed picture of John with the attached one of Phoebe face down on the dresser. Three days ago she yearned to have his arms around her. She wanted to hear him tell her how wonderful she was one more time. She felt so betrayed. She wanted someone to talk to; someone who would be honest with her and help her get back on her feet. There had been too many lies.

She thought about her doctor, but she didn't have time to listen to Tina's misery. She thought about her Pastor. He was a good man, but she didn't want someone to pray over her. She wanted someone who could *hear* her, *really* hear her, the way it used to feel when John listened to her. Now it felt like that was only sympathy. Was it just another rescue? She had blocked out the messages John had shared with her about who was *always* listening to her, *hearing* her, waiting *patiently* for her to ask for help.

An image of her mother came to her mind. She picked up her phone. Her finger hovered over "Mom." Tina looked at the clock and laid the phone down. She had no car. She couldn't kill time by going to the store. It was only 4:00 p.m. There was no dinner to cook since the girls were bringing Chinese. She felt so listless, floating along in what felt today like a useless existence. She wasn't even tired enough to go back to sleep before work. Aimlessly, she walked to her bathroom and stood staring at herself in the mirror. She turned on the water in the tub, poured in a generous scoop of epsom salt, and undressed to take a long soaking bath.

The girls showed up around six. Cathy was excited to have some attention. Carson got home a little early thinking he could get a chance to talk to his mom. She took the keys from him, informed him the cat still hadn't come inside, and walked out the door. He went outside to look for Sheba. The girls argued about what movie to watch, two of them wanted to know what *Carson* liked, hoping to lure him into joining them. They gave in to Cathy and agreed to watch *50 First Dates.* Cathy chose it so Carson would beg off, but she was wrong. He was bored and in the mood to watch something he had never seen. The girls were overjoyed, but carefully acted nonchalant. Carson called several times, but still no Sheba.

Tina went home Sunday morning to a silent house. The kitchen was clean, as was the living room. There was Sheba's food, waiting in the bowl. She had planned to go to church with Carson. Instead, she decided to leave a note for him on the counter. The excuse of a headache worked for explaining her behavior and got her out of cooking breakfast. She went to her room, undressed, and climbed into bed. When she woke in the afternoon, she felt groggy. She hadn't set an alarm and had slept hard. Faint voices came from the kitchen, so she put on her robe and pushed herself back into the world of the living.

Carson and Cathy were sitting at the counter. They stopped talking as soon as they heard her doorknob turn and stared at her when she walked into the room. Earlier, Cathy told Carson about Tina taking the chime down, and he shared concerns he already had. They agreed something was wrong but neither knew how to get Tina to talk about whatever it was.

"Is there a problem?" She met their questioning expressions head-on. "Did anyone find Sheba?"

Carson was first to speak up. "I got up and went to church. You weren't up so I figured you were gettin' caught up on sleep. Then I saw your note. We were tryin' to be quiet. Mrs. Cross brought Penny home, and Natalie offered to stay and help find Sheba. They went out lookin' for her. They've only been gone about thirty minutes. I was wonderin' if you wanted me to go get some groceries."

"No, I'd like to go in a few minutes. I'll get dressed. I still have plenty of time to cook. What do y'all want for supper?"

Carson turned to Cathy with a *maybe she really was only tired* look. She returned a similar raised eyebrow expression.

"I guess whatever's easy that you don't mind making, Mom, or you can tell us what to do and we can make it. Carson's been rubbing it in that he's learning to cook and I'm not, so I guess it's time for me to show him a thing or two. I'm tired, but it's not that hard, is it? At least not if we do it together. I'm going to bed early, but we've still got to eat. Maybe we should be asking what *you* want for supper."

Tina laughed and shook her head. "Did I wake up in an alternate reality? I'll tell you what, let's start a new tradition. Let's make Sunday afternoon our time to cook together. It's about time we scheduled a dedicated time for a family activity. Maybe we can add a game or a movie on Sunday nights when I don't have to leave for work. This afternoon, we can start with something super easy, like taco salad. I already have some meat I cooked and seasoned in the freezer. Do we have any of those good blue corn chips? Sour cream . . . tomato . . . lettuce . . . I think we have everything else . . ." Tina's voice trailed off as she rummaged through the cabinet and the produce drawer in the refrigerator. She turned to give her smiling children a thumbs up and she thought to herself, "I know I can do whatever it takes to put this family back on track. I've done it before, and I can do it again. I just have to stay focused."

"Carson, you can start by opening a can of black olives and cutting them up. Cathy, go grab the freezer bag of meat seasoned for tacos, it's labeled. Put it in a bowl in the sink and let the cold water run on it for a few minutes." Tina's new project was underway. She had always been good at shifting her attention when things were too uncomfortable. This was something she knew how to do. Avoidance via redirection . . .

Penny and Natalie came bursting through the front door with Sheba.

Tina was relieved, "Yay! You found her! Natalie, call your mom and see if you can stay for taco salad if you want to, or I can take you home if you'd like. Where in the world was the cat?"

"Mom! There's a man named Mr. Harris two blocks over," Penny was out of breath from running the best she could wearing the boot and she was talking fast. "You remember that grey house that was for sale for a long time? He lives across the street from it. The man who lives there now, in the grey house, just moved in. We were walking down the street calling Sheba and he came out on his porch—the new guy who just moved in, not Mr. Harris—and he asked us what we had lost. I said we were looking for my cat, a big white Persian. He said, 'Come see if this cat I found is yours.' Mom, I remembered when you told me about people tricking kids to go into their house or their car to show them puppies or to help them find something, so Natalie and I stayed right beside each other on the sidewalk and told him what she looked like. He said, 'Come up here and look at the cat.' I told him I wanted to call the cat and he could open the door. If it was her, she would come. He was weird, Mom. I got one of those bad feelings. I didn't think he was going to do it, so I yelled really loud, 'Mister you better let my cat out of your house,' and another man came out to the sidewalk from the house across the street and asked what was going on. I told him that man on the porch told us we had to go up to his house to see if the cat he had in his house was mine. He said, 'You girls stay right here,' and he went up there. The man on the porch had gone inside and he wouldn't answer the door. We couldn't hear what Mr. Harris said, but suddenly, the door opened, and Sheba practically flew out of there. She shot under the bushes and we had to crawl under there and drag her out. Mr. Harris said, 'You girls get on home.' He told us we probably should stay off that street. He told me to tell you his name was Mr. Harris and he was going to call the police and report what happened."

Tina, Carson, and Cathy were dumbfounded. They looked at each other as if to say, "What else could happen in this family right now." Tina decided she needed to tell Julie before things got blown out of proportion, so she called. Natalie's parents came over to get the whole story first-hand. They went ahead and took Natalie home so they could drive by there and Natalie could show them which house it was. Mr. Cross wanted to talk to the police also. Tina was ready for life to slow down. The *family food night* as they decided to call it, was a success. When Tina left for work, she reminded them to make sure the doors were locked.

29
When ... Finally!

The special family time impacted all four of them. On a few occasions, one of them questioned what they would be cooking next weekend. Tina patted herself on the back for changing the course of the way things had started to move. The old routines that still functioned ran like clockwork. By the time Tina got home from work on Tuesday morning, she was back in the old sleep pattern. She chalked up her reaction to her visit with Gwen to being exhausted. She got the children off to school, including Cathy who was doing so well the doctor said she could sit in class, but no gym, no getting overheated, and *definitely* no swimming for two more weeks, and then only some laps.

Tina went to her closet and stared at the rack of old clothes. She hadn't bought anything new in what seemed forever. She wondered what she was thinking when she agreed to go out. She had no idea where they were going. Laughing to herself she thought, "I could dress for work. I wonder what he would think if I wore scrubs to dinner." The image of a possible look on Greg's face brought an audible laugh. "Hmmm, I'll go with classic and simple." She pulled out a pair of black pants hoping they still fit and grabbed a white cotton shirt; then stuck the shirt back because she didn't want to iron. She put the black pants back and took out a pair of khaki pants. A black, lightweight long sleeve knit top she had forgotten she owned looked perfect—that would work with black flats and her pearls. Done. She could wear that anywhere. Now she could sleep without worrying about what she would wear. A ponytail would have to do. Before she got in bed she called and scheduled Penny's therapy appointments. Then she called Martha Miller next-door to see if she could borrow her car next week. Tina hoped she could eventually talk Martha into selling it.

When her alarm went off, Tina was already lying awake dealing with a bit of anxiety about going to dinner with Greg. Maybe her mom was right. Was she too vulnerable? Even worse, was he looking for someone to rescue? That subject was bothering her more than anything else given the new information she got last week from Gwen about the man she thought she knew. Now she didn't know if it was her own judgment that was faulty or if John had an agenda she never understood. She preferred to believe none of that mattered. Even if he had loved Ruthie, she broke the deal by lying and showed a side of herself he couldn't accept. That only said something about *John's* morals and ethics. So what if he *was* lonely and heartbroken that night in the coffee shop. There was no crime in that. She certainly was sad and lonely. It was just two weeks after her abusive marriage ended with her husband's suicide. None of that meant anything about the love that grew between her and John. She didn't have money, she wasn't due to get some big inheritance, and there was no logical explanation to make her believe she was second best. She had mulled it over for five days now. No matter how she looked at it, she simply had to accept it.

The issue that remained was what to do about this girl? Gwen suggested Phoebe had nowhere to go but to live with Tina. Could she really consider taking in this child to become a single mother of *four*? She needed to get up. She couldn't dwell on this.

Cathy called and asked if she could go to the club and watch practice. Tina made an executive decision that it was too soon. Cathy didn't need to breathe any of the chemicals, not today anyway. She agreed to talk to the doctor to see what he thought about it, but for today all arrangements were already made. She was pleasantly surprised when Cathy didn't argue.

Tina stood at her bathroom sink and inspected her face in the mirror, debating whether to wear some make-up. She didn't want Greg to get the idea she wanted attention. She only used a little blush, some light mascara, and lip gloss. She decided that was good enough. When she walked out of her room into the kitchen, Penny was leaning against the doorframe, glaring at her with her arms crossed.

"My goodness, Miss Priss, what's *that* look for?"

Penny simply turned and headed for the stairs.

"Penny, come back in here and talk to me."

Tina could tell Penny's reply was coming from somewhere on the stairs.

"Why are you dressing up and going out with that policeman?"

She went toward the entry so she could see her daughter.

"Penny, I'm going to have dinner with another adult. The same as when I went for coffee one afternoon last week with an old friend from high school, remember? I know you don't want me to be gone from home, Honey, but sometimes moms need an opportunity to have grown-up conversations that don't have anything to do with homework, groceries, or housework. I'm only going to supper. I'll be back to get the car before I go to work, I'll kiss you goodnight, and I'll kiss you when I get home in the morning just like I always do. There's nothing for you to be worried about. I promise. You and Cathy and Carson are the most important things in my life."

Penny came back down the steps to Tina's out-stretched arms.

Greg parked in the driveway and walked up to the front door right on time. Tina felt a little like she was back in school, intentionally waiting in the kitchen until he rang the doorbell so she wouldn't appear too anxious. She greeted him, asked if he thought she needed a wrap, took his word for it that she didn't, and called to Cathy and Penny that she was leaving.

Greg had already decided where he wanted to take her. He pulled into a spot in front of Luigi's, where they had anything from salad or pizza by the slice to Penne Puttanesca or Chicken Carbonara. Luigi's had been around for a long time, so it felt like it was a safe choice. Tina was delighted. After they ordered, she remembered she wanted to tell him about the man with their cat on Sunday afternoon. While she was relating the story as Penny had told it, he got a serious look on his face.

"This is the street about two blocks over from you? Did you go over there?"

"No, I didn't go. Penny had Natalie with her. Her parents came and heard the whole thing and Bill Cross, Natalie's father, went over. Bill couldn't get the guy to come to the door. It was a man from across the street who told Penny and Natalie to go home and not to go near there. I think Penny said his name was Mr. Harris. He was the one who went up and got the man to let the cat out. He told Penny he was going to call and report it."

"That's George Harris. He called us to report the incident. There's much more to the story. I can't discuss it. I wish I could. At some point I'll be able to, but for now keep Penny close to home. No roaming the neighborhood alone. Well look at that. Here's our dinner."

Tina tried several times to start that conversation back up, but Greg shut her down each time. The rest of dinner was pleasant, but there were no fireworks. Tina hadn't thought there would be. She was relieved it appeared to be mutual. It was comfortable and nice to feel like an adult anyway. Greg walked her to the door, and she thanked him for a nice evening. Except for the polite comment he made that they'd have to do that again sometime, that was that. As Tina walked into the house, there were three sets of eyes on her. She laughed to herself as she went to her room shaking her head to change for work.

The rest of the week was basically uneventful. On Thursday they had a cake and ice cream to celebrate Cathy's actual birthday. Tina surprised her with a birthstone gift, a small emerald pendant that had belonged to Tina's grandmother. Cathy was preparing for exams and looking forward to the school year being over before Memorial Day, even if it meant school starting again mid-August. She would be joining Carson at Weatherford High, where she had already been signed to the swim team. She had expected to start the next season already holding the District title—stupid pneumonia.

Penny was excited to be moving up to middle school, grateful Cathy would no longer be there. The hours she spent with Mr. Quintana continued to be the brightest spot in her day. She had been learning about how middle school works. The yearbook and newspaper committees sounded like things she might want to sign up to do. Another day was marked off the calendar on the wall by her desk with a big red X. She circled the Wednesday of the last week and put a star. Then she wrote "Orientation 5:00." On the next day she wrote "Grad/Dance" and added a little heart. On the Tuesday of that week she had written "BOOT OFF." Thankfully, the therapy on her ankle wasn't as painful as they told her it would be. On Friday in big letters she put "NO MORE SCHOOL." She flipped ahead to June and wrote "NATALIE" on the 18th and drew a cake with eleven candles on the 21st and wrote "ME." Penny stepped away from her calendar and admired all the red on it. It looked like an important month already half-way gone.

30
A Twist of Fate

Saturday morning everyone was up early planning to go to the swim meet and cheer for Cathy's team even though Cathy was unable to swim. It was hard for her because this chance to win District had been her goal for so long, but she was forced to accept reality. Tina and Carson both reminded her of all the progress she had already made and convinced her she would be even better by next year. There was no reason to think her chances of swimming in the Junior Olympics were over.

The meet was scheduled to get underway at 9:00 a.m. Cathy came downstairs with sunscreen and ball caps for everyone and found Tina standing in the kitchen looking out the window with a puzzled expression.

"What's wrong, Mom?"

"Maybe it's only me, but the air looks funny. I know that sounds crazy but come look at the sky. Were we expecting a front?" Tina went to the French doors and stepped out onto the deck with Cathy close behind.

"Wow, it's a weird color Mom. You're right, it's sort of yellow."

"Not good! Cathy, go turn on the weather. See if they're saying anything."

Carson came down when Cathy was turning on the television.

"What's up?"

"Carson, look at the radar on your phone. Mom's out on the deck."

"What's everybody doing? Why aren't we going?" Penny came into the living room.

"Sit tight Penny, Mom thinks the sky looks like somethin's goin' on. We're checkin' the weather. We'll go in a minute . . . *or maybe not* . . ." Carson's voice raised when his radar app connected.

"Hey! Oh no!" Cathy yelled from the living room.

"Y'all come look! It's getting even more green! It looks like a tornado sky! Cathy, did you find anything?" Tina called from the French doors.

Cathy came running out to the deck with a frantic look in her eyes.

"Tornadoes Mom! There's a tornado warning on the screen. It's saying there's a whole line of weather and it's moving in our direction. They said yesterday it didn't look bad but this morning it's blown up big with hail!"

"Hey y'all—look at this radar! *Wow!*" As Carson turned the face of his phone to share the image on his screen, the sirens from the tornado warning system started blaring. Just as suddenly, he lost his signal.

The sky was darkening. The wind was starting to blow in gusts with leaves and things flying around. The tops of the trees jerked and swirled erratically. Tina yelled, "Y'all get inside!" She motioned for them to go and pulled the drapes in front of the doors and windows.

They knew this drill. In this part of the country you had to know what to do and how to do it quickly. They headed to the space up under the stairs that was their lowest and safest place in the center of the house. There they sat huddled together to wait it out. Sudden blasts of wind and heavy rain repeatedly hit the windows and shook the walls of the house. It was like the water was being blasted at the house by someone pointing a fire hose at it, then it sounded like a spray of bullets being fired from a machine gun.

Tina nodded, "There's the hail! Thank goodness I put the car in the garage when I came home this morning." They sat together for a good thirty minutes and prayed for their safety and for their community. Finally, the noise from outside stopped. Tina was relieved they never heard the train-like roar. Tornadoes were not that uncommon. It always amazed her how they could appear suddenly and leave almost as quickly.

The onslaught of Mother Nature, as devastating as it can be, also serves as a fast cleaning out of old dying limbs, piled up leaves, and structures that have seen their last useful days. The string of storms moved across the area like a toddler having a temper tantrum. It came on with little warning and was wild and unrelenting, but when it was over it was completely over. As fast as the sky had turned green then black, it was blue again and the sun was shining.

Carson drove Cathy over to the pool to survey what had happened since they had no service. The streets were scattered with limbs, moss, and garbage cans, and there were a few downed trees and damaged cars and porches. People were already out cleaning up, and overall, at least this time the community had been spared the worst. Unfortunately, the pool at the swim club didn't fare so well. One of three tornadoes had scraped across a nearby building and scattered large amounts of debris across the property and into the Olympic-size pool where the meet was to have been held. The officials determined the meet had to be rescheduled. If at all possible they had to find a date that would still fall within the required timeframe to count toward District.

Cathy's teammates turned to look at her. They all knew how important this was for her, and they welcomed her strength for the team events. With a broad smile, Coach Benning gave Cathy a high-five and said, "You better ask your mom when you're allowed to start practicing."

That afternoon Coach Benning stopped by the house to let them know the meet was rescheduled for June 2nd, one week after school was out. Dr. Harmon had already given Cathy permission to start back swimming in another week, but only laps for the first week and she had to continue her breathing treatments. That would give her one week of swimming hard to build her stamina back up. Cathy vowed to get enough sleep and to eat right. For the next week she asked to go to the gym with Carson every afternoon so he could help her with her leg strength and gradually add a little cardio. She was going to have a chance after all; she didn't want to blow it.

On Sunday Cathy went with Carson to the gym after lunch. When they put their bags down to stretch, Cathy flipped her t-shirt over her head and tossed it onto her bag.

"What do you think you're doin' Cathy? Put your shirt back on."

"I have on a sports bra, Carson, it's for *exercising*. Good Lord, what's wrong with you?"

"No, I'm not okay with you bein' half-dressed in here. Look how those guys are lookin' at you!"

Cathy looked around. "I look like every other girl in here, Carson. You don't have a problem with my swimsuit, so what's the deal? You afraid I'll get more attention than you, Mr. Muscle?" She secretly liked that he cared about her and wanted to protect her. Kenny and Jerry walked up just in time to hear Cathy's comment. Jerry laughed. She noticed Kenny hadn't taken his eyes off her.

"Not funny, Cathy, you're *thirteen*, not twenty-three. Put your shirt on or I'm takin' you home." Carson was adamant.

"Fine, but I'm fourteen, *Dad*," Cathy pulled her shirt back over her head.

Carson's friends had been going to the gym with him and Mr. Branson liked the idea. He was considering joining also. Jerry was getting into it. Kenny couldn't do much yet, so he was taking it easy. Carson told Kenny he thought he was spending a little too much time looking at his baby sister.

That night they celebrated the rescheduled meet with a pizza delivery instead of cooking, then decided the *family food night* would still be good every other week. Tina was disappointed, but at least they ate together. She was determined to get it going every week eventually, but conceded it wasn't the best timing to try to start something new at the end of the school year. Tina managed to get an entire week of work in without another disaster, not counting the tornado.

31
The Lucky Wonderful Week

As Sunday rolled around again, Tina insisted they do something special. They cooked baked Ziti with roasted asparagus and garlic bread. The house smelled like an Italian restaurant and everyone went to bed full and ready to finish up the school year with a good last week. Tina felt great about the effort they all made to help and have fun together. Even if it was only a few hours that week, it was better than it had been for much too long. She had made plans to borrow her neighbor's car on Monday, finally for something other than therapy. She planned to pick Penny up from school for a surprise shopping trip.

Tina had the school send Penny to parent pick-up, which upset her at first. With everything that had gone wrong lately, Penny was afraid something else had happened. It only took her a minute to get excited once she knew she and her mom were going shopping.

"Would you like to wear a dress, Penny? Or would you rather find some dressy pants?" Penny looked at the racks of clothes, frustrated that the cuter things were in larger sizes.

"All the things that fit me look like kindergartener clothes. I hate being so small. I wish I could find something to make me look a little bit older."

Tina took her by the hand and started out toward the exit. Penny saw a look on her mom's face she didn't recognize. She wasn't sure why, but she thought she might be in trouble.

"I'm sorry Mom, I'll stop complaining. I promise. Really. Can't we still look?"

"Yes, but we're going somewhere else. I have an idea. Let's go, okay?"

They got in the car and Tina headed to a shop she hadn't visited in six years. When the car stopped, Penny looked around. She didn't think she had ever been here before. It was right on the side of the street, not in the Mall or back behind a big parking lot. There were pretty pots of big red flowers outside the door and a black and white striped awning out over the window where welcoming mannequins wore sunglasses and fun summer outfits. It looked like a wonderful place.

"This, Penny, is a boutique. I used to shop here when you were a baby. They carry things for ladies and girls, but not like the department stores. This kind of store is a little more expensive, but they have beautiful things, and there's always a sale rack. I haven't bought anything new for myself either, not in years. We, my dear, are going to treat ourselves."

"Yay! It's girls' day!" Penny practically skipped into the shop and came to a screeching halt when she saw a pair of palazzo pants. They were tiny, like her, but they looked so grown-up. They were a soft grey-blue like the sky on a rainy day, and there was an off-white blouse with lace and ribbons hanging next to them. Penny finally stopped staring and looked around in wonderment at all the things in the store. They had a chandelier and there were oriental rugs on the floor. There were bags, scarves, cool necklaces, and clothes were hung all around; not on big, round, crammed racks. She had never seen anything like this place.

"Well would you look at that. Palazzo pants. We couldn't have hoped to find anything better." Tina smiled confirming Penny's interest, then looked at the sizes and took the girls' 6/8 and the matching blouse and put them in the dressing room. A salesgirl Tina remembered from when she shopped there before came over to welcome them. Tina told her how glad she was to see she was still working there. Penny watched the animated interaction. This was all new to her, and Tina realized this was something she should have been doing with Penny all along. Instead she took the easy route, shopped, and put things in Penny's drawers or closet. She felt as though she was waking from a six-year-long spell like *Sleeping Beauty*, but she wasn't sure who or what played the part of the apple poisoner that left her asleep for so long. She wondered if maybe she had done it to herself.

"Are you looking for something special?"

"I think we may have already found something Chloe, it is Chloe, isn't it?" The salesgirl smiled and nodded. "This is my daughter, Penny. She's graduating this week from fifth grade, and there's a dance that afternoon. I'm going to chaperone, so I'd like to look nice, too. I haven't bought anything new other than scrubs in years."

"Nice to meet you Penny, congratulations on graduating. I saw you looking at those palazzos. I'll bet they're going to look great on you. What did you do to your foot?"

"I fell off a rock in the creek and it landed on my ankle! It got dark and nobody knew where I was, so God had to come and pull me out of the water. *Never* think it's a smart thing to have a secret place to go. And today is the last day I have to wear this boot." Penny excitedly explained her ordeal.

Poor Chloe wasn't quite sure how to respond to all of that, so she looked at Penny and then at Tina with big eyes and an open mouth, then said, "Oh, my goodness, that sounds like a big ordeal. I hope it's better soon, Sweetie." She turned to Tina, "And what can I help *you* find? I'm so sorry, I don't remember your name."

By now Tina was shaking her head and laughing. Penny watched her wondering what was so funny. Tina winked at Chloe and smiled.

"It's Tina, Tina McKenzie. I think I'd like to find some nice pants, maybe linen, and a top that looks like it isn't ten years old, and I'll be perfectly happy. This is Penny's big day. I don't want to upstage her."

"How would you do that, Mom?"

"I don't want to take any attention away from you, Honey."

"But you need to look really beautiful so Mr. Quintana will notice you."

Tina gave Penny a questioning look.

"What does Mr. Quintana have to do with Thursday?" Tina asked Penny. It dawned on her this might be that secret plan Penny had going on in her head.

"Oh, did I forget to tell you, Mom? He's the academic sponsor for the dance. Isn't that *great?* You'll get to spend the whole afternoon with him. May I go try on those pants now?"

Tina shooed Penny toward the dressing room. Now it was Chloe's turn to laugh. She had been watching this mother-daughter interaction with obvious delight.

"You've got yourself one special little girl, don't you? Who is Mr. Quintana?"

"Unbelievable. It looks like my child is playing match-maker. At least she has good taste. He *is* one *handsome* man. Maybe I need to think twice about what I'm looking for after all . . ."

Penny came out of the dressing room looking adorable. The outfit looked like it was made for her and she was glowing. Tina was looking through the racks when Penny spotted a red blouse that Tina was about to pull out. They both agreed it was exactly what Tina needed.

"Mission accomplished, Penny. We are going to look great. Wasn't that fun? The only other thing we need to do is go get haircuts. How about we do that tomorrow after school?"

"Mom, I love having special time with you!"

Tina pulled Penny close as she opened the car door for her.

Penny went to school on Tuesday without the boot. Mrs. Miller had no problem letting Tina use the car again, so after school they went for haircuts. Tina felt so competent being able to get things done in the afternoon, she decided to ask again about the possibility of buying Pete's car.

Pete and Martha Miller lived in the house next door when Tina and John bought their home. They were a sweet couple in their eighties. Mr. Miller passed away last year, and Tina made it a priority to check on Martha every few days. They only had one son who had retired and moved to South Florida. It seemed to Tina he made little effort to visit, but she didn't know the whole story. Tina had asked Martha if she would sell Pete's car, but she hadn't been ready to let it go yet.

When they got home from getting haircuts, Tina pulled the car into the driveway next door and headed up the walk to return the key. Martha was sitting in a rocker on her porch, smiling at Tina.

"I'm going to miss this place and your sweet family, Tina."

"What are you talking about? Please tell me you aren't moving away."

"Robert called me today. You remember my son, Robert, don't you? He has bought a different home down in Florida. He said he's been worried about me and wants to have me where he is. He bought one that has an apartment attached to one side of it with its own carport and its own side entrance. It's in a neighborhood with mostly older folks, *and* it has a pool. He's coming up soon to help me pack and move me down there." Martha was beside herself. "He said there's only room for my one car and I told him I only *had* one. He asked what happened to his dad's car and I told him I already found the right home for it. I think you need to take that car of yours and get it out of my driveway." Martha was beaming and began to giggle. She looked happier than Tina had seen her look in a year. It was such a relief hearing Martha's son wanted to take care of her.

"Martha! I was on the way over to see if I could talk you into selling it. You don't need to *give* it to me. That's ridiculous. Let me buy it."

"Tina, I watch you take care of those children and work crazy hours and find ways to keep that home of yours in beautiful condition; add that you're always over here check-ing on me like I'm your mother. You deserve some help, and I'm in the position to give it. So, my dear, don't argue with me unless you want to hurt my feelings."

By now Tina was in tears. She couldn't get over Martha's generosity. She bent down and gave her a big hug. There were no words.

"When's Robert coming? I'd like to come over and help you go through things so you'll be ready for him. Men throw things out without asking. You're going to need to have some of it packed up before he can question you. At least let me do that."

Martha giggled and gave Tina a thumb's up.

"He'll be here in two weeks. I want to donate a lot of it unless there are things you or the children would want. He said I have one bedroom, a small living room, and a nice roomy kitchen and laundry. I told him I need the measurements so I can make good decisions and not try to take more than I need to be comfortable. Without Pete . . .," Martha's eyes were beginning to tear up, "It's been lonely over here. I'm grateful to have had a sweet neighbor like you. You've made it so much easier, Tina."

Tina was squatting beside her, holding her hands. She hugged Martha again and told her she would come over tomorrow afternoon after she got up, then headed toward home to start dinner almost forgetting to take the car to her own driveway. Then she remembered orientation and let Martha know she would be tied up until Friday.

When Carson and Cathy pulled in, Tina was just getting out of the car. They looked at her and made questioning faces. Tina dangled the key and pointed at the car. Then she pointed at herself and danced around in the driveway. Martha watched from her porch, laughing. Carson got out of the Subaru and did a little dance mimicking her, dangled his keys and pointed at the Subaru then at himself. He waited for confirmation with a questioning look. Cathy got out and asked if everyone had lost their minds. Carson ran to Tina and they hugged and jumped up and down. Tina said he better go next door to thank Martha, but he was already headed over there before she could complete her sentence. Martha told Carson she was moving, and he told her he'd be over on the weekend to help. She was beaming, blowing a kiss to Tina and Cathy. Penny heard all the noise outside and came out to see what was going on.

"Why's the car back over here, Mom?"

"Sweet Miss Martha is letting us keep it!"

"Yay! Now you can pick me up from school more often." Penny waved and smiled at Martha. "Wow, this has turned out to be our lucky wonderful week!"

As they walked into the house, Tina could feel her phone vibrating.

"Hello?"

"Hi Tina, this is Beverly Greene. I wanted to check on Penny and see how things are going."

"Things are wonderful, Beverly. How are y'all doing up there?"

"Oh, we're fine. Glad school is about over. Listen, I heard about a little church camp for girls in Alabama. It's up north of you, near Tennessee. They don't advertise much because it stays full by word-of-mouth from their church. I took a chance and called to see if they have any sessions this summer for two eleven-year-olds. They have two sessions when our girls could be together. One is right during Penny's birthday, and the other is over the Fourth of July. It's for two weeks. Any chance you would consider letting Penny go? I sure would love to find a way to keep the girls connected."

"Oh wait, let me keep walking back to my room where I won't be overheard. We just came inside from celebrating. My neighbor has given me her late husband's car. Can you believe that? An unexpected blessing, but now I've got to pay for insurance, and with a teen driver in the house, it's out the roof. How much does the camp cost? Goodness, for *two weeks?*"

"Tina, I've been looking and pricing camps. Some of them are two grand a week. Outrageous. I couldn't believe it when they said the cost was twelve hundred for the two-week session, and that includes *everything*. And it's close enough for you to drive there. I could fly with

Sally to Birmingham and rent a car, and we could take them together." Beverly was talking so fast it made Tina's head spin.

"It sounds like you've been doing some figuring," Tina laughed, "I need a few minutes to think about how I could pull it off."

"I bet your mom would help with some of it for Penny's birthday. I can loan you part of it if that would make it work. They told me they would give me an hour to let them know before they showed those spaces as available. I think this must be the time of year all us last minute people try to figure out something for our children for the summer. Which session should I tell them to give us?"

Tina took a deep breath, "Penny already has a surprise she doesn't know about yet for her birthday, so it'll have to be the fourth, if that is okay with you."

"I wouldn't have given it to you as an option if it wasn't. Alright then. I'm calling them back right now. I'll send the deposit for both and we can work out the details later. I'll give them your address to send the paperwork and list of what she'll need to take. I think I'm more excited than they will be. I'll talk to you again soon. And you need to order some iron-on name tags."

Tina thanked Beverly and wondered how she was going to work camp into her budget. She still had some of John's life insurance money set aside, but she hoped to keep that for real emergencies. To be realistic, this wasn't an emergency. She felt the old doubt creeping in, slinging thoughts of failure around in her head, calling her stupid.

"I'm not going to do this today."

She sat on the side of her bed, closed her eyes, and bowed her head. Tears ran down her cheeks before she even began to pray. "Father, I'm so tired of feeling lost. I'm tired of always either running or hiding. I need help. I know I should focus on being grateful for how even the terrible things that have happened lately have turned out to be wonderful, but I need you to take this fear and dread from me and hold me. I can't do all this on my own. Thank you for my children, for protecting Penny, for healing Cathy . . . for all the things you do to get my attention. Thank you for Miss Martha—for putting it on her heart to give me that car. Forgive me for thinking I could do it by myself. I need your help, Lord. I need you to show me what to do about this girl named Phoebe, John's daughter. She is always in my mind, those eyes, looking at me—looking through me. I want to do the right thing, but I don't always know what that is. Please help me know. I need a sign."

Tina stretched out on her bed and stayed there for a while staring at the ceiling before she got up to start dinner.

32
Conclusions

Carson and Cathy had both taken exams during the past week, so they were enjoying a laid-back last week of school. Cathy was finally swimming laps to build up her endurance, but she was missing her afternoons at the gym. She especially missed spending time with Kenny.

Carson was enjoying more freedom with the car and spending as much time as possible with his friends. Things had happened fast. Their dad filed for divorce and their mom moved out. With the Beemer totaled, Mr. Branson bought two used Civics for Kenny and Jerry for their birthday a few weeks early, one silver and one gold. He spent more time at home, and Jerry told Carson his dad had said he was ashamed about how he handled his embarrassment. He was humiliated by their mother's behavior and had accepted responsibility for it. He was hurting so bad inside he ran from the situation, not realizing how much it was hurting his boys. Now, even though they had their own cars, they were spending more time together than ever, and still joining Carson at the gym. It looked like Mr. Branson was doing his best to step up as a dad. He wished that could happen for Luke.

Carson tried to include Luke, but he seemed bound and determined to take a different path. Luke's mom sort of dropped off the radar and his dad wasn't happy about suddenly having to be a dad again. Luke's stepmother was only twelve years older than him. She kept no secrets about being more than a little put out that she had to play Mom to this boy she didn't want to know and didn't particularly like. He was a big inconvenience for her life as a trophy wife. Luke's pain was obvious but not to him. He struck out at every person who even tried to be nice to him. Carson could see how Luke's beliefs from years of neglect were popping up and directing his behavior. Luke was sure he wouldn't be liked because he believed he wasn't good enough and wasn't lovable; so he set himself up to be rejected. No one wants their basic beliefs to be shattered, even when they are negative. Not liking who you are can sometimes feel more comfortable than not knowing who you are at all. This is where faith makes a difference. Without faith, it is difficult for anyone who has felt rejected or betrayed to gain self-acceptance. Belief in the possibility of change is necessary.

On Wednesday afternoon, Tina took Penny to the Riverside orientation where they were greeted by Mr. Quintana. It looked like it was going to be a good fit for Penny with opportunities for the school newspaper and a writing club. Penny didn't seem intimidated at all about going to the larger school, or even about her size, but it brought back terrible memories for Tina.

Her therapist had told her how parents' emotions are affected when their child reaches the age the parent was when they experienced problems. She explained that sometimes the parent will project their own feelings onto their child and assume they feel the way the parent had felt. Thinking back, Tina had to say she agreed with that concept. Karen died when Tina was eleven. Now that Penny was turning eleven, Tina's emotions had been all over the map. It had become apparent she expected middle school to be terrible for Penny.

Tina was so unhappy then, and her parents were in turmoil and emotionally unavailable. As her eyes were finally opening, Tina began to wonder if maybe those other girls weren't as mean to her as she wanted to believe they were. Was it possible she had looked for someone else to blame for her misery? Maybe she had invited the negative reactions—sort of a sick confirmation of her beliefs about her worth. The one thing she *was* sure of was that she loved her children enough to look deeper into her own issues. She wanted to be confident and available so she could be a better mother. She looked down at Penny and admired her enthusiasm, curiosity, and bravery. She knew a good mother would want to nurture that loving, courageous spirit.

Tina was glad she had managed a few nights off so she wouldn't have to juggle so much on Penny's special day. It was finally Thursday morning and she was driving Penny to school. Carson and Cathy gave her a card at breakfast, but they planned to surprise her and be at the graduation at ten.

When they got to school, Tina went down to help Mr. Quintana set up for the afternoon festivities. She couldn't help but notice how he looked at her. She was grateful Penny told her he would be there and glad she had taken a little extra time to look nice. There was something about this man. She wasn't sure if it was that she had been alone for such a long time or what, but she had this sensation she hadn't felt in years in the pit of her stomach. Her mom always insisted there were no coincidences, and she hadn't felt like this when she went to dinner with Greg. Tina decided she needed to treat this situation as *possibly* important, but she was determined to proceed with caution. No matter what kind of feelings she had, she would need to get to know him well enough to know if she genuinely *liked* him.

The graduates were excited. The ceremony was nice, and the lunch included their families. Tina was sure this wasn't the same food they had every day that Penny complained about. After lunch, the teachers took them back to the classrooms to gather their remaining belongings before they came back down for their dance. She wondered why they bothered to call it a dance. No one danced. They stood around in little clusters talking and laughing. The refreshments were unnecessary since it was so soon after lunch. It didn't really matter if it made sense since they were enjoying themselves. Tina was trying extremely hard not to be judgmental, but she would have done it differently.

While they were standing around, she and Mr. Quintana had an opportunity to get better acquainted. He insisted on being called Hugo so he didn't feel like he was at work. Tina was determined to keep her personal life private for now. Penny had shared with him that he had the same quote her grandmother had given her. It sounded like there were quite a few details Penny had kept to herself. Tina had worried Penny was telling him all sorts of things about her family, but apparently that wasn't the case. Tina was relieved she didn't have to either explain problems or live up to expectations. She hoped he felt the same way.

Dismissal was the usual time even though many of Penny's classmates had gone ahead and checked out with their parents. As the group dwindled, Tina watched Bobby Taylor sitting by himself. She had looked around for Rhonda but hadn't seen her there. She walked over and sat down next to Bobby.

"How have you been, Bobby? Do you remember me? I'm Penny's mom."

Bobby gave her a nod and a weak smile, but no eye contact.

"I thought I'd see if there's anything you need over here."

"No, I'm okay." Bobby said, flatly. "My mom couldn't get off work, but it's okay, she said she's proud of me."

Tina's heart tightened. "Alright then, I wanted to make sure. Congratulations on graduating. *I'm* proud of you, too."

As Tina stood to walk away, Bobby gave her an odd look.

"Why would *you* be proud of *me?* You don't know anything about me. I'm the one who made Penny want to run away. I figured you *hated* me."

Tina swallowed and took a deep breath. He was obviously miserable. Why would he think that was his fault? She wondered what Penny might have said to him and she wasn't sure this was the time or place to deal with it, but she was sure *something* needed to happen.

"Well, Bobby, no one told *me* it was your fault, and everything turned out fine. I think there must have been a misunderstanding. I'm sorry you've been thinking that."

She headed back over toward the table with the punch and saw Penny watching her. Then she saw Hugo Quintana watching her, and thought to herself, "Looks like drama has started already in elementary school." She motioned with her index finger for Penny to come to where she was.

"What were you talking to *Bobby* about, Mom?" Penny was groaning.

"I told him congratulations and that I was proud of him after he said his mom had to work. Then he said something interesting. He said he thought I must hate him because it was his fault you ran away." Tina had a stern look on her face. One of those *I want to hear the truth* looks.

"I never said it was his fault. Honest, Mom. Since I got back to school after being gone a week, he hasn't talked to me at all. I thought maybe he was mad at *me* for something." Mr. Quintana could hear enough of the conversation to be interested and moved closer.

"I wonder if *now* might be a good time for you to ask Bobby why he thinks that." Tina said, and Mr. Quintana nodded.

Penny gave him a quick look. Then voiced an exaggerated sigh and stood. With slumped shoulders she headed over to where Bobby was sitting.

Bobby saw her walking in his direction and looked away. They couldn't quite hear the conversation, but there was some headshaking and some shoulder-shrugging, and then Penny sat down beside him. Tina watched as they talked and was moved to tears when Penny reached over and squeezed Bobby's hand. Then she stood and walked back to where Tina and Mr. Quintana were standing with big smiles.

"Everything's fine now. Is it close enough to three for us to go home?"

"I couldn't be prouder of you than I am this very minute!" Tina said as she hugged Penny. They told Mr. Quintana goodbye and headed home.

"Yay, no school tomorrow for the graduated fifth graders. Can Natalie come over?"

Tina smiled and thought to herself the summer was going to be different than she ever would have dreamed. She couldn't imagine what kind of ride it was going to be. She felt like she was going into Space Mountain at Disney World for the first time; riding a roller coaster in the dark!

"Of course, Natalie can come over. But they already left. Let's go call her."

That night, Penny and Natalie turned on the tv and were playing Backgammon while they waited for the news to go off. Cathy was still at the pool and said she had a ride. She was staying a little later since daylight savings time had started. Tina was in the kitchen when she heard the girls yelling for her to come quick to the living room. They were pointing at the news, yelling, "That's him! That's the man who had Sheba!"

Tina ran in and turned up the volume. She only caught the tail-end of the report, but she got there in time to see the mug shot of a middle-aged man. There was an investigation and something about this man being linked to two missing children in Birmingham. They had been looking for him for questioning when he disappeared. Now he was in the local jail and being taken back to Birmingham. Tina felt sick when she heard it, realizing someone like that was right there in their neighborhood.

"I told you I got a funny feeling, Mom. He was weird, wasn't he Nat? You think he would have grabbed us if that man across the street hadn't come out?"

"No, he couldn't have grabbed us because we were smart. We stayed together and we stayed out on the sidewalk."

Carson got home as the mug shot was on the news. He looked around, then asked if Cathy was home yet. He wasn't sure if he was supposed to pick her up, so he had gone by the Club. Someone told him she had already left with a guy and she wasn't answering her phone.

"A *guy*?" Tina asked.

"That's what they said. I figured you would know."

Just then they heard laughter at the door and in walked Cathy and Kenny.

"Dude, don't be picking up my sister without telling someone." Carson bowed up and raised his voice.

Cathy looked like she was about to scream as she glared at Carson but took a deep breath and gained her composure. She could feel Kenny starting to bow up, too. She reached over and put her hand on his chest and turned to Tina, hoping her mom would take control of the situation. Cathy had no idea Carson would have that reaction.

"Hi, Kenny. I'm glad *you* are the mystery guy who gave Cathy a ride. I'm so glad you've recovered from your accident like you have. You sure had us worried. We had no idea who picked Cathy up from the Club. I hope that explains Carson's reaction. Now that Cathy's at an age where she has friends who drive, I'm going to want to know who she's with. I don't think that will be a problem for you, will it?" Tina was doing everything she knew to patch things up before they got torn apart.

"I'm sorry, Mrs. McKenzie. I didn't know she hadn't told you I was bringing her home. I'll make sure to call you myself." Kenny was talking to Tina, but kept looking over at Carson, who was finally calming down.

"Well, you boys are good friends, and I know you both have Cathy's best interest at heart. I'm going to assume this is resolved and I'm sure Carson's relieved she was with one of his friends."

Carson was grateful Tina bought him some time to calm down. He reached over and shook Kenny's hand and apologized for his reaction.

Tina left the room to make a phone call.

"Hello"

"Greg? Did you know that was going to be on the news tonight?"

"Not until I was watching it."

"Were you going to call and let us know?"

"Tina, the few things I know I'm not at liberty to discuss. I told you that last week. Don't let Penny wander around the neighborhood alone. I'm sorry if you think I should have told you more, but that's the best I can do. How's Penny doing?"

"She's fine. The boot's off. She graduated and she's ready for middle school. Everything's good. I hope you're well."

"Yeah, I'm fine. A lot of paperwork. You all take care of yourselves. If I learn anything I can share, I'll be glad to let you know."

"Okay. Well, we'd appreciate that. Take care." She wasn't sure why that conversation annoyed her so much, but it did. There was something going on with him. There was a familiar feel to the tone of his voice, like a pot about to boil. She decided not to think about when she had heard that tone before.

33
Uncharted Waters

Hugo Quintana was cleaning out his temporary office at Carver Elementary and moving things back over to his office at Riverside Middle School. He glanced at the clock and noticed the time. Three days ago at this time Penny had cheerfully come through that door, excited to tell him about a shopping trip with her mother. That thought caused him to sit down and reflect on how Tina McKenzie handled the awkward situation between Penny and Bobby yesterday. He was touched when he saw her reaction to Penny squeezing Bobby's hand. Getting to know Penny spoke volumes about her upbringing. He imagined Tina must be an exceptional mother.

His work brought him into contact with so many frightened and angry children in this harsh world. Some managed to come out the other side of trauma with positive beliefs, and others seemed determined to self-destruct. Wanting to know what made the difference kept him going back year after year to work in the schools. He was convinced that being raised in a family that taught morals and compassion made the greatest difference for many of them. He prayed for the students but had to be careful about praying *with* them. Hugo Quintana struggled with his willingness to deny his personal beliefs for the sake of his job. He wasn't sure how to do anything about it and still work in a position to help troubled children.

Penny's family had certainly had their share of traumatic events, yet they kept finding a way to overcome and move forward. He wanted to get to know Tina better. He was grateful he had not been asked to "counsel" Penny, so there would be no ethical conflict. A knock at the door brought him back to work wearing a thoughtful smile.

Late Thursday night Tina sat at her computer debating her next move. She wanted to go back to school. When Penny was a baby John encouraged her to take college classes. She was within only a few courses to finish her two-year degree in general studies. Diving into a major would mean more difficult classes and more expense. She wasn't sure she was ready to invest the time and money, especially since she wasn't sure what career interested her most.

She wanted at least to take an online course that would set her up to be a better provider for her children. She wanted to find something she could do that would allow her to schedule her hours around her children. It had been the other way around for too long. The few afternoons with Penny had been so meaningful. Now Cathy had a swim meet coming up. Tina envied other parents with normal nighttime sleep schedules. She hated having to take time off work because there wasn't enough time for sleep if she spent time with her children. They were growing up so fast; she had already missed too much. She researched different trainings for medical billing since she already had a surprisingly good feel for that.

Now she needed to learn how to market herself. As she scrolled through different sites, she came across one for learning how to build a website. That got her thinking. If she could learn to do her own, she could do it for other people, like the billing; or who knows, maybe she could teach other people how to do it. She loved working at her computer more than just about anything. Then she went to the site for the Community College. When she clicked on the tab for financial aid, there it was. Grants. She hadn't needed one when John paid for her classes, so she had no idea how it worked. It couldn't hurt to go there and ask. She scanned the calendar. Tomorrow was Friday with Monday a holiday. She found the school calendar and it looked like they would be there tomorrow until noon. Then she realized it was after midnight. "Looks like I'll be doing this today. Step one of my plan: find funding to go back to school. Maybe today is the day I'll find out if I'm on the right track."

Tina called the Community College to ask about getting a grant when she woke up. The woman she spoke with was kind, but not knowledgeable about financial aid. No one from that office was there and an appointment had to be made. She was encouraged to look online at the courses offered so she would have an idea of what she wanted to study. Tina hung up and decided to go over there anyway and walk around, get a feel for what it would be like to go back to college, and maybe get a catalog before the office closed at noon; that way there would be time for a nap. Taking so many nights off in the past month had her internal clock totally messed up. She went ahead and threw on some jeans and a t-shirt and went out to find Penny watching cartoons and eating cereal. Carson and Cathy were at school for their last half day.

"Hey you, sixth-grade cutie pie. Want to ride over to the college with me to pick up a catalog?"

"Yay, another girls' day? Sure."

"Finish that cereal and run brush your teeth so we can go. I need a nap when we get home. I work tonight." Tina put the cereal bowl in the sink and met Penny at the door as she came galloping down the stairs.

The week dragged on and everyone tiptoed around Tina's sleeping hours. Now that school was out, Penny was ready for a summer of adventure. She had no idea about the things already planned for her, but she was doing some planning of her own. She wanted to figure out how to get permission to go out with her metal detector, and she needed a ride to the library to check out a book about pennies. It was a perfect summer project. She wasn't sure where she would be allowed to go, but there had to be somewhere. Natalie was all for it, but she wasn't allowed to go anywhere at all, especially after their experience with the cat stealer. Penny wanted to go look by the creek. She had heard there were Civil War battle sites nearby and she thought there would be good stuff to find. Unless Carson would take her, she didn't see that happening. Maybe he would take her for one day as a birthday present.

Carson had asked Mr. Hyatt several times when he could possibly be hired to work at the gym. Mr. Hyatt was concerned about liability and didn't want to hire anyone under eighteen. Carson realized he would have to make some choices. He planned to look for people who wanted a private trainer to go to the gym with them and help them train. Mr. Hyatt made it clear Carson wasn't allowed to promote private training while he was at the gym since he wasn't employed there. Since Jerry had been joining him to work out, Carson felt the gym owner had grown distant. He wondered if Mr. Hyatt's friendship with Luke's dad had become a problem. Carson wasn't interested in competing as a bodybuilder and wouldn't need the gym as a sponsor, so he was no longer sure how he could reach his goals. He needed to find a way to advertise and get private clients. He thought about looking on the internet. He remembered Jerry making a comment that his dad had considered setting up a gym in their garage. He had an idea. He headed out to his car and gave Jerry a call.

This was the last week left to practice before the swim meet. Cathy had taken it easy like she had promised through Saturday after the last half-day of school. Then the count-down had begun. She had to do everything she could to be ready. This was her chance. There was no way she was going to allow herself to be distracted, especially with almost blowing it and ending up with pneumonia. This was one of those things that caused people who wanted her attention to throw their hands up and walk away.

Even though she was only fourteen, most of her friends had been in a relationship at least once—not Cathy. She had liked some boys and had some crushes, but she wasn't going to put her own goals aside for a boy when she was quite sure he wouldn't do the same for her. Kenny asked if he could come watch her practice. She told him no because she wanted to stay focused. She really liked him. If he didn't understand he wasn't the boy for her. Then Kenny said he understood. He said he would wait until the meet and he would be in the crowd cheering for her; afterwards, if she had time to hang out that would be great. She didn't know what to think. Other than her family, no one had ever made her feel that important. She had always had to tell *them* that. And then she was usually accused of being self-centered or conceited, which was not true. She was blown away at the thought of there being a boy out there who understood her drive and admired her determination. Even thinking about the possibilities was messing with her focus. She needed to set this aside and visualize the pool, the water, and winning. She closed her eyes and saw herself on the podium.

At 3:45 on the Friday before the meet, Tina woke to her phone vibrating on the bedside table.

"Hello?"

"Hello Tina, this is Hugo. I hope I'm not calling at a bad time."

"Oh, no, not at all, I'm doing a few things around here before I go to work tonight. How are you?" She was yawning and trying to sound awake.

"I'm well, thank you. I've finally finished moving back to my real office over at Riverside. It's been an interesting experiment. We hope it will make the sixth-grade transition easier. It's a difficult age . . . but enough of work. I wanted to tell you I appreciated you being at the dance last week. I admired the way you handled the issue between Bobby and Penny. It made me wonder if you've done this type of work before."

"You really must be kidding, right? It's just parenting," Tina laughed. There was silence. "Oh, I'm sorry, I guess

I assumed all the time you and Penny spent together she probably told you my life history. I didn't mean to sound rude. Ending up a single mom with kids who had a tough start drove me to therapy and parenting classes."

"No, perhaps it wasn't an appropriate thing for me to come out and ask. I was an only child raised by my father and I have no children. I suppose I'm curious. Child development fascinates me. Penny didn't share much of anything about family except things about her father. I think she appreciated having an opportunity to talk about him with someone who didn't know him. She's a brilliant child, by the way, but I'm sure you know that. I considered the time we spent in my office an opportunity and a privilege."

As she listened, Tina was wondering how she could be having this conversation and it feel so comfortable and natural. "That's kind of you to say. Yes, I know she's one of a kind. She's never bored, that's for sure. She always has some kind of project planned."

"I'll bet she does. What is she doing over the summer?"

"She has no idea yet. Her birthday is June twenty-first, a friend's mother is taking them to Birmingham to a book signing with G.M. Plessy, their favorite author. That would be enough by itself, but it's not all. She's going to camp for two weeks. Her best friend since diapers moved last August. Her mom found the camp and made a lot of the arrangements."

"That sounds wonderful. So, what about you? Any special plans for summer?"

"Me? Well, not really. Cathy, my middle child, has a swim meet tomorrow. I won't be sure what the summer holds until we know if she wins District. If that happens, she'll have a chance to compete in the Junior Olympics. They say it's probable, but she's just recovering from pneumonia."

"I wonder why I didn't hear more about Cathy. I knew she was in the hospital for tests, but Penny didn't share much more. I don't ask a lot of questions in situations like Penny's."

"I could've guessed," Tina laughed. "An ongoing competition. Cathy turned fourteen two weeks ago. Penny has a brother also, Carson, he's sixteen."

"I actually know Carson. Well, he doesn't know who I am, but I see him in The Beat, and sometimes at the gym. He's only sixteen? I would have thought a little older."

Now Tina's curiosity was up. He shops at The Beat. He knows Carson. And Penny didn't talk about Cathy?

"Yes, Carson is the serious one in the family. He keeps us all straight."

"So, I was wondering, I'd like to spend some time with you. I was hoping we could make plans to go out."

"I'll be honest, Hugo, I was hoping you would ask." Tina's entire body was tingling, and she felt like a sixteen-year-old being asked out for the first time. It was all she could do to keep herself from giggling. She heard herself say what came out of her mouth and she couldn't believe her ears. Before she could say anything else she pinched her own arm to remind herself to shut up. She shuddered at the idea of what in the world he must think.

"Well, I'm pleased to hear that. Now I guess we need to think of where and when. I have something to check on. May I call you tomorrow?"

"Of course, I love suspense. I'll look forward to your call. Keep in mind I go to work at 8:00 most nights, so I sleep part of my days. I absolutely *must* change my summer schedule now that school's out. I even went to the college last week to get a catalog and look into a grant."

"A good friend of mine works out there. Have you ever taken a test to help you determine your interests? They can be helpful for finding a good fit for you."

"No, I never have. I'm good at a lot of things, but I don't know what to do about it."

"Well then, I can help you with that. It can be fun. There are so many ways to use talent and skills that most people never think about. After watching you with Bobby and Penny, I would think something like Human Resources, counseling, or even teaching would be a natural fit, but that may not be what you would enjoy. There are a number of ways to get ideas. Enough of that today. Plenty of time for that. I'll give you a call tomorrow afternoon, okay?"

"Okay, sounds great. I'll look forward to it."

"Yes, me too. And good luck to Cathy tomorrow."

Tina had been on her bed while she talked. She rolled over grinning from ear to ear. Summer was looking better and better. She hoped he was right that there would indeed be plenty of time for that.

As she was getting up, the phone buzzed again. She laughed, thinking it was him calling right back, then realized it wasn't from a local number.

"Hello?"

"Hi Tina, it's Gwen, please don't hang up."

"I'm not going to hang up, Gwen. I'm not sure what I can do, but I can at least listen to whatever you feel you need to tell me."

"Thank you. I wondered if you had given any thought to Phoebe."

"Are you kidding me? She's practically in my mind all the time. How could I not give her any thought?"

"Tina, the situation has gotten worse. Bob's parents are trying to get a court ordered test done to prove she isn't his child. They want the boy and not her. They are heartless. I realize they are hurt and angry, but to take it out on a child? It would be one thing if she was some incorrigible monster, but she's sweet and kind and intelligent. She's so well-mannered. What I'm going to ask may really freak you out, but I have to anyway. Would you be willing to get Penny to let you do a mouth swab for a sibling DNA test?

Without John's DNA it won't be as conclusive, but it should be enough. If something happens to her grandmother, she could end up in foster care with no other next of kin."

Tina was dumbfounded. Part of her wanted to scream into the phone and tell this crazy woman to go get a life and adopt the child herself. But then Gwen would have baggage, so that couldn't happen. She wondered what Gwen's reaction would be to that, but Tina wasn't that kind of person. Her heart went out to this child, and actually, to Gwen, too. She wasn't sure if it was the smart thing to do, but she knew in her heart it was the right thing. But, how in the world would she explain the mouth swab to Penny?

"Yes, Gwen, but what do I have to do? I'll have to come up with a good reason. Where do I get one? When are you going to be in town, or how can I get it to you?"

"I'm here until Sunday. Oh my God, thank you. I knew you were a good person. I knew you had a kind soul," Gwen was crying as she spoke, "I have a home kit. I don't know . . . maybe if you tell her you are doing Ancestry? I'm at my mother's. I can drive over right now and put it in your mailbox."

"Would it be possible for me to take it to your mother's late tomorrow afternoon? Cathy has a swim meet tomorrow and I'm not going to get much sleep, so Sunday I'm not going to want to see anyone or be waked by anyone. Besides, it just dawned on me that Sunday's my birthday!"

"Of course, of course, whatever works for you, Tina. I'm so grateful, anything that works for you. My mother's house is at 3750 Gilcrest. Not too far from you. I'll make sure one of us is there tomorrow afternoon. Thank you, Tina, bless you. And Happy Birthday!"

Tina sat and stared at the wall.

Less than ten minutes after they hung up, Gwen's car stopped for a minute in front of the house. Tina walked out to get the mail.

34

Ominous Dreams

Moses had been up on the camp property most of the month getting things ready for the summer. There were the usual things he had to do every year, like clearing out old branches and raking the paths clean; there were also minor repairs, like loose screen door hinges and creaking floorboards.

He liked this new Pastor Patrick. He was a lot younger than Pastor Matthews and he was dedicated to doing the Lord's work. He was interested in hearing all about Moses' life in the woods and he got excited when he learned how much Moses knew about gardening. At first the Pastor wanted to learn more about what they needed to do to grow some of their own food for the camp. Then he had the idea to offer gardening as one of the classes. That earned Moses' admiration.

"It looks like we are in for a full house all summer. It's only May and there are hardly any openings left. I'm glad you were able to come up and help us get things ready, Moses."

"Well, I'll tell you, when I heard I had to come up and talk to a new man, I was worried. Yessir, I was worried. I love comin' up and doin' whatever I can to serve the Lord. Bring the young'uns up right. That's what's important. When you ast me to come and stay my heart took off singin'. This is the kind of work keeps me young and strong. That's right, young and strong. I'll be happy to do this as long as you'll have me."

Sometimes when Moses talked while he was happy, which was most of the time, he sort of laughed his words out. The first-time people heard it they weren't always sure how to take it, but once they got a feel for his rhythm, it was hard to listen to him without smiling along with him. He was just a man, but he was also joy, alive and walking on legs. And as joy went down the path with a rake, humming along, Pastor Patrick watched him stroll away, thanking the Lord for putting this man in his life.

It was a rainy afternoon, and the bunk felt good under his tired back. The breeze blew through the screen and the patter of the light rain falling on the tin roof made for a tranquil break. Moses lay there with his eyes closed, resting and enjoying the softness of the damp air. He thought about his mama and how he always felt safe with her. He wished for a day snuggled up close to her and her lilac smell, with her arms around him like when he was a boy. There were days he wished he had children of his own, but there was something in him that told him there were things he didn't want to allow to go forward. He never knew where he came from. He didn't have to know. He did know there was something he had to go take care of on his next break from work. It would be important for him to find David Bradley's daughter, Ruth. She had handled several things for Moses since his mama died.

Moses also knew the dreams he'd been having since he came to the camp were different. He saw her face, the one from the creek, the one who looked so much like Leah Bradley. He believed that had to be a sign. Now there was another one; there must be a connection. Almost all the dreams ended when he looked at his hands and they disappeared. In the most recent one he could no longer see his feet. Invisibility. Wouldn't it be grand . . .

35
Turning Points

Saturday morning and round two of preparation for the swim meet, Carson took Cathy to the pool at 7:30 and came back to the house. Tina cooked breakfast and couldn't help looking out the window several times to check the sky, which was a beautiful, cloudless blue. With sunscreen, visors, and bottles of water in a bag, the family headed out to cheer for Cathy. Kenny and Jerry were already there when they arrived. There was a larger crowd than Tina had expected considering it had been rescheduled into summer vacation.

Cathy swam in the first relay, the 200-yard Medley, and her team won. Other members on Cathy's team either won or placed in the medals in most of the events. Overall, they were holding their own. Cathy placed third in the 50-yard Freestyle and felt so exhausted afterward she wished she hadn't tried that one. Her last and most important event was yet to come, and it required a tremendous amount of endurance. The 500-yard Freestyle had always been hers. She wasn't sure she had the strength today. She lay down on the bench and practiced focused breathing and visualization like her coaches had taught her, while she waited until a little closer to time to swim to warm up.

Her event was getting close and Beth Benning looked at Cathy with concern.

"You know you don't have to do this."

"I know, Coach. But inside I know I have to give it a shot. If I don't win, I'll know I wasn't ready. But if I don't try, I'll never know. Besides, it won't kill me."

"I get it, Sweetie. Go do it then! We're all behind you, proud of you for fighting so hard to come back."

Cathy went out and stood under the shower, rubbed her arms and legs, and shook her muscles loose. When the 500 was called, she took her place in her lane and readied herself. The rest was a surreal blur. She had been focusing on the quote Gramma had given her. She imagined the earth and the water trembling as she moved it out of her way and pushed herself forward. Her legs felt electric with the strength Carson had helped her add at the gym. Focused on her rhythm and her breathing, she saw and heard nothing. Where the other swimmers were didn't matter. This was her race and she was swimming against herself and only herself. Lap after lap, she touched, she turned, she swam with all her might. Then she touched for the last time. The shouting and screaming from the crowd and her teammates came into her awareness. She blinked as she saw hands touching the wall beside her. She looked up. She had won.

Tina watched as Cathy lifted herself up enough to reach over and high-five then hug her competitors in the lanes beside her, then she laid her head on her arm. Her shoulders heaved. Tears ran down Tina's face as she shakily held the phone, facetiming Carol and screaming. The cheering crowd was such a joyful noise! When they jumped up, Tina told Penny and the boys to stay in the stands until the end of the meet to show respect to the rest of the competitors, but that didn't stop the waving and screaming and kiss-blowing. With eight or nine events still to go, Cathy stayed down with her team, cheering them on, but looking happily up into the stands from time to time.

Tina couldn't help but look back at the last two months and wonder what could be next. Life was moving at the speed of light. Even though she sometimes felt like she was being slung off a spinning top, she was determined to hang on.

Today, however, she was exhausted. Tina called the clinic and asked if there was anyone who could trade shifts. Samantha had already called and asked if anyone wanted off, so the one-day swap was approved. Sam was wanting to change permanently to night shifts. Tina requested switching to the day shift, and it would be sent to HR on Monday for consideration. It was a stretch for Tina to think they either valued her enough to keep her on her terms or she could quit. Could she really let herself consider that? She wasn't sure where the surge of confidence was coming from. Maybe watching Cathy's determination was rubbing off on her. Maybe she was finally waking up.

Tina could barely contain the excitement of the possibility of changing to days. She was making good money doing all the billing that had gradually been added to her stack. It was obvious she was doing a good job because she was paid based on the payments she recovered for the doctors. That it could be done from home was the best thing about it. Tina suspected Dr. Harmon was responsible for getting several of the new accounts for her.

"Woohoo! I'm not working tonight. Let's all go out to celebrate," Tina said once things were completely over and the group was waiting for Cathy to change and come out. Carson looked over at Jerry, who acted nonchalant, but then he glanced at Kenny, whose eyes were glued to the door to where Cathy was changing. Tina realized there must be other teenage plans. Her feelings were a little hurt, but she looked at Penny, who was expectantly waiting to hear where they were going. Tina laughed a little and decided it would be fine.

"Okay, I get it. I won't ask y'all to change your plans. Tomorrow is Sunday and life has been so crazy I forgot it's my birthday! I'm already scheduled off, so I'm going to insist on grilling out and turning our family night into a combination celebration for Cathy's victory and a birthday party for me. Y'all can invite a few of your friends." Everyone agreed that sounded like a great idea.

"Looks like it's you and me, Miss Priss. I don't know about you, but I'm hungry." Being called that made Penny mad before, but she was beginning to like it when Mom said it with a smile.

"Can we go get barbecue? I want some of that camping stew and corn on the cob." Penny expressively licked her lips and rubbed her stomach.

"Yum. That sounds good," Tina said, almost tasting it.

Then Tina remembered she needed to do something about the mouth swab. She wasn't sure how she could pull off leaving something at Gwen's mother's house. She looked at her watch and saw it wasn't as late as she felt—then she got an idea. She didn't want to put it off and give the sample to Gwen personally.

"It's still early and I'm sweaty. I think I'd like to go home and change, how about you?"

"Okay with me." Penny smiled. She was liking it when Mom asked her opinion. It made her feel important, like how she felt about things mattered.

When they pulled into their driveway Tina saw Miss Martha over on her porch.

"Hi Martha," she called loud enough for Martha to hear her. "Cathy won her event at the swim meet! Penny and I are going out for barbecue, would you like to join us?"

"That's wonderful dear. No thank you, I'm having my nighttime cereal in a little while."

"Okay, well, we're grilling tomorrow night. Maybe you can join us. I'll be over tomorrow after church to work on that packing." Tina waved as she went inside.

Tina freshened up and Penny came down after changing. Tina acted like she had a surprise.

"Penny come here a minute," she reached in the drawer and pulled out the kit. "I ordered DNA kits to see our ancestry, you know, like we see on tv? Yours is the only one that came so far. Let's go ahead and do it so I don't forget." Tina followed the instructions she had studied the night before and swabbed Penny's mouth. "Good. Now I can send this Monday."

She then sent Penny to use the bathroom before going to the restaurant.

Penny obligingly left the room. She was used to the bathroom drill. Tina quickly reached into the *just in case* drawer and pulled out a large greeting card, slid the kit inside, and sealed it shut. Penny came back in as she was writing GWEN on the front of the envelope.

"What's that?"

"My friend Gwen's birthday is next week, just a few days after mine. I got a little something for her and I want to drop it off to her at her mother's house since it's on our way," Tina said with a smug smile.

On the way to the restaurant after dropping the card off, Tina's phone buzzed.

"Hello?"

"Hi Tina, Hugo. Do you think you might be able to get off work on Friday night? There's a play I'd like to take you to see. *Greater Tuna*. It's a two-man performance by a couple of my friends. It isn't until 7:30 and there's no matinee scheduled. Oh, and how did Cathy do?"

"She won the 500! That will take her to regionals, and I'm fairly sure it also qualifies her for Junior Olympics, but I think I already told you that. A *play*? Crazy name but that sounds wonderful. I think I may have found someone to swap schedules; I'm hoping I won't be pulling the all-nighters anymore. She asked to swap tonight, so Penny and I are on our way to get some barbecue. Say," Tina looked over at Penny, who was trying awfully hard to figure out who Tina was talking to, "I'd love for you to join us. We're going to that little mom and pop called Uncle Bud's up on the highway."

"I'll meet you there. See you soon," Hugo said enthusiastically.

"Great!"

"Who's coming, Mom? Please don't let it be that *policeman*."

"No, Penny, it's not Greg. I don't think you'll mind this person joining us."

When they pulled into a parking spot, Penny saw Mr. Quintana getting out of his car.

"Look Mom, Mr. Quintana eats here too. Hey . . . wait a minute . . .," Penny practically spun around in the seat to look at Tina. "*Really* Mom?"

Tina laughed and nodded her head.

The barbecue was delicious.

The company was even better.

36
Calm After the Storm

On Sunday morning Carson and Cathy cooked a big breakfast to celebrate Tina's birthday. The bickering that often happens before church was practically non-existent and the family made it to the 9:30 service, which was Carson's favorite. He was sure it would be perfect for his mom's special day. It was a more contemporary service and he raved about the music. Tina was old fashioned and didn't think she would enjoy it, but once there she decided she felt more connected to Spirit. Finally beginning to realize making some changes could be positive, she was sure that wouldn't be the last Sunday they went to that service.

That afternoon, Tina and Penny went over to help Martha sort through some of her things. She had gotten the measurements of the rooms and had tags hanging on the pieces of furniture she was keeping. A truck was already scheduled to pick up the pieces she was donating. Martha was remarkably organized. Tina hoped she would be like that when *she* was turning ninety. Penny told Miss Martha it was her mom's birthday and Martha surprised Tina with her silver tea service and a beautiful antique vase, insisting Tina, the daughter she never had, would appreciate it much more than Robert would. Tina was totally overwhelmed and was only just realizing how much she was going to miss her precious neighbor.

The backyard cookout was perfect. Penny asked her mom to invite Mr. Quintana, but Tina explained she wasn't quite ready for that. Penny invited Natalie. Her parents stayed for a while when they brought her over to spend the night. Cathy invited Susan and another girl from her team to come, too, since there was that gross crush going on. As to be expected, Kenny and Jerry were there. Even Mr. Branson came by for a while. Tina was glad she had brought the wind chime back out. The warm afternoon and the laughter of young voices were exactly what she needed. Carson had asked Luke to join them though he doubted he would come. He not only came; he brought his guitar. They had been playing together every now and then, and Carson had shared some things with Luke that had helped him feel more *normal.* They played for a while as it got dark with the flames leaping from the firepit and licking the early summer night air. Carson admired the pit he had dug out and lined with old brick.

Carson turned to Luke, "You ready to play the one we wrote?"

Luke smiled and nodded.

"I had the lyrics pretty much written, but I couldn't have finished the arrangement without Luke's help."

They moved to where they could sit side by side, and everyone else gathered around to listen. "We call this 'Oh Father, Father.'"

They played and sang:

Along the broken path this weary seeker travels
With hopelessness and fear my tangled life unravels
Alone in the damp and dark I stand and wait
For the sun to rise again, for the opening of the gate

Oh Father, Father, take this pain from my heart
This hopelessness and fear are tearing me apart

In my lonely hours of sorrow and despair
I long for a miracle, for a song to fill the air
For you to take me home someday and bathe me in
your Grace
And wash away the remnants of shame and disgrace

Oh Father, Father, lift this burden from my soul
My life's falling apart - I want to give you all control

I come to you Lord, with faith in your promise
To prepare a home for me, a place of peace and solace
So provide for me, your child, a shelter from the storm
Where you will hold me close, and keep me safe
and warm

Oh Father, Father, let me understand my gifts
The seed of my faith grows, the strength of my trust
shifts

Oh Father, Father, shine your Light; expose the lies
That from this fertile soil joyful blessings may arise

The summer was off to a good start. The negative events of the past two months were finally becoming blurry.

37
Life Goes On

School had been out for three weeks. Mr. Branson liked the idea Carson had pitched for him about setting up a gym at the Bransons' house and let Jerry and Carson run it like a private club. He agreed under a few specific conditions, all of which he was willing to back: Carson needed to go to a training that would get him an applicable certification, and Jerry would have to take a business and marketing class online. Mr. Branson said he would take care of necessary licensing. He stressed the importance of the boys going to talk with someone from the Small Business Administration so they would understand what's involved in starting a business. Meanwhile, they could have a small number of paying members coming to use the gym. Once they proved they were willing to take on the responsibilities, Mr. Branson would consider opening a gym in town. The boys decided there was nothing holding them back and it was too good a deal to ignore. Carson gave up his job at The Beat and talked his boss into hiring Luke to take his place. Once they got started, they understood why Mr. Branson was so serious.

Kenny had impressed Beth Benning. She hired him to work as a lifeguard for the recreational hours at the Swim Club for the summer and provided the training for his Red Cross card. It turned out he was a strong swimmer. Cathy thought he should try to get on the school team. He and Cathy were considered a couple by their friends. Cathy was sticking to her preparation for her next level of competition, and the high school team was already starting their practices a few days a week. Staying focused on swimming and having a boyfriend was harder than she expected.

At the clinic, Sam switched to night hours, which opened a daytime receptionist position. Tina and the others worked out a schedule making two of them full-time and Tina and another girl who wanted to work part-time filled in all the holes. Tina had her billing job on the side. Provided it didn't interfere with her work, she could do it there or at home. It all worked out in time for her to go with Hugo to the play. She was having no trouble getting used to the idea of being involved with him. She decided to wait a little longer before having him over to the house. It was obvious he wanted to spend as much time as possible with Tina, but he was also willing to give her the space and time she needed. It was a refreshing change for her. She hadn't told her mother about him yet. She also still hadn't told her mother or Hugo about Phoebe Kendrick.

Since the school year ended, Hugo had worked short days through the first half of June, and now he was off for most of the summer. He went to the college with Tina and introduced her to his friend who worked in guidance and financial aid. Tina couldn't believe all her options, and she found the vocational test to be fascinating. The results revealed her love for problem solving and for helping others achieve success. She could imagine having a job helping people discover what they would be happy doing. She felt she needed to clarify her own path first. She applied for a grant to complete more training in medical billing and for several certifications in computer technology.

Hugo was trying to talk her into going for a degree, especially since she was almost half-way there. Tina wasn't ready yet to commit to a long-term plan, at least not for college. They were getting to know each other and found they liked a lot of the same things. Tina wanted to take her time to make sure her own life was on track and to do life right this time.

38
Kindred Spirits

Penny thought and thought and came up with the perfect special request for her birthday. She didn't want a traditional party. She wanted to go to Galaxy Drive for a picnic and take the metal detector to have a treasure hunt. Once she presented her idea, even Cathy thought it would be fun and asked if she could help plan it. Penny thought it might be a trick, but Tina convinced her she should give Cathy a chance to earn some trust.

Plans were made for Penny to go on June eighteenth to the Cross' house for Natalie's birthday party. Julie invited Penny to stay the following day, too, then pretended to have something to do in Birmingham. She told the girls they could ride with her and go to the zoo if there was time. That sounded like a great idea. The party was fun and the next day they went to the movies. Penny thought about going home, but then she remembered the zoo. On the morning of the twentieth they drove to Birmingham.

"What do you need to do there, Mom?" Natalie asked.

"I need to pick up a dress I ordered a few weeks ago to wear to your cousin's big formal wedding in August. It finally came in and it might need to be altered. I told them I'd pick it up there since they have a seamstress there. Once I try it on, I'll know if we have time for the zoo." That sounded reasonable enough and seemed to satisfy Natalie, but she didn't remember hearing about a big fancy wedding.

They got to the mall and found the parking lot to be crowded. Once they found a space, they headed into the entrance in that section of the mall. There was a long line of people. There were mostly girls and a lot of them were around Penny's and Natalie's age. They looked around wondering what was happening, then Natalie noticed her mom was smiling.

"Do you know what's going on, Mom?"

A tall, slender, bookish-looking girl of about fourteen who was already in line practically spun around. With a big smile, she said enthusiastically, "It's the big book signing! G.M. Plessy is here! Her new book is out, *Finding the Fatal Flaw.*"

Penny and Natalie turned to each other and held hands, jumping up and down squealing.

"Mom, you tricked us! What a great birthday present! How did you know?"

"I saw it in the paper several weeks ago. We've been keeping it a secret."

"My mom knows, too?" Penny asked.

"Of course she does. She was in on it with me."

The girls were silly and giddy, and the line was finally moving at a crawl.

"Are we really going to *meet* her? In *person?* And we can get one of her books? With her signature in it?" Natalie asked her mom.

"Of course! That's what happens at a book signing. She will ask you your name and then she will write 'To Natalie', and sometimes they say other things, then she will sign her name, and you will own a first edition copy of the book, signed by the author. And I imagine I can take a picture of you with her."

It took close to an hour to make the turn and see the table where the famous author was sitting. They were sort of coming up from behind, and when they were close enough to see, Penny grabbed Natalie's arm.

"Look! there she is," Right then G.M. Plessy turned, and Penny saw her profile. "Oh, never mind, I don't think that can be her. She doesn't look anything like the pictures on her books."

The girl in front of them turned to Penny and spoke authoritatively, "She *never* has her picture taken from the side, *that's* why she looks different to you. She only allows photos from the front. She *hates* her nose, and she hates her *name*, too. *That's* why she uses her initials. Her name is *Geraldine.* I read it in an article. There was an interview with her and that's what she said."

Penny was stunned. Her nose was long, but it wasn't ugly. Penny thought she was pretty. For a moment Penny felt sad. Geraldine Plessy was famous and her books were wonderful. Why wasn't that enough? As they inched closer, she decided how she wanted her book signed. Natalie's mother had taken care of purchasing the two books and handed them to the girls. Natalie was first and told the author her name. The inscription read, "To Natalie, you can never read too many books. With Love, G.M. Plessy." Now it was Penny's turn.

"My name is Penelope and I plan to be a writer, like you. I'm in a club called the Star Writers. Could you say something about that, please?"

She gave Penny a long, knowing look and a kind smile, then put her hand on Penny's and closed her eyes for a few moments. G.M. Plessy looked like she had a sudden idea, then she asked Penny's last name.

She wrote in Penny's book, "To Penelope McKenzie, Star Writer, Words can hurt or heal, use kind ones generously. With Love and Shared Passion, Geraldine M. Plessy." Then, looking right into Penny's eyes, she whispered, "Only for *you*." Then she gestured to Penny and Natalie to come behind the table and stand beside her for Natalie's mom to get the picture of them all together.

Penny's hands were shaking when she was handed the book. She wasn't exactly sure what had happened. There were only two other times in her life she got that feeling that she remembered. One was when Daddy held her and told her about the stars, and the other was when God stood behind her and told her he was there to save her. She knew none of that would make sense to anyone else. It didn't matter. Whatever it was, she would never forget for as long as she lived how special she felt just because of who she was.

By the time they headed home, the zoo had been forgotten. Both girls were quiet and thoughtful during the drive. Julie Cross dropped Penny off at her house.

When Penny went inside, everyone was there. The teenagers had been planning the treasure hunt and they listened to her tell about what happened at the mall. She didn't try to explain or make a big deal about it. Instead, she let them tell her what they had planned.

Tina was upstairs and called to Penny to come up to her room. When Penny walked into her room, she saw that her mom had taken all her special things out of the trunk. She began to panic, but Tina quickly explained it was all safely on a shelf in the closet and it was temporary. Penny had no idea what this was about. Tina opened the trunk, and her clothes were packed in there, along with a flashlight, a journal, and some sheets and towels.

"What *is* all this, Mom?"

"I've been ironing nametags in your clothes this week while you've been at Nat's. Tomorrow's your picnic, the next day I work, and then we relax on Saturday to get ready for your biggest and best birthday surprise." Penny's stomach started doing the crazy flip-flops. Tina continued, "Sunday morning you and I are loading the car and driving to the mountains to meet Sally and her mom. You and Sally are going to summer camp for two weeks!"

"*Whaaat?* Camp? You're *serious?* Camp!" Penny was screaming and jumping up and down. Carson and Cathy were standing at the bottom of the stairs cheering for her. Penny shouted, "Mom! This is the *best* summer. I've wanted to go to camp my *whole life!*" She grabbed Tina and hugged her. Then she backed up and looked at her mother with a profoundly serious expression. "But what about Natalie? She'll feel so left out."

Tina was touched that Penny was concerned about her friend. It was in moments like this she knew she had done a lot of things right. "No, they have a trip planned to Disney, so she won't feel left out at all. Y'all will have plenty to tell each other when you get home. And you don't have to keep it a secret tomorrow at the treasure hunt either because her mom's telling her about her trip right now."

"You're so *sneaky*, Mom."

"Sometimes moms have to be. That's how we have extra fun."

39
Treasure

While Penny was at Natalie's, Carson had messed around with the metal detector. After he put fresh batteries in it, he tested it out with things in the yard. Once he knew it still worked, he and Jerry went to a junk place on the highway and bought old metal things. They found a silver fork, a candlestick, an old piece of chain that was maybe gold, a thimble, and a ring. They went up to Galaxy Drive with posthole diggers. Once the junk was in the ground in random places, they packed the dirt back down hard. Then they took pictures of where they put things to make sure they would know she found all of it. The plan was for there to be several gallons of water and wet wipes since the event was going to be a dirty mess.

Cathy and Kenny took charge of the food and decorations. They had bags for things that were found, some silly pirate hats and eye patches for Penny and Natalie to wear, and a cooler loaded with sandwiches and bottles of water. They got the folding yard-sale table from the garage, taped white craft paper to the top of it, and provided a box of markers for everyone to write Happy Birthday on the tabletop. Cathy picked out a chocolate chip cookie cake. Since they were going to be out in the heat most of the day the thought of hot buttercream icing was just too gross.

Tina had been busy getting Penny's things ready for camp. She was grateful the older kids decided to be a big part of the plans for Penny's party. She wanted to invite Hugo to join them, but it had only been a month since the school dance. Even though she knew Penny would love for him to be there, she decided against it. She planned to introduce him to Cathy and Carson while Penny was at camp.

On Saturday morning Carson and Cathy loaded everything in the Subaru and went to Galaxy Drive to set up. Tina and Penny went to pick up Natalie on the way. Jerry and Kenny were going to meet everyone there. The treasure hunt was going to be everything Penny had asked for.

She knew there had to be good stuff up there, and she was beside herself. This was better than she had dreamed it could be. She and Natalie wore their pirate hats and eye patches and couldn't stop giggling while Tina took pictures of them posing with their shovels and buckets. They impatiently headed along the hill with the metal detector. Carson and Jerry kept a close eye on where they went, hoping to steer them close to where things were buried. The detector started buzzing, and the light was blinking. It made a loud signal when Penny swung it back and forth over the spot. Once they narrowed down where to dig, Natalie dug into the dirt with the small shovel and they heard a clink.

"You hit something Nat, dig some more dirt out."

Natalie lifted a shovelful of dirt. Nothing yet. She stuck the shovel back in and another clink. She lifted out another shovelful, and there it was. Penny's eyes got big. "Look! Look! It's something long and dark!" She reached down and picked up a long pile of dirt, knocking it loose to expose a tarnished silver candlestick. "Wow! Look Mom! Look, everybody! We found treasure!"

Jerry dug his elbow into Carson, and Cathy hooked her arm through Kenny's, smiling. Tina took pictures, and the hunt was on. The girls worked at it for a couple of hours before they gave in and took a break to eat a sandwich. Natalie's parents came out to join in the festivities and the girls showed off their goodies, including an old silver spoon, a thimble, a ring, and some things that looked like buckles and random broken metal objects.

Carson checked his phone to see what they hadn't found yet, and it looked like they already had everything. The big question became how to get her to stop without ending up disappointed if there wasn't anything else out there. "Why don't we go ahead and have the cake, Penny?"

"Okay, but I want to look down by the creek. I want to go down where I was on the bank. If there were soldiers around here during the Civil War, I bet they would have been down closer to the water. After cake can we go down there and walk along the creek with the detector?"

Carson and Jerry looked at each other as if to say *really? are we doing this all day?*

Tina looked right at them and said to Penny, "Why sure, Honey, I bet Carson and Jerry will take a walk down there with you. First I want you girls to go for a short walk over to where there are some big bushes." Tina winked.

Cathy turned to Kenny and spoke up before Carson could answer, "Kenny, don't you want to go down and see if there's anything there? I know *I* do."

"*Really* Cathy? *You* want to go down there with us?" Penny was thrilled.

With that, they made the relief trip and washed their hands. They all had a slice of the cookie cake and Penny opened her gifts. Natalie gave her a new journal. From her family there was a book about the history of pennies, another one about the values of pennies still expected to be out there somewhere, and plastic sleeves made to fit into a notebook to protect and catalog coins. Jerry and Kenny gave her big magnifying glasses that lit up and fit on her head so both her hands could be free to hold coins and write notes. It was perfect! Penny saw right away those glasses would come in handy for her late-night writing. Finally, everyone headed down the hill, except Tina and Natalie's parents, who watched from the top.

Natalie insisted Penny should do all the rest of the treasure hunting; it was her birthday, after all. About half-way down the hill the detector started buzzing. Jerry looked at Carson, who shrugged his shoulders and shook his head.

"I need your help, Nat. Here, you hold the detector." Natalie narrowed down the spot and Penny started digging. It was deep, but loud. She dug deeper and felt the shovel hit something hard. Both girls were digging, and whatever it was, it was long. Finally, they got enough dirt out to pull on it. Penny called out, "Somebody big come here and help us. I think it's some kind of gun."

Carson scrambled over to where she had been digging and after one look yelled, "Y'all! Come look at this!" The others gathered around as he took the small spade and carefully kept digging around the edges. "You're right, Penny, it looks like a rifle. Let's be careful gettin' this outta here."

"You keep digging that out, okay? I want to go a little closer to the creek." Penny and Natalie headed off with the metal detector and Cathy followed.

Carson didn't even answer. He was intent on getting the whole thing out without damaging it. The excitement was infectious. Natalie's dad heard them and came down to help.

"That's a Civil War musket, boys."

While they were brushing dirt off what was left of the gun, they heard the detector beeping again. Penny and Natalie were on something else and they hadn't gone far.

Penny stuck a stick in the ground where it buzzed and kept moving. Another beep, this one had a different sound. There was supposed to be a guide on the detector that explained the different sounds, but it was missing. Penny took the detector and moved it around where she was standing. It made different sounds over an area about two feet square. Penny and Natalie looked at Cathy, who looked at Kenny.

Cathy was having so much unexpected fun. "It sounds like there's more than one thing here. Ken, can you go up and get one of those other little shovels and a gallon of water and bring them down here?" As he headed up the hill Cathy was already on her knees shoulder to shoulder with Penny. "I had no idea this would turn out to be so exciting. Hey, bring a bucket, too," she yelled. Kenny motioned a thumbs up.

Cathy took the small spade and started taking dirt off the surface while Natalie manned the detector, every now and then swinging it over the top of the area. Cathy flipped dirt out of the hole and Penny sifted through it.

"I feel something hard."

"Make a pile 'til Ken brings the bucket, then throw it in there." Cathy took charge.

"Here's something else," Penny was rubbing something, "I think it's a coin."

"Here's the bucket." Ken set it down by Penny where she could put clods of dirt in it.

Natalie swiped over the spot again. "Listen to that!"

"Scrape some more dirt out, Cathy." Penny's voice was shaking with excitement.

Cathy dug a big glob from about ten inches down in the hole and lifted it to the surface making a pile of dirt. Penny ran her fingers through it, "Hey, this is heavy." She was shaking the dirt loose from something, "It's a ring! It's a ring!"

"Put it in the bucket, that thing is still beeping, there's more!" Cathy said.

Mr. Cross, Carson, and Jerry had gotten out of the dirt and had it up at the picnic table inspecting it when Ken came up for the bucket and told him the girls had found several things. They followed Ken down to where the girls were, so Tina and Julie went down, too.

There was quite an excavation taking place. The bucket was filling up with chunks of dirt the detector said contained metal. When they had it all out of the ground, Ken took it up to the sidewalk to pour water on it to avoid a muddy mess where they were digging. There were several buckles. Mr. Cross said cloth and leather would have rotted away in the damp earth, so they probably had been on a pack or satchel at one time. There were coins, a fork and spoon, a shallow bowl, a small frame that probably had a picture in it at one time, a chain, a pipe, and a man's ring. Penny felt a wave of sadness as she studied the personal items. She went with Cathy and Natalie a little farther downhill and closer to the creek. There was a flat, grassy spot under a large Willow that looked inviting.

"Can somebody dig where I put the stick? Halfway between where we found the gun and the rest of the stuff," Penny called up to Carson, "I promise, we're just looking one more place."

Jerry grabbed a shovel and plunged it into the soil where Penny had left the stick. It wasn't far down when he heard a loud clink. He lifted a large shovelful of dirt to the surface. "It's a rusty knife, like a Bowie knife. Look at that." He took it up to the table and poured some water on it to wash it off.

When Natalie eased the detector along a flat area of ground there was nothing.

"Keep walking, Nat, this looks like a place I would want to sit," Penny said as she moved her arm in a sweeping motion across the area. "Can you smell that? What is that? It smells so good. I think I could sit here and write all day."

Natalie moved closer to the tree under the edge of a bush with clusters of small, light purplish-blue flowers. "I think it's these, Penny." Natalie pointed at the flowers. The detector started beeping again.

"I knew it. I just *knew* it." Penny took the spade and started slowly digging, taking about an inch of dirt off at a time. When she was about eight inches down, she hit something hard. It was a root, but there was something else right beside it that was white and smooth. She used the spade and her fingers to brush away enough to reveal the face of a broken, empty-eyed doll. "Oh, my goodness!"

Cathy and Natalie crouched close to see. Natalie turned the detector on again. The beeping was just off to the side of the doll. The three girls carefully worked together to unearth the treasure. The corner of a metal box was exposed. They scraped and brushed and slowly uncovered enough of the box for Penny to pull it up out of the ground. The box was only about three inches wide and five inches long, and it looked like thick rusted metal. When she knocked more dirt off, it rattled. Penny looked up at Cathy and Natalie. "Wow," She turned it over, "It has a drawer."

The drawer was stuck, sealed with tiny roots and hardened soil. Cathy tapped on it to make the crud break loose. Finally, it wiggled. Cathy took the box from Penny to get a better hold on it and jiggled it until it started to slide open. The three girls sat and stared at what they had found. Inside the box there was a small rock shaped like a heart, another rock that looked like some type of crystal, an oval gold locket, and three coins. Cathy said the crystal looked like it came from a geode.

They put the things back in the drawer and worked on getting the doll out of the ground, but it turned out to be only the head. "I know it's creepy, but I want to keep it, there's something about it . . ." Penny picked up the head and studied the empty eyes. Cathy gathered the box and digging tools just as Tina came down to tell them it was time to finish up.

"Would you look at that! What's a lilac bush doing down here? I've never been able to keep them alive. Doesn't it smell wonderful, girls? I don't know what it is, but there's something about lilacs." Tina broke a piece of the shrub off and held it to her nose to inhale the fragrance.

"Look at this stuff, Mom." Penny held out her new treasure for Tina to see. "And there's stuff in the drawer of the box Cathy has, too. There's a locket that looks like gold and two rocks and three coins; and one of the rocks is heart shaped. This all must have been special to some little girl a long time ago." Penny was flushed with the excitement.

"Let's take it all up to the street. Time to pack everything up." Tina motioned for them to head up to where the cars were parked. They joined the others and showed them the latest goodies. "Anyone know who owns this land?" Tina looked at Bill Cross.

"I'm pretty sure it belongs to the state, but I'm not positive."

Jerry said, "I can ask my dad to look into it."

"That sounds like a good idea. I'm not sure about who has rights, and some of this might be valuable. I don't think too many people need to know about it right away." Bill was looking at Tina.

"We really found *treasure!*" Penny turned to Cathy and gave her a big hug. Dirt was everywhere. "Can I call Gramma and facetime her and show her all our booty?"

"Aargh. Wash your hands off first, then call her." Tina had put the eye patch on. She laughed and put her phone on the table for Penny. "I think we need to take all this home and clean it up, then start some research on the property and the things you found. I can get with Mr. Branson while you're at camp. I don't know if it's even legal for us to be out here doing this. Who knows, there may be a lot more. We still have things to do to get you ready for camp, and the Cross' have to get ready for *their* big trip, too."

Cathy held out her hands. "Well, I know one thing. I'm ready for a shower. This was fun but I feel gross."

"I'm supposed to invite you over to our house. Dad's grilling steaks." Cathy gave Ken a big smile and a thumbs up.

"Well it's only four, what are y'all doing for dinner tonight?" Tina turned to Julie, then looked at Carson and Jerry.

Julie looked at Bill, "I don't know." Bill shrugged.

"I have a date."

Everyone turned and looked at Carson. "*What?*" Cathy gave him a wink and said, "Well? With *who?* Tell!"

"You don't know her. Someone I met at the gym."

"Her name is *Someone?* That's an unusual name," Cathy teased.

"Okay. Fine. Her name is Jillian, and I also know her from school, but she's a year ahead of us."

"Jillian *Barnes?* Oh man, you *dog!* She is *hot!*" Jerry couldn't contain himself. Carson turned red as a beet.

"Can we go back to Uncle Bud's, Mom? Maybe you can invite Mr. Quintana." Now *all* eyes with raised eyebrows, especially Cathy's and Carson's, turned to Tina.

Tina took a deep breath as her eyes darted from child to child.

"It's okay, Mom, we already know all about him. You know Penny can't keep a secret." Cathy grinned and so did Carson. Penny drummed her fingers and looked up in the air like she was watching a fly, humming, her mouth pinched tight.

"It isn't a secret, I just didn't want it to turn into a big deal, not until after the swim meet and Penny's birthday at least."

"I think Uncle Bud's sounds like fun. Why don't you call your friend and we can all plan on going around six o'clock? That way we can go get cleaned up." Julie smiled. Tina had told her a little, but she had been waiting politely.

"Alright. Fine. We'll see y'all there, but make it 6:30, with or without Hugo. Yes, I *will* call him. And Carson, I doubt you'll want to, but you're welcome to join us with Jillian."

Carson laughed. Then he saw Tina's face. "Oh, you're *serious?* Um, I think that might be a bit too much fam for the first date, Mom. Maybe next time if there is one."

Dinner was wonderful. Hugo met them there. One more layer of the poison apple spell was gone.

40

Unforeseen Puzzle Pieces

Tina and Penny were on the road, driving to the camp. Beverly decided not to fly. They were on their way from her cousin's house in North Carolina where they had visited for a few days. This way she would have her car and turn it into a vacation for herself, too. The plan was to meet at the camp around 2:00 that afternoon.

"The GPS says we're only fifteen minutes away. I think we must have camped near here Penny. This all looks familiar."

Penny was watching the GPS and the turns, hoping to see a sign. "It says we're turning left up here, Mom . . . look, there's a sign, Wellspring."

"It sure is, Honey, looks like we're in the right place." The road took a quick turn and went sharply uphill. Tina followed as it snaked its way up the mountain. "Wow, it's really up here. My ears just popped." The road finally leveled back out and went into an area that was not so dense. "The flowers sure are pretty up here. I can't believe the size of these Rhododendron bushes."

As they circled around, there was a big welcome sign and an archway over a wide double iron gate that said WELLSPRING with a pretty cross above it. There were several cars parked off to the right and a sign that said Registration with an arrow to the left. Tina parked and they headed over with Penny's paperwork.

Inside the screen doors there were rows of picnic-type tables, and signs above. They found the table with the L-Q sign and got in line behind another camper signing in. The lady was pointing to lists of names in different cabins and Tina and Penny tried to hear what she was saying to get an idea of what they would be doing. When it was their turn they stepped up to the table.

"Hi there," the sweet-looking lady with little round reading glasses on the end of her nose said, "what's your name, honey? I don't recognize you—you must be a new camper."

"Penny McKenzie. Yes ma'am, this is my first time here." Penny told her with a big grin.

Just then Penny heard her name and turned to see Sally running toward her. Big hugs all around as Tina greeted Beverly. They handed over their paperwork and got instructions about where to take their things. All the cabins were named for trees. Penny and Sally were in Cedar. It was the largest cabin. There were four bunk beds on one side, a walk-through bathroom with toilets, sinks, and showers, and four bunks on the other side. Sally and Penny picked their bunk and agreed to switch top and bottom half-way through, with Penny up top first. Once their beds were made and everything unloaded, Tina and Beverly said their goodbyes. As they were walking out, Tina did a doubletake, trying to place a girl on the other side of the cabin who looked vaguely familiar, but she couldn't imagine who it could be.

It was a small camp, but it appeared to be up to date and clean. They had a big pool. It was also on the river, with canoes lined up on the shore. Tina could see the archery range across a field. It looked like there were badminton and volleyball nets and a few tennis courts, too. Registration had been held in the dining hall called Chuck Wagon, where they also had chapel. On either side of the dining hall there were two different big fire pits with logs surrounding them for sitting. They chatted as they walked to the cars.

"I think we need to find one of these camps made for grown-ups." Tina laughed.

"I'd be right there with you. I loved camp when I was a kid." Beverly said.

"I loved it, too. I think this will be a good experience for Penny. She was worried about wetting the bed, poor thing. It almost never happens anymore, but we bought her some pull-ups to wear under her loose pajamas just for sleeping. We made sure no one would be able to tell."

"At some point when we get back to your house, I want to hear all about the things that happened when she was missing, okay?"

"Sure. It's quite a story, and still a mystery, but then we don't do anything half-way in our family, do we? This spring was wild. My co-workers started calling me Lemony Snicket."

The drive back to Tina's was only about an hour and a half. When they got there, Tina found a huge bouquet of flowers on the kitchen counter. "Look at those," she said as she crossed the room. She pressed her face into the flowers and inhaled deeply, lingering before she lifted the card out. It said "Thinking of you, H." She held the card to her lips with her eyes closed and the corners of her lips curled, then looked at Beverly through the corner of her eyes and smiled.

"I believe you're glowing, Tina."

"I know I am on the inside, that's for sure. How about a glass of wine out on the deck? I bought a bottle since you'd be here."

"Sounds wonderful. A perfect way to start my grown-up vacation."

Penny and Sally were having a blast finding their way around and getting their activity schedules. This was their only chance to make changes. The one thing Penny didn't have that she wanted was Drama. Sally had Drama and didn't have Badminton, but Penny did; they were at the same time, so it was a perfect swap. There were mostly girls who came every year. Everyone seemed nice.

After supper they split up into two groups, the twelve and overs and the under twelves, and that's how the two campfires were divided. The campfire was where they learned the camp songs and had prayers every night called vespers. Cedar girls were all nine, ten, and eleven. So many good things for Penny to record in her new journal.

Tomorrow morning they would swim to determine what level they were, and afterward they would start their other classes. Penny spent as much time as she was allowed to write before lights out. It was an exciting day and she was tired. She made sure to write down the names of the girls she met, hoping that would help her remember.

On Monday morning the big bell was clanging, letting them know they had fifteen minutes to get up and head to Chuck Wagon. Penny learned quickly that most of the girls referred to it as simply Chuck.

"What's breakfast like?" Penny asked Carly, the girl from the bunk beside them.

"It's okay, there's always fruit and cereal, oatmeal, and bacon and eggs. Every now and then we get pancakes and sausage, and on Sunday they have biscuits and gravy."

Penny looked over at Sally and licked her lips. Sally nodded, "Sounds good."

After breakfast they changed into their swimsuits, grabbed their towels, and headed to the pool. Penny noticed she wasn't the only small girl. There was Jill on their side of Cedar who was about the same size as her, and another girl in Cypress someone said was twelve who was even shorter. Penny didn't feel like she stood out at all. She was beginning to feel more confident. She held her own at the pool and proved she was a safe swimmer. That helped, too.

Swimming took up most of the morning. Thankfully, there was still time for arts and crafts where they designed a tile mosaic trivet they would make and take home. Then there was lunch, followed by a quiet hour to either nap or read. Penny wrote about camp so far, and about how excited she was to be going to her first drama class after the rest hour. Only three people in her cabin were going to afternoon Drama that was held at Chuck: Penny, Diane, who was two bunks over, and one girl from the other side Penny hadn't met yet.

"How do you have time to go change between Drama and Canoe?" Penny asked Diane on the way to Drama.

"Oh, you'll figure it out. I usually wear my dry swimsuit under my shorts, then I only have to change afterward."

Penny hoped it wouldn't take long to know the tricks and the shortcuts. She had seen a few of the girls run down trails between the cabins. She wasn't sure where they went, but she was looking forward to exploring.

They walked into Chuck and the Drama group was gathering by the stage. There were ten girls in the group. They sat in a circle and introduced themselves: Gina, Diane, Penny, Ginger, Ruth, Zoe, Annabella, Sarah, Phoebe, and

Rebekah. Their counselor, Meredith, was from Pine and was a Theater major at Florida State. Penny had no idea camp counselors were college students, but she imagined it might be something she would want to do. Meredith had brought a play for them to perform this session. She had adapted it from a different play for the girls at Wellspring. It was about a camper who was lost, and the theme was Jesus, the Good Shepherd. She called the play *Seek and Find*.

Meredith lined the girls up by size; Penny was the smallest. Then she matched them by hair color and characteristics into three groups she called families. The idea was to make the story believable with good casting. At the end of the class she gave out lines to take to the cabin and practice for a reading on Tuesday to decide who would be cast in each role. Penny was in a family with Phoebe and Ginger.

After the class, on the way to change for Canoe, Penny and Phoebe walked to Cedar together. Phoebe was the girl from the other side of her cabin. "I've never done acting before. I plan to be a writer," Penny said.

"I've been in a lot of plays. I got involved with the theater when I was seven. I just auditioned for a movie part two weeks ago. That's cool that you write. I think if I don't get discovered as an actress, I'd like to be a screenwriter, or maybe be a director." Phoebe was so confident.

"You auditioned for a movie? Wow, I think that's so awesome. I've been studying character development and point of view, but some of the things I've read are about making my stories cinematic. I have to go to Canoe now, but can we talk about writing and acting later?"

"Sure, sounds fun. Don't forget we have some lines to practice."

Penny went to Canoe class. She was suddenly feeling a little more grown up and whispered to herself, "This camp is so awesome. Such cool girls. I'm so glad I got to come. This place is going to change my life."

41
Mysterious Ways

Tina and Beverly were enjoying re-connecting.

"I miss you being close, and we sure do miss Sally."

"I miss the laid-back life here, but I have to admit, there are so many opportunities up there, especially educational things for Sally. Great restaurants, plays and concerts— there's always something going on down on the Mall and in the museums and galleries."

"Yeah, I'm sure. I'm such a homebody though, I wonder if I would even go."

"We don't as often as we should. I keep thinking maybe when we're more settled we'll take advantage of things. So, tell me more about Hugo."

"Hugo . . ." Tina sighed and got dreamy-eyed, "I'm not sure how it happened. Well, yes I am, but it's embarrassing. Penny. It's all because of Penny playing matchmaker. Well, not really, but she was the catalyst. We never have managed to completely understand what happened in April. Then Cathy had pneumonia, and Carson's friend was in that terrible wreck. It's crazy, because despite it *all*, things are wonderful. Actually, better than ever."

"You told me once your first husband's death was a blessing in disguise. Otherwise you never would have met John."

"I know. Then this crazy thing with Penny, and now Hugo. And something else has happened . . ." Tina shared the meeting with Gwen and showed Beverly the picture of Phoebe. Then she stopped for a second when something crossed her mind, "No, no way . . ." She shook off the thought.

"You believe her?" Beverly sounded skeptical about Gwen's motives.

"I have no reason not to. She hasn't got anything to gain from it." Tina picked at her cuticles. "As much as I'm enjoying this, I'm really tired. I've been tired a lot lately. I think I'd like to call it an early night. What are your plans this week?"

"I'm going to Montgomery to see an old friend tomorrow and staying a few days. After that I'm taking it one day at a time. Didn't make definite plans since I didn't know what you had going on. I can come back here, go to Atlanta, even go back to my cousin's 'til time to get Sally. Whatever works."

"Well, I'm working tomorrow. I'm only part-time now at the clinic, but I'm doing a good bit of billing. That's my bread and butter. Hey, I didn't tell you I've applied for a grant. Hugo's friend at the college is helping me. A long time ago I found a book my mom had, something like *I Could Do Anything if I Knew What it Was.* I laugh because that's exactly how I feel now. I want somebody to help me figure out what I can be when I grow up."

"No better time than now!" Beverly raised her wine glass to toast with the last sip.

"I guess I'll see you in a few days and we can regroup. I want you to see Cathy and Carson, and I want you to meet Hugo. I'll be honest, his name is a little bit weird. I keep wanting to call him Hugh, but I don't want to hurt his feelings. You'll like him. He's like a refined John."

Beverly made a goofy face at Tina. "Explain *that* comment."

"It's hard to explain. He likes so many of the same things. He was going to major in Astronomy, for goodness' sake. You remember John's obsession with the stars, don't you? John played the guitar. Hugo? The violin. And he wants to learn to play the cello. John physically rescued people, Hugo does it in the office as a counselor. John wore jeans, Hugo wears khakis. He works out but instead of lifting weights he does things like yoga and spin class. Maybe it would help to tell you he was raised in California by his father. Does that make any sense?"

"Actually, yes. Perfect *stereotypical* sense. I bet he has more refined features, too."

"*Exactly!*"

Beverly laughed. "Wasn't it you who liked that crazy tv show called *Fringe*? The one about alternate reality and the duplicate people?"

"Stop it! It's not *that* weird. And yes, that was me. I'd still love to get the DVDs of that. I liked it even better than *X Files* and *Dr. Who*. I'm turning in. I'm still not adjusted to normal sleeping hours. I go to work at nine tomorrow morning. I'll already be up with coffee made by seven. Penny's room is ready for you when you're ready. If you need anything else, you know where I am." She blew a kiss to Beverly, then changed her mind and came back and gave her a hug. "I love seeing you, my friend."

It was already part way into week two at camp. Penny and Sally had fallen easily into the camp schedule like it was second nature, and both planned to beg their moms to return next year. Sally loved the sports and Penny's favorite part of the day was Drama. She was excited when she heard they were adding gardening next summer. Meredith told Penny she was a natural and she cast her as Phoebe's little sister, with both playing the lost campers in the play. Meredith loved it when she found two people totally unrelated who even had similar mannerisms. She could cast them as relatives and it would be believable. She said casting people who didn't have any similarities as siblings was one of her pet peeves. Penny was thinking theater might be her next direction. This girl Phoebe was only six months older than her, but she was smart, and living in the city had given her advantages Penny never had. The coolest thing was that they would be doing the play for the parents on the last day.

During the week Tina had been in touch with John Branson. He had done a preliminary check on the property. It was odd. Most of the surrounding property belonged to the state. The land where they had the treasure hunt was part of about one hundred acres owned by an individual. The deed was being held elsewhere. Apparently, there was a transfer of ownership in progress. John said he would let Tina know as soon as his office got more information.

Beverly came back for almost a week, then decided to go to North Carolina until time to pick up the girls. After she met Hugo, she wholeheartedly agreed; even though it was weird, he was a refined version of John. Tina was loving the fact that nothing crazy was happening and she was getting plenty of normal sleep for a change.

The only issue Tina and Beverly had with the camp was the scheduling of the end of session activities. The program for the parents was on Friday, but the girls weren't scheduled to go home until Saturday. For anyone not local, which was just about everyone, that either meant lots of driving or a hotel room, which also meant lots of driving since there were no nearby hotels.

"So, we're expected to be there at 8:30 in the morning, stay most of the day, then go find somewhere to stay so they can have their last night with their friends, then go *back* and get them on Saturday morning?" Tina called Beverly to see what she had decided to do. When she thought back about the camp she went to growing up, it must have been that way.

"Yep, I think that sums it up." Beverly didn't really care since she wasn't trying to juggle a job.

"I don't remember reading that in the brochure, do you?" Tina asked.

"No, but when I found out, I booked a room for us. It's only thirty minutes away. It'll be fine." Beverly could tell it was stressing Tina out. "I booked it for two nights so we'd already be close Friday morning. I just assumed you would come up and stay with me Thursday night after work so we could go over together."

"Sure, that sounds good. This might be one of the reasons it's a less expensive camp. But hey, if they're happy and safe I guess it's worth it. Send me the info and I'll go ahead and pack and come straight up after work."

Thursday night Carson called Tina shortly after she had gotten into the hotel room. "Hey Mom, I wanted to let you know when I brought the mail in there's a slip that says you have a certified letter and you're gonna have to sign for it."

"Does it say who it's from? Sometimes our carrier fills those out like she's supposed to."

"It just says 'letter' and then it says 'Randolph'."

"Ugh, okay, put it on the counter. I'll go to the Post Office Saturday if we're back by twelve, but most likely it'll have to wait 'til Monday. Thanks for letting me know. Everything else okay at home?"

"Sure. Everything's fine. Tell Penny hey. Love you Mom, see you Saturday."

"Okay, I love you too, Carson."

"Problem at home?" Beverly couldn't help overhearing.

"You remember me telling you about Gwen and the sick grandmother in Atlanta? It looks like I've got a certified letter from Mrs. Randolph waiting for me. Beverly, what *am* I going to do?"

"I'd be talking to an attorney, pronto. And not judging, just asking, have you told Hugo about any of this?"

Tina looked at Beverly, biting her lip and picking at her cuticles. "No. I haven't even told my mother."

On Friday morning Tina and Beverly left the hotel and went to the camp. As it turned out, parents from far away didn't necessarily come. Tina could understand why. The music and demonstrations of what they had learned was sweet, but not that big a deal. Penny let Tina know she was going to be in a play after lunch, and she disappeared back to the cabin while the moms were watching Sally play badminton.

Penny ran to Cedar and looked through the screen, then went inside, looking for Phoebe. She wanted to take Phoebe to meet her mom, but she hadn't been able to find her. "Has anybody seen Phoebe?"

Marcia, Phoebe's bunkmate, was packing. "She lost her locket. She said she was wearing it yesterday when y'all went on the hike. It wasn't around her neck this morning and it's not in her stuff. She was crying. She went to look along the path. She said she's not coming back until she finds it."

Penny turned and took off running down the trail. They had gone where they weren't supposed to go yesterday. It was considered too dangerous and was off-limits. She was trying to remember which paths they took. They had gone to the big hole at the ravine on the way to the gorge. Penny was getting one of those bad feelings. The farther she went, the more she wished she had found someone to go with her. But why hadn't she found Phoebe yet? She was almost to where they stopped and sat to talk.

"Phoebe . . . Phoeee . . . beee . . ." Penny yelled as loud as she could. She stood still and listened. She heard something behind her and whipped around, but nothing was there. That was the direction of the ravine where they had gone. She moved cautiously toward what she thought she heard. It was like she was being pulled that way. She called out again, "Phoebe? Are you out here?" She got closer to the edge and heard a crying moan. Holding onto a limb, she leaned way out. Down below in the ravine she could see her on the ground. Her left leg looked twisted. "Phoebe! Oh God! Phoebe! Are you okay?" She backed up quickly when she felt the limb bend.

Phoebe moaned. "Penny? You found me! Oh, Penny, I think my leg must be broken."

"I'll go get help. Did you find your locket?"

"Yes, that's how I fell. I guess it caught on a branch when we leaned over to look yesterday. It was just a little way down and I thought I could reach it. I lost my balance. I never should have come by myself."

"After we get you out of there, I'll have to tell you about my rescue in April." Penny spun around to leave and almost ran right into a tall, thin, very old man. He just stood there, smiling at her, with a strange joyful smile. She stared, speechless, then got up the nerve to speak. "God?"

"No, Apple, I'm not God, but He sent me."

"But you saved me in the creek."

"Yes, I did do that, I did indeed. *He* sent me. And He sent me here today. He's been showing me. You be still and sit right here."

Penny felt a chill run down her spine. "Shouldn't I go get some help?"

"Help is already here, yessum, and more on the way." Just then he lifted his chin and looked toward the sky.

Penny heard a helicopter in the distance. She stared at him and watched as he held onto roots and vines and slowly worked his way down into the ravine. He was so old . . . how could he do that? He pulled a mirror from his pocket and flashed it in the sun at the helicopter, which moved closer, hovered above, and filled the air with sand and leaves. Penny covered her eyes. She tried to peek between her fingers and watched in disbelief as the helicopter lowered a basket down into the ravine. Penny stood back because there was so much sand in the air, then watched as the basket was brought up right beside her. A man leaning out of the helicopter yelled and motioned to her to get in. There were steps made of rope she used to climb up and over the side where Phoebe was. Penny tried to look down into the ravine but couldn't see the man. She hadn't seen him climb out, either.

Gently, the basket was raised up over the tops of the trees. Penny held Phoebe's hand and told her it was going to be okay, and before they realized where they were, they could hear cheering. Penny lifted herself up to look over the side. "Phoebe! It brought us to Chuck! This was a more exciting search and rescue than that play!" That brought a smile to Phoebe's face, even through her pain. Sally was with her mom and Tina. Penny waved as Tina's hands covered her open mouth. The basket was set down and Penny climbed out, telling them Phoebe's leg looked like it was broken. Two men lifted Phoebe out.

"Penny, my locket! It's in the basket."

"Wait!!" Penny yelled and climbed back into the basket as the helicopter hovered. "I got it!" After she climbed back out, Penny looked at the man waving the helicopter off. "Wait! What about the man who helped us? He's still down in the ravine."

The man looked at his phone and looked back at Penny. He sent a message to the helicopter and waited. Then he turned back to Penny with a questioning look. "They received an all clear." He waved the helicopter off. "Now just waiting for the ambulance."

"But they *left* him! Wait, that's not right . . ." Penny was beginning to cry, "you can't just *leave* him there . . ."

Tina hurried over and put her arms around Penny, who was totally confused about where the man went. She had dropped the locket down into her pocket. Tina could tell she was upset. "What is it, Honey, what's happened?"

Tears were streaming down Penny's cheeks. "Mom, it was God, but he told me he wasn't, he said God sent him. God sent him to save me from the creek and today sent him to save Phoebe. He called me apple. He climbed down into the ravine. He put Phoebe in the basket."

"Phoebe!" Tina felt a jolt of incomprehension and awe all at once.

"She's right there, the one from our cabin. She fell in the ravine trying to get her locket and then God, I mean the man, was there. He came out of nowhere and he was standing behind me and he went down into the bottom and then she was in the basket. But they said he wasn't there. Where did he go, Mom? Where did he go?" Penny was getting agitated.

While Penny was talking, Tina looked at the girl they had put on a blanket on a picnic table with the camp nurse tending to her. She *did* recognize her, the girl she saw on the other side of Cedar. She hadn't imagined it was possible. It really was Phoebe Kendrick. How could this all be happening? Her mother would simply shake her head at a time like this and say there are no coincidences. And the same man? On a mountain an hour and a half away from where he rescued Penny in April?

"*Mo-om*? Please look at this. I don't understand." Penny was holding an open locket in her hand, staring at it. Phoebe's locket. "Why would Phoebe have a picture of Daddy in her locket?"

42
Least Expected Blessings

The ambulance took Phoebe to the hospital, which wasn't far from the hotel where Tina and Beverly were staying. They went ahead and left the girls at camp for the night once Tina got a solemn promise Penny wouldn't go anywhere but to Chuck or Cedar, and Tina took the locket for safekeeping.

On the way to the hotel they stopped to get an early supper. Once they were in the room, Tina decided to call Gwen. She answered on the first ring.

"You know Phoebe is at Camp Wellspring?"

"*Tina?* No, Phoebe has been injured and she's in the hospital overnight. How would *you* know about camp?" There was a bit of a slur in Gwen's speech.

"She and Penny were in the same cabin. I was there when the ambulance took her. She had lost her locket. Penny kept it for her, but Penny looked in it."

"I'm not sure I know about a locket. What does that have to do with anything?"

"It has John's picture in it." Tina let out a long exhale. "Who's picking her up?"

"I am. I'm at the Holiday Inn near the hospital."

"This has surpassed strange. My friend Beverly and I are here, too."

Laughing, Gwen said, "Nothing strange about all of us being at the only decent place to stay near the camp. I'm in 216. Come have a drink and unwind with me. I just got back from the hospital a little while ago."

"Okay, we'll be there in a minute." Tina hung up and looked at Beverly with big eyes.

"We'll be where?" Beverly was wide-eyed and shaking her head.

"You are *not* going to believe this," Tina's hands were shaking. "Gwen is in room 216. She wants me to go have a drink with her. You're going with me, come on."

Beverly was shaking her head. "Really? Why do you want *me* there?"

"Because this can't be real, and I need a witness. *Fringe* is looking like normal life. Also, because I'm not sure what direction this conversation is going to go. I'm sure she's been drinking. I may need you to get me out of there."

"Just don't push me into some parallel universe and leave me there, okay? Promise?"

They walked out and down the hallway, laughing.

Gwen had opened her door and was waiting for Tina.

Tina greeted Gwen and introduced Beverly. "Carson called last night to tell me I have a certified letter waiting for me when I get home from Randolph."

"Rhoda sent you a letter. She wanted to make sure no one read it but you. There's nothing legal in it or anything. They don't have the DNA results yet. She wanted to thank you for allowing it to be done. She also wants you to know she had a trust fund set up for each of the children with the life insurance and home insurance money she got after the fire. She's old and ill, and she's afraid you might not want the financial burden of another child. That's pretty much the whole thing. She asked me to read it before she sent it." Gwen's affect was flat. She got up and walked across the room, took the paper wrapper off another glass and scooped a few ice cubes into it. She opened the bottle of scotch and gestured toward Tina with the bottle. Tina shook her head.

Beverly said, "Go ahead and pour me a short one, thanks."

"You keep referring to her as old, but she's Ruthie's mother. How old could she be?" Tina asked.

"She adopted Ruthie. Ruthie's mother died from an overdose when Ruthie was a baby. Rhoda was Ruthie's great aunt. I was adopted, too. That's how my mother and Rhoda met. Rhoda's 85. I guess that's not always considered so old anymore, but she has health problems. She survived breast cancer but now it's in her colon. She knows she won't likely beat it this time. Does that answer your questions?"

"Yes, it does, and I'm sorry she's had such a difficult time. I suppose my questions sound rude, but it helps to have a better understanding of the whole situation. I know you tried to tell me more before. I wasn't ready to hear it. How bad is Phoebe's leg?" Now that she had more clarity about Mrs. Randolph's reasons for worry and fear, Tina was more concerned about Phoebe's future.

Gwen smiled. "Not too bad. Nothing complicated, no pins or surgery. She was lucky." It was obvious Gwen had been drinking for longer than the last thirty minutes.

Tina took a deep breath and shook her head. "I hear myself saying things like that . . . 'not too bad, could be worse, we're fortunate, it's a blessing.'" she looked off into a void space as she spoke. "It seems my life has been a parade of blessings camouflaged as tragedy. At this very moment my life is the best it's been in decades, and yet

I have no idea what each day is going to throw at me. It reminds me of a commercial several years ago about life coming at you fast. For me, it's more like I'm riding on one of those things that spins really fast on the playground, and if you don't brace yourself exactly right, you fly off and land in the dirt. As much as it wears me out, I'm not sure if I know how to function any other way anymore." She turned and looked into Gwen's eyes. "I'm not sure you can identify with that, can you Gwen?"

"No, Tina, I can't. It's okay. You go ahead and call me out. I deserve it. I love this little girl, but *I'm* not a *mother*. I'm a quitter, Tina. I'm one who looks for the quick and easy way. You? You're that woman who takes it in stride and chooses the difficult path. It's like you know where the best reward is, but you're not even looking for one. I envy you, but I don't think I have it in me to sacrifice for a child. Maybe because no one ever sacrificed for me."

"But that's where you're wrong, Gwen. God sacrificed plenty for us, you included. He sacrificed His son. Jesus accepted the deal and gave His life to prove to us how much our real father loves us. I'm sorry. I hope I haven't offended you. That wasn't my plan. I'm glad you trusted me enough to come to me with the truth. Now that I know, and now that I've seen *this*," she pulled out the locket and laid it on the table, "now that *Penny* has seen it, it can't be denied or brushed under the rug."

Gwen picked up the gold, heart-shaped locket and opened it. She smiled back at the rugged smiling man in the photo, "I wonder who Ruthie told her it was?"

"Maybe you should ask Phoebe. I don't know. How do we explain to two girls, just six months apart in age, that the same man fathered them both and loved both of their mothers? He never knew about Phoebe, and if he had, Penny would have never been born. And if he hadn't tried to go upstairs to save Ruthie, they both would still have their Daddy."

"If you want me to take it to the hospital and ask in the morning, I will. If you want me to go ahead and tell her everything, I will. I was her mother's best friend. I've known her all her life. Whatever I tell her, she'll believe. If you don't want to have her live with you, I'll try to keep her. I love her. But I love her enough to know that she would probably be happier with a biological sister and a mom like you than she would be with me."

Beverly sat quietly, holding her drink, and watched with tears slipping out of the corners of her eyes.

Tina reached over and pulled Gwen close, and then hugged her. "I think you should tell her; but do her a favor and be sober when you do." Tina turned toward Beverly to say it was time to go, then had another thought. She turned back around. "There are still six weeks left before school starts again. She already knows Penny. I think she should come for a visit."

Gwen grabbed Tina and hugged her tight. "I have to go up to the camp and get her things in the morning before I get her from the hospital and take her to Atlanta. They said the counselor and other girls would pack her things. I'd like to meet Penny."

"I imagine Penny is one of the ones doing the packing. Listen, I have people I have to share all this with. Up until now, Beverly is the only one who knows any of it. I'd be lying if I said the idea of having her with us hasn't grown on me. John would want me to care for her and make sure she knows she's loved. And the way this has taken such a bizarre twist says to me that this is part of God's plan. I guess we have to let it unfold."

Two Weeks Later

Penny was pacing back and forth, watching through the sidelights of the front door. Carol had driven up for a visit and was in the living room with Carson and Cathy.

Hugo and Tina were out on the deck. They had just finished arranging a vase of flowers they cut from the yard. Tina sat down in the glider and picked up the stack of mail Carson had handed her. "Bills . . . junk . . ." She slapped a few down without opening them, then stared at one that looked official before slicing it open and sliding the contents out. Tina blinked as she tried to understand what she was reading.

Hugo looked up and saw the look on her face. "What is it?"

"I'm not sure I understand. It's from John Branson's office about the property up off Galaxy Drive. Does this say what I think it says?" Tina handed Hugo the letter with shaking hands.

As Hugo read the letter his expression matched Tina's. "It says Penelope McKenzie is the owner of the property, and you, as her mother, are her representative. What?" They were flabbergasted.

"How could that be, Hugo? Who would just *give* land to a child like that?"

"You'll need to get more information from John; but if this is correct . . . wow . . . how crazy!"

A shout came from inside the house.

Tina and Hugo smiled and went in through the French doors.

Penny turned toward the living room and yelled to Tina, "She's here!" Then threw the door open and ran down the walk, yelling, "My sister Phoebe is here!"

Phoebe ran from Gwen's car to embrace Penny.

Things are not always as they seem.
We are works in progress.
It is never the end . . .

Author's Note

After twenty years in several small businesses and a few failed marriages, I returned to college for a dual master's degree in Counseling/Psychology and School Guidance. My employment during my registered internship with the State of Florida Department of Health involved going in-home over a six-county region to counsel children who were at risk of either hospitalization or involvement with law enforcement. This was a last least restrictive chance for children who had not progressed using outpatient services. I was humbled daily by these children and their families who allowed me to become a part of their lives.

Once I became a Licensed Mental Health Counselor, I opened my private practice. Almost immediately, I found myself immersed in cases which involved trauma. I had thought this was only a problem with the more severe cases where I had been working; but no matter the presenting issue, from physical pain and deteriorating health, to relationship problems or mood disorders, some form of trauma appeared to be a common denominator, and it appeared to be a much too common problem. I became obsessed with learning all I could to be able to help these souls whose bravery was, and continues to be, inspirational.

I continued my studies and earned a board certification as an expert in traumatic stress in 2002. As a trauma therapist, I enhanced my education fervently. I sought to learn ways for my clients' discomfort to be alleviated. I attended trainings and conferences for every modality I believed might be promising, and then found ways to integrate them into my counseling style. My goal was to help my clients reach *their* goals: to feel *normal*, to have a greater capacity for joy, and to find and accept their authentic selves. As I look back at the chain of traumatic events in my own life, I believe I have been guided along my past path to be prepared to do the work I am meant to do in the place where I am meant to be; where my gifts have been rekindled to fulfill my soul's calling. As tragic as some of my recent losses have been, blessings abound.

The Scent of Safety is not intended to be a memoir. As is true for most novels, my characters are an amalgam of personal experience, of friends and family members, of stories from my precious clients, and some are from my wildest dreams and imagination. In my practice I learned more about myself from my clients than I could have ever hoped to learn. At risk of sounding repetitive, I give them credit not only for my personal growth and healing, but for helping to keep the passion for seeking truth alive in my heart.

Since his creation, man has tried every way possible to control his environment, his fellow man, and his own destiny. This drive has fueled conflicts throughout time. From a scientific perspective, the history of joyful triumphs coupled with painful tragedies, has been inherited for generations in the form of cellular memory—a database in our DNA. To this inherited database, we add sensory experiences from before birth and during early childhood. We then add daily experiences to formulate beliefs about the world and our relationship with it. It is on these beliefs that we base our sense of self and our life's decisions.

There are many theories about the nature of man and his ego-driven, futile attempts to direct the future. This is the behavior I believe the creator expected, which seems to me to be a relatively universal concept, but with countless variations. Most major religions include principles within scripture; most include a creator and valued behaviors, such as truth, honor, obedience, kindness, and compassion. For Christians, there is a mandate to love, accept, and pray for others. Salvation is not offered for a life free of sin, but for the confession of sin, and for faith and trust in God's promise of love and salvation through expressed belief in his son, Jesus Christ.

I believe that when faith in a higher power is followed and allowed to awaken, there is a call to action that is like a seed in the depths of our souls. Faith in a promise nourishes the seed and grows courage to overcome adversity; it urges us on, rather than allowing us to hopelessly give in to fear and accept defeat. For me, this is a proof of God's existence. Without Him there would be no moral compass, no need for compassion, and no hope for the future.

We rarely know what others have endured, what beliefs and past experiences drive them, or how their view of reality differs from our own. Things we believe to be true simply may not be. The effects of trauma can be seen daily all around us. One touch, one smell, or one sound may set off an emotional reaction that seems irrational; yet one look, one word, one act of kindness, can make a difference in the life of someone who is struggling.

Take time to acknowledge challenges faced by others by practicing gratitude and compassion. Do it because it is the right thing to do, despite the fact you may never see its impact. Do it because you are where you are supposed to be, and it is what the creator asks of you. Do it for your soul's sake, for that is the one thing you must never compromise.

References and Credits

Tina – Ron's Office:

In researching the quote known commonly as Einstein's definition of insanity, "Doing the same thing over and over and expecting different results," I discovered it is not actually an Einstein quote.

The book, *Codependent No More: How to Stop Controlling Others and Start Caring for Yourself*, by Melody Beattie, first published in 1986, is an excellent and well-known self-help book.

Penny:

The poem Penny takes down from the shelf is an excerpt from *Evangeline: A Tale of Acadie*, by Henry Wadsworth Longfellow, 1847.

Six Steps to Making a New Start Author unknown other than scripture from *The Bible*. This folded paper was in my own father's wallet at the time of his death in 2009. Numerous searches yielded no information about the source.

Missing:

When Tina deals with panic and a flashback, she uses vague elements of several protocols. This is NOT intended to be instructional and it is by no means a suggestion for readers to attempt this on their own. I highly recommend seeking a therapist who uses one or more energy protocols. Some worth researching are: EFT (Emotional Freedom Technique), EMDR, Lifespan Integration, Rapid Resolution Therapy, Matrix Reimprinting, and Neurofeedback. These are several I personally learned and used, there are numerous others.

When the nervous system is over-aroused, it can help to take steady breaths with longer and slower exhales than inhales. This helps to shift from the Sympathetic to the Parasympathetic.

Gramma!:

The Hidden Messages in Water, by Dr. Masaru Emoto, Atria books, 2005. This is a fascinating book documenting the research of Dr. Emoto using high-speed photography to show the profound impact of positive and negative thoughts and statements on the development and formation of water crystals. Keep in mind that the heart and brain are about 73% water. Amazing book.

Quotes by Isabel Allende are numerous on Pinterest and Etsy. I feel I covered her as the author of the quotes adequately within the story, but I wanted to add this. After reading her lengthy and detailed website and biography, I was even more taken with her passion for her work. There is no question why she has been honored with so many awards. Consider checking out her website and her many brilliant and moving books.

The song Carson sings for Gramma is "Just Be Held" by Casting Crowns, a contemporary Christian rock group. It is a single on their 2014 album, *Thrive*.

Turning Points:
Hugo invites Tina to a play titled *Greater Tuna*, which is the first in a series of four two-man comedic plays by Ed Howard, Jaston Williams, and Joe Sears. My husband took me to see this delightful play for our first date.

Calm After the Storm:
Lyrics for "Oh Father, Father" were written by the book's author, 2020.

Mysterious Ways:
Tina mentions a book her mother had long ago. *I Could Do Anything If I Only Knew What It Was* by Barbara Sher was first published by Dell in 1995. It was ahead of its time and continues to have valuable information, despite the shift in the direction of electronic media.

Front cover photography is by the author; the model is Emma Herring.

Acknowledgments

This novel is the result of who I have become over almost seven decades. My acknowledgements must include more than people directly involved with the writing and publishing process.

I might never have completed this book without the loving support and encouragement from my brilliant husband, Jody, the rock to whom I attached my kite string twenty-five years ago. Thank you for your steadfast belief in me. You remind me daily of who I am inside.

I was blessed at birth with kind, gentle, and generous parents, Martha and Tom Bingham, who taught me the meaning of unconditional love and raised me to be honest and compassionate by setting an example of patience and strength through faith. I trust they are smiling.

I am grateful to God for entrusting me with three precious daughters: Rachel, my advocate in Heaven, Diane, whose unrivaled determination and dedication to family is always an inspiration, and Sarah, who has given me an understanding of the true meaning of the Serenity Prayer. P.S. Let your light shine.

My marriage gave me two sons, Shaun and David, who welcomed me into their lives and taught me about boys in time for me to prepare for grandsons, as boys were a rarity in our family.

Until they came along, I couldn't fathom loving anything or anyone as much as I love my girls, but there is something magical about grandchildren. Audun, Henry, Alec, Emma, Ace, and Zack, you are my reasons to stay healthy and young at heart!

A grateful thank you to Pastor Denvil Farley, of the Port Charlotte United Methodist Church, for your undying dedication to God, to your beautiful family, and to your congregation. Your Mothers' Day 2019 sermon, the first Mothers' Day after my eldest daughter lost her battle, was a specific message that felt like it came to me directly from God. It came as confirmation I am where I am supposed to be, doing what He wants me to do. On that day, the flame was fanned.

I would like to thank Kary Oberbrunner, of Author Academy Elite, and the Igniting Souls Tribe for the support that is always readily available. It is indeed a fellowship like no other. Thank you to Esther, Valaree, and Lorrie. The members who have impacted my life and given the needed encouragement to stay the course are too numerous to list.

I will never know if any of you see this, but there is a special place in my heart for the many people who came to my office and allowed me to be present with you while you walked through the valley and fought your demons. You are my heroes. Your courage and your willingness to remove the shroud and face your fears was unsurpassed. You will never know what a gift you gave me. You provided inspiration and strength when the time came that I needed it the most.

Above all, I am grateful for my sister, Holly. You have always been my greatest cheerleader, no matter what, forever reminding me to lean into Jesus. Thank you for loving me, laughing with me, trusting me, and for allowing me to shamelessly share my deepest and darkest fears. You have been the best big sister anyone could ever hope to have.

Next from Sue Bingham Herring:

Do Unto Others

Raveled Tapestries Book Two
Anticipated publication in 2021

Is it time for you to seek truth and find peace?
I would love to help

For more information:
www.suebinghamherring.com

Check out the services I offer, which include my
newsletter entitled "All Things Health,"
a free assessment, and opportunities for consultation,
coaching, and counseling for individuals and adults.

CPSIA information can be obtained
at www.ICGtesting.com
Printed in the USA
FSHW011829311020
75418FS